I hope you
enjoy Katie's
book

The Chronicles of Articia

Children of the Dead

K.D. Enos

Aventine Press

ISBN: 1-59330-781-0

Library of Congress Control Number: 2012911719
Library of Congress Cataloging-in-Publication Data
The Chronicles of Articia/ K.D. Enos

Printed in the United States of America

Special thanks to,

Editor: Joan M. Flaherty, Maynard MA
Illustrator: Dylan McCusker, Westford MA

For Shauna Lee Cotte, thank you for providing the spark that helped Katie to become a remarkable person.

Table of Contents

Divided We Fall

"The children have been born." Meriab Coralm, the healer, spoke at a whisper to the Oracle.

The Oracle nodded.

"So the prophecy is true!" Duke Marquin shook his head as he entered the antechamber of the royal birthing room. He picked up the boy and looked into his eyes, "They must be separated for the sake of the kingdom. They cannot be allowed to know that more than one child was born to the queen today."

Meriab frowned uneasily, "This is treason, Duke. Be cautious. It may be safer for them to stay together. The king will never allow you to separate his children." The Oracle nodded in agreement.

Duke Marquin shook his head, "The king does not have to know. It is best for the kingdom and children if they are separated." The Oracle was about to speak but was cut off by the duke.

"It must be done. This is all I will hear on the matter, they will not stay together!"

The Oracle and the healer walked back into the birthing room to tend to the queen. The duke swore and turned to his advisor. "Prepare a squad and a nursemaid to transport the children to my northern estate. We will decide where to send them after things have settled."

His aide responded uneasily, "Milord, the healer, and the Oracle will protest; they will be difficult."

"FIND A WAY!" The duke stormed out of the room.

The aide weighed the duke's command and called over the night guard. "Arrange transport immediately." He looked into the birthing room; the queen had been unconscious since the first child was born. Was she unaware that she had birthed more than one babe? He looked at the healer and the Oracle …

Training Grounds

Dominic, the crown prince of Articia, sighed inwardly as he stood before the two stubborn children with their arms crossed. Both had coal-black hair and stormy, gray eyes, unlike his and the king, their father. They were no longer the same height, as they had been as toddlers. Nevertheless, they were definitely twins, in all the worst ways. The only other difference was their gender—by far the most important factor in most of the kingdom of Articia. Dominic stared at the training room wall. The tapestry draped there was an important part of the royal training program. On it was the map of the entire kingdom of Articia and beyond.

The tapestry showed the regions of the kingdom as it stretched widely across Greater Articia, Which is the largest known kingdom; Articia dominated the neighboring lands of Martenic, Cyrus, and Husteria, as well as the Dulst city-states to south and the Mildanar tribes to the north. Within the great kingdom were many farming communities, nobles' estates, and of course the city of Articia, where the king resided.

To Dominic's right stood his younger brother, Prince Aleczander, with arms crossed, lips puckered, and a very serious, angry look on his face. It conveyed his great disappointment at the world for displeasing him. Dominic had to chuckle. Even though Alec was a mere eight years of age, it did not hinder the power in his glare, whether he was looking at his older brother and the heir apparent of Articia or not.

Next to Alec stood his twin sister, Ava, looking like the beautiful goddess Adara herself. In fact, he often pondered how much his little sister resembled the statue of the deity in the great Temple of Adara. Dominic had seen it only once, when he took his first pilgrimage to the rolling hills of Westwood just north of the Adaran River.

He remembered that trip fondly; he had traveled with his family to the noble estate of Sir Dale of Westwood for the first time. The summer festival was one of the largest he had ever attended. Priestesses and priests of the goddess as well as people from all around the known world traveled to Westwood to participate.

The Temple of Adara was a remarkable structure. Built into the hillside, the temple entrance was only visible from the east. In the center of the temple was a large opening to the sky and under the opening was a twenty-foot statue of Adara cradling a baby in her arms. During the summer solstice celebration, the moon passes over the opening and lights the statue, bringing the goddess and the child to life, or so it seemed.

Dominic remembered how feminine Ava had seemed then in her party attire. Today Ava was in the borrowed tunic and trousers of her brother, which were rather tight since she was now an inch or two taller than Aleczander. Ava had crossed her arms in a ridiculous attempt to look as angry as her twin was, but in her eyes, Dominic saw pleading.

Dominic could see that she intended to train with Alec and any other option would be unacceptable to Ava. The heir apparent turned to his brother Tristan for help, but Tristan, who had recently turned twelve, just shrugged his shoulders and shook his head. Dominic would receive no help from Tristan today.

The stubbornness of the royal twins was common knowledge in Castle Articia. Three years ago, when his mother had told them Ava was not to take the same classes as Aleczander from their private tutor, they didn't move from their chairs in the dining room for a whole day. Eventually, the nursemaids carried them off to their room when they fell asleep. This continued for many days. The queen finally decided that for both their welfare and the well-being of everyone in the royal hall, Ava would take lessons with Alec.

Now, on his eighth birthday, when he was to start his training to become a warrior prince of Articia, Aleczander had arrived at the training grounds … with his sister. When she refused to leave and Alec refused to let her go, Bryn, the weapon master, called for Dominic and Tristan. Only they could sway the course of the twins when they set their mind on something.

"See what I mean?" Bryn chuckled.

"With her determination and stubbornness, she would make a good warrior." Dominic meant this as a jest, but it put an idea in his head.

Dom turned to speak to the weapon master and saw mischief reflected in Tristan's expression as well. "Train them both then. Just … don't tell father." Tristan smiled at Dominic as they turned and left the training grounds.

Bryn watched the older brothers leave and was only slightly surprised. He had learned to expect the unexpected from the sons and daughter of King Henry.

The triumphant twins, already in an uproar over the change in events, were arguing about who got to practice with the sword first. Bryn looked at them, and being the good weapon master he was, saw the great leaders and warriors they would both be, if only the Fates allowed.

Bryn had been in service to King Henry for over thirty years. Born to a family of farmers, Bryn joined the army of for the king after he lost most of his family to the same plague that took many of Articia's citizens and most of its royal family. He had spent a dozen years as a foot soldier, rising through the ranks unnoticed by the royal family until the Battle of Mildanar Steppes.

In that battle, Bryn was the captain of the cavalry of the famed One Hundred and was fully engaged in a skirmish with goblin riders when he recognized that King Henry's flank had been weakened by a focused goblin attack. Unwilling to yield his position, he split his forces with a command to hold the line and secured the king's flank. His action turned out to be a pivotal point in the battle because the goblin horde had overcommitted to the flanking maneuver and the king was able to rally and rout the goblin forces. King Henry had been very young, but very savvy, at the time of the border wars. He immediately recognized that his inexperience was not a benefit to the battlefield. Had the young captain named Bryn not recognized the weakening flank, the battle could have ended in disaster.

Henry was impressed with Bryn's tactical knowledge and mastery of many weapons and made him the Captain of the Army, the highest military rank in Articia. Knowing he could not effectively lead the armies of Articia forever, Bryn spent many years training some of the brightest officers of the line so that someday he could step down from his post.

The current captain of Articia's army was one of those protégés. However, King Henry was not able to let his longtime friend and comrade to leave his side so he asked Bryn to stay and teach his children weapon mastery and tactics. He wanted his children never to be in a position of desperately needing a "Bryn" on the battlefield.

Bryn looked at the king's youngest children and sighed. He knew this pair's reputation; this truly was going to be the biggest challenge of his life. At that moment, he wished he were back on the field of battle.

As Alec ran toward the training equipment in an attempt to get to the sword first, Ava reached out with her magic and caused her brother to trip. He slammed to the ground as she casually walked over to pick up the wooden sword.

"I am ready to train now," Ava declared.

Bryn smiled as he helped up Alec who was clenching his fists in anger at Ava's actions, "Why yes you are, my young warrior princess," Bryn replied. *Though I am not sure that I am ready to train you*, he thought.

. . .

Ava had started to show magical ability at a very young age. They say that when a child is around two years old, a time that most parents call the challenge years, children start to become more independent and stubborn. For Ava and Alec, these years were especially difficult because the twins were particularly independent and stubborn. On one of the more memorable days of the royal twins' activities, their nursemaid, whom they both adored, had to leave the castle to tend to an ailing parent. Of course, the twins would have none of it and did not truly understand the need for the nursemaid to leave.

It was at this time that the royal family learned of Ava's magical ability. When her tantrum erupted, they noticed the change in her immediately. As she made a fist, her eyes started to change colors and swirls of wind surrounded the grounds. No one is sure if things would have gotten out of control that day because a rather powerful mage named Brendan, the royal scribe, was in the yard and intervened. He managed to distract Ava with a colorful pyrotechnics display.

After little Ava's remarkable expression of power, things got very interesting in the castle and Brendan spent many years working to teach her restraint and control, at least as much as was possible for the remarkably stubborn child.

...

The twins trained with Bryn for many years after that first day, each with their own special talents. Ava was very adept with the sword, and with her innate magical ability, she was able to enhance her movements and responses to the point where even Alec's growing height and weight offered him no advantage when he sparred with her. Alec had grown to a fit young man, which was quite a change from the early days when Ava was the stronger and larger twin.

Bryn explained to the siblings that the changes were part of the natural development of the beings of Articia and that "the goddess Adara made the females of all species stronger than the males when they were young so that they could defend themselves against the males, who were wilder and more aggressive. When the females were old enough to defend themselves, the males of the species would get larger and stronger, mostly to defend themselves from the aggressiveness of the mature females." Ava thought this was rather funny, especially since she was still better with the sword than her brother Alec.

Alec's skills were much better suited to the longbow and horseback arts. His jousting skills had already earned him honors in the local games. However, Alec's skill with the longbow is what earned him renown in the kingdom. During the annual Artician festival, warriors and artists of many forms had come to the capital to compete in the games. The tournament, hosted by King Henry's cousin, Sir Dale of Westwood, who is celebrated as one of the best archers in Articia. Now that Alec was fourteen, he could compete in the games. It would be the first test of his archery skills in a formal contest.

The archery contest ran all day and required precision and stamina. Hundreds of archers started the contest that morning, including Alec. Most of the younger archers were eliminated from the competition early for lack of stamina, but Alec successfully completed every round, besting all his opponents until he reached the final round; for this, he was to compete with Sir Dale, last year's champion.

As champion, Sir Dale had the honor of calling the first shot of the match. He started by calling a long shot, hoping to end the contest quickly and assuming incorrectly that the young prince would not have much strength left to pull back the bow to reach the target.

Alec just smiled, for he knew he had not yet reached his limit. Alec was very clever for someone so young but he had had a great tutor in Bryn. The weapon master had spent a considerable amount of time preparing Alec for the archery contest, giving him a clear strategy for managing the length of the archery competition. Whenever Alec had honors in a match, he would call a closer shot that required more precision so that he could save his strength for the challenges later in the day.

Sir Dale shot first, reaching and striking the target easily. Alec followed; hitting the target as well, but not as close to the center as the shot of Sir Dale. Alec now had honors and called a closer, more precise shot in which he pulled the closest mark. Remarkably, the contest continued for forty rounds, the maximum allowed under the rules of the game. Alec had managed to obtain a draw against the best archer in the kingdom.

Sir Dale bowed to the young prince, "Remarkable job today young master."

"Thank you, Sir Dale. I learned much about competition in our duel today; someday I hope to finish the games as the victor," Alec said as he bowed to his father's cousin.

"I am sure that will someday be the outcome," Sir Dale stated as he patted Alec on the back. "I will do my best to give you competition each year, but for now I must withdraw. I have yet had a chance to sample the fares of this festival and have much catching up to do," Sir Dale finished as withdrew from the grounds. Alec smiled, for he knew Sir Dale's reputation with the noble women in court and he knew well what Sir Dale was planning to sample.

"Well done, Alec!" Bryn called, smiling. "You have brought much honor to your family and me on this day."

"Thank you, Bryn. I am sure I would not have lasted long in this contest without your sage advice," Alec responded. "But let us go out and experience the fares of the festival, too. It has been a long day of competition and I do not want to miss out on all of the merrymaking."

Alec and Bryn left the contest grounds, heading toward the festival's main thoroughfare. Had they been more aware of their surroundings, they would have noticed the dark-cloaked figure in the dispersing crowd. This figure had been taking special interest in the activities of the young prince.

...

Ava had returned early from the festival, unwilling to lose her independent training period. Only in the late evening or during festivals, when the castle was deserted, could she sneak into the armory unobserved. She used the time to practice with the sword called Last Kiss. As far as Ava knew, no one in the castle knew she had trained with one of the royal swords of Articia. The young princess worked hard to maintain that secret, despite the constant call of the magical sword.

Ava could still remember the day she first heard the summons of Last Kiss. It had only been a few years after she started weapons training with Bryn.

"Ava!" whispered an unknown voice.

Startled, she looked all around and saw none of the chambermaids or other servants of the royal house. Ava continued walking, thinking that she must have imagined it.

"Ava, come to me!" the voice beckoned.

This time Ava stopped dead in her tracks. Now she was afraid, not knowing what to think, but she felt drawn to the armory's door, which she had passed many times. Ava opened it apprehensively, and peered inside the circular chamber of the royal swords of Articia.

"Hello," Ava whispered. "Is anyone there?"

There was no response, but the unseen force she felt drew her to the center of the room. The door slammed shut and the force of the darkness surrounded her being.

"Ava, we are predestined to be bonded!" Ava heard the musical voice again as she moved closer to the source "As it was at the instance of the forge, heart to hand and hand to heart, the soul of the sword chooses its wielder."

Ava found that she could not speak, she could not respond to the call of the sword, as no words would come when she tried to communicate with the unknown spirit of the blade. On the northeast side of the room, the bright light of a glowing sword flashed in her eyes and her soul. As the sword continued its song, Ava's feet continued to move toward the glowing object despite her fear.

"From warrior to warrior, heart to heart, and soul to soul I have passed. I am the last touch of the lovers and the first glimpse of fear in my foes. Mastered by none, and feared by most. Independent and free, our souls have touched queens and princesses but no man-child can wield or control our spirit. Behold Last Kiss! I am your confidant, your partner!"

At the last word, Ava grabbed the hilt of the sword and pulled it out of its stand, holding it up over her head, pointing to the ceiling of the chamber. Tears were streaming from her eyes as the emotion and power of the sword bonded with her soul. The power of the blade surged through her arm and into her whole body. Light flooded from the glowing sword and lit the room. It was then that she noticed the radiant glow of the other swords in the chamber.

"Today we stand in service of the goddess and the light!" exclaimed the spirits of the remaining royal swords.

When the sword paused in its message, Ava was compelled to turn its point downward as she dropped to one knee. Ava then bowed her head and reveled in the newfound union with the sword.

She was not sure how long she knelt on the floor as the sword communed with her soul, Last Kiss replaying its battles and glories and revealing the souls of the rare women warriors previously bonded to Last Kiss. Then the final statement from the sword came and it almost broke Ava's heart.

"From this time on, we will speak no more; it is now the time of Ava and the building of her soul bond. Though I will feel right in your hand, you will not hear my song again, for it is now your song that must be heard. No one should know of our bond, though the day and time of its revelation is not far from this moment."

Ava was compelled to return the sword to its stand.

"As it was from the first warrior, so shall it be with each to follow. Come to me when you can, and I will train your mind and your soul. You are still so young. The time is near when we will draw our first drink of blood, and that will be the day of sorrows."

The sword went silent, and the light disappeared from the room. Ava fell to the floor and cried herself to sleep.

. . .

Ava grasped the hilt of Last Kiss, feeling the silk wrap of its handle. She lovingly pulled it from its stand. The young princess started immediately into the drills that looked like an intricate dance.

Ava found her time with Last Kiss too fleeting; she was pleased that this time she would be able to stay and work longer than any time before and strengthen the bond with her sword. When an hour had passed, Ava realized that the midday was waning and soon she would have to ready herself for daily training. She loved to train, but today would be a short exercise. Later in the day would be the banquet.

Today's celebration was the climax of the summer festival. However, this year's festival was especially exciting because tonight's banquet would celebrate Dominic's First Excursion. It signaled the time when Dom, having reached the age of twenty-one passes of the four seasons, would first go out to travel and explore the kingdom on his own. How Ava wished she could travel the kingdom. Ava thought of adventure and how exciting it would be to leave the confines of Castle Articia.

As Ava started to put Last Kiss into its holder, she stopped. It was just a feeling; she was not sure why, but today she was going to bring Last Kiss up to her room. She sheathed the sword and headed out of the armory.

3
A Deal with the Darkness

The dark citadel, hidden under Coal Mountains, was a remarkable structure. Even the goblins that occupied the caves above did not know of its existence. For more than a thousand passes of the seasons, the sorcerers of the darkness had been developing and perfecting their dark arts. Lately, the sorcerer master of the dark arts had been very busy building their plans of domination. In all that time, the only thing that had truly concerned them was the birth of the royal children.

"So the accursed offspring are fourteen now," the master of the darkness questioned the scribe.

"Yes, master, their day of birth has now had fourteen passes." The dark scribe responded. "It has caused quite the stir amongst all of the practitioners and the demons as well."

"Yes, I can see how the demons would be concerned. They do not like the balance that the children's existence represents." The dark sorcerer crossed the room and started turning the pages of a tome that rested on a stand in the middle of the chamber.

The chamber was the place where the citadel's master performed the strongest of the dark arts. It was a round room with obsidian black walls. For those who knew of their existence, the barely visible runes etched into the walls represented all of the classes of the dark arts. The runes circled the most powerful symbol of the dark deity, the head of a dire wolf.

The master of sorceries is the most powerful of the dark practitioners and occupies the chambers at the highest level of the citadel. Had the citadel been on an open plain, its four identical sides rising to a single point would have been observable, its form, and shape, of the dark citadel, known only by the practitioners who carved it out of the base of the mountain with their dark magic.

The master sorcerer flipped through the pages of the tome. "I remember a story in the archives about demons of significant power. Summoned to signal a catastrophic event, certainly an appropriate answer to the problem we have with the children. Those beasts would be a worthy match to their growing power."

"Have you the magic to summon such creatures?" the scribe queried.

"No, it is beyond my power. But I believe that if we align with the demons that have taken residence here on our world, we should be able to find a way to bring the demons through the rift between our worlds." The dark master turned to the scribe. "I have found this incantation, which may help to bring about the unbalancing." As he found the page, the practitioner stepped aside to allow the scribe to view the book. "What do you think?"

The scribe stepped up to the podium to read what the master had found. "Hmm, it is an interesting option. Clearly a good match for our situation, but can we control the beasts?"

Many years before the discovery of magic, demons had entered the world of Articia. They caused havoc wherever they passed. It was not until the elves of the other world arrived that Articia found some peace. The elves and the demons have an uneasy truce. When the people of Articia discovered magic, they learned that they could control some of the weaker demons and imps, but the more powerful demons worried the master sorcerer and his scribe. He would need an alliance with the lord of the demons if his plan were going to work.

"I think with the help of the demons already in our domain, we should be able to bind them," the practitioner said as he crossed the room and grabbed a scroll from his desk. "Take this to our contact in the demon territory and we will see if we get a positive response."

The scribe took the scroll and left to accomplish his dark task. He could not help but think that this proposal had the ring of disaster about it. If they could not control these new demons, it could mean the destruction of Articia.

The master continued to read the tome to look for additional clues to creating an unbalance that would give the darkness more power. *King Henry's brood is troublesome, especially the young princess,* he thought. *Her reported power is immense. We will have to eliminate her soon before she matures and has the ability to take the citadel down.*

...

"Baron Gerund, you take great risks meeting with our kind," the demon in the center of the chamber said to the lord of the northern wastes. The demon stood a full twenty hands tall, much larger than the man who stood nervously beside the great beast. It seemed rather impatient with the man from the north. "We have not had our morning meal yet and you know we prefer man meat to any other sustenance on your world."

"I appreciate that you have not succumbed to your natural instincts and have accepted my request for an audience," the baron responded. The baron was tall for a human but seemed like a dwarf standing next to the demon. "I have a proposal for you and your kind that I think you will find agreeable."

"You assume too much, human. Our kind rarely finds our dealings with your species to be agreeable. But I will tolerate you for the moment; it might be interesting to hear how you think we can have any kind of alliance." The demon stopped walking and stared down at the baron.

"You know of course about the birth of the royal children. They have now reached the age of fourteen." The baron was on the verge of terror having the demon stare at him; it took all of his willpower to keep from fleeing from the chamber.

"Yes, we felt their arrival long ago. It created quite the uproar here in our domain. Do not think that we are not aware of the relevance of their fourteenth year," the demon replied.

"It created quite a commotion amongst my allies as well. We have come to like our current position and our authority, and the

larger royal family threatens our lifestyle." The baron moved
back a step to put more space between him and the demon.

"We care not of such things; your human politics are trite
and meaningless to us," the demon responded.

"Yes, but you do care about the royal family's relationship
with the elves of the Vale. An alliance with me and mine is an
alliance against the elves and the dwarves."

The demon considered the words of the human at his feet.
How he despised their existence. The demon thought of the weak
truce they had with the accursed warriors of the light, though
the elves and the dwarves were not natural Artician beings, they
were loyal to the Artician king. The elves had come in pursuit of
the demons. The dwarves had arrived by accident. Being miners,
they had come through the rift in search of rare metals and could
no longer return to their own world. Both races had become a
thorn in the side of the demons.

"Go on." The demon seemed more interested now.

"Our practitioners of the dark arts, our mercenary soldiers,
and the noble families that do not support Henry would join the
demons and goblins against the royal family and their allies. This
alliance will give those who support the dark lord an advantage."
The baron finished, waiting for a response from the demon.

"Your proposal is intriguing, Baron, but I foresee a problem,"
the demon cautioned.

"What problem?" the baron asked.

"The youngest children of Henry must die before my kind
will take action to usurp the throne of Articia."

"We have a plan in place to eliminate the royal children; it
has already been arranged," the baron replied. "My people have
had our eyes on Henry's heirs for years and have started moving
to eradicate the brood."

The baron noticed the demon had raised eyebrow and heard
him murmur, "So you think you can exterminate the whelps."
The demon crossed the room so quickly that the baron, caught

off guard, howled as the demon grabbed the startled baron with one of its enormous hands and held him against the wall.

"It will be interesting to see your people at work. I will give you this one chance to get the job done." The demon dropped the baron to the floor. "I suggest you leave our domain before the feeding frenzy begins." The demon left the baron shaking on the floor as it exited the main chamber.

...

"So, do you think they have any chance of successfully completing that task?" the lesser demon asked as it stepped out of a hidden clutch in the wall of the room.

"No, I think they will fail miserably. They do not know what they face in the brood, and when they return to report their failure, we will be able to bind them to us. Soon they will come to beg us to complete the task that they cannot." The demon looked away as if scanning something a great distance away. "And they cannot even guess the great deception that has been placed in front of them."

"Our dark lord will be pleased," the lesser demon noted.

4
A Hidden Conspiracy

Alec grasped the wooden sword tightly despite the renewed pain that shot up his side and his arms. The red welts on his body were the cause of his discomfort, but he still lifted the sword to block his sister's attack in his attempt to receive no more bruises. Alec preferred competing with his sister at archery, or horseback riding, in which he was particularly talented. Nevertheless, here he was again, in the training yard taking another beating from his sister Ava. Alec had become an excellent swordsman, mostly thanks to Bryn's training and his dislike of the injuries he received from training with his sister. They learned early from the many sparring contests that Bryn arranged; the only people in the castle that could best him with a sword were his brothers Tristan and Dominic, the king himself, his sister Ava, and of course Bryn. In fact, Alec cannot remember anyone who even caused Bryn to break a sweat in competition.

Ava swung to his left, her sword making a loud thwack against his sword. His fingers instantly went numb. *How is Ava using magic to do that again!* He thought. The wooden swords they used for practice did not make the same satisfactory clang as the swords that clashed in battle, but they could still cause pain. Grunting with effort, he ducked again and aimed low for her legs. As agile as ever, she jumped the sword and came crashing back on the attack.

His feet skated across the gravelly dirt as his breath came quickly. Feinting to the left, he tried to trick Ava by coming under her swing. She pretended that his action fooled her until the last second when she backed up and quickly came up under his sword. It was one of Ava's signature moves, and he felt stupid for falling for it every time despite his knowledge of the tactic. His sister used the same strategy when she played chess, sacrificing her queen just to make the final checkmate with a pawn.

Ava stepped into his swing and was about to disarm him but Bryn intervened. "I almost forgot; you two need to get ready for the banquet your parents are holding for your brother's coming-of-age ceremony. Go now, or you'll be late."

Ava groaned, irritated that the spar ended just before her victory. Alec grinned, silently thanking the gods for his escape from additional bruises on his hammered body.

They hurried up to their bedchambers. The castle had a secret passage from the training ground to the sitting area of their rooms. The twins had discovered the dank and long-forgotten passage many years ago. It became important for the twins to use this route to the training grounds so that Ava could avoid being discovered running about in trousers. Her regular antics had already caused a stir among the royal staff. Seeing Ava in nontraditional attire for a princess of the realm would have sent the castle inhabitants into pandemonium. The servants tolerated much from the young twins, but they were traditionalists and would not be able to tolerate the princess walking the halls of the castle in her brother's trousers without a specific decree from King Henry.

The passage ended in the main room in the twins' bedchambers. Their father had tried to put them in separate lodgings years ago but had given up when they had both refused to eat, sleep, or do anything until the abomination ended. Instead, a door was constructed, at Ava request, between the two connected rooms so they could still be together. It allowed each of the siblings to have private space.

Aleczander washed from the basin and donned a royal blue tunic with ruffled sleeve ends; he always loved the light swoosh the fabric made as it slipped over his head. Most of Alec's clothing, including the tunic, is imported from the markets in Cyrus. The merchants of the eastern shore sold fabrics that folklore said to be sewn from the silk of remarkable worms raised by the elves of the Vale. His trousers and cape were fine-looking ivy green. He pulled on his favorite black boots. Looking in the mirror, he had to admit he looked good. *Look out ladies, here I come*, Alec thought as he attempted to pull a comb through his black curls.

He swore under his breath as his comb was stuck in his mass of hair. Alec stopped fussing as Ava took the comb from his hands and gently teased the curls out. "Patience is a virtue, little brother."

Alec smiled at his younger sister. He was her elder by only a few minutes, and he thought, *Even though you can still pummel me with that sword of yours, I can now out lift, out climb, out ride, and outrun you.*

Ava had washed her hair and brushed it out by the fireplace to dry it. It was still quite cold in Articia despite winter's waning. Once the season made it uncomfortable to set a fire, it would be more difficult to dry her hair; she would have to allow much more time to ready herself for castle events.

When her hair was clean and dry, it naturally curled and waved beautifully past her shoulder blades and down her back. Her midnight blue gown and deep green cloak were identical in color to his garments, so they matched. Ava looked in the mirror quickly. She never spent much time admiring herself in the reflecting glass; it was a functional device. Like her clothing, her brush, her comb, it served a purpose—to ensure that she would be presentable in court. Otherwise, she never really concerned herself with her looks. Though she did make the mistake once of asking Alec about her appearance. He completely misinterpreted her request; she had only wanted to know if she was presentable, but he had pulled out one particularly embarrassing love letter from a baron's son and read it aloud to her. It reminded her why she was not particularly fond of the note or its author.

Ava, your face was beautiful to gaze upon,
your cheekbones high and flushed with color
and seen with spotless complexion.
You full red lips curved in a smile,
straight nose curved only slightly,
not pudgy but not overly long.

Your chin is delicate but strong,
almost like iron-filled glass.
Your eyebrows are, like your hair,
jet black, but not too thick.
Your eyes, a stormy gray
were always hinting a smile.

Ava knew she was stunning and held herself like someone who knew it. However, that was the absolute worst poem she had ever gotten from any of the noble courtiers. "Alec! Where did you get that?" *Why did I keep it?* "Give it to me now!"

"Sure," Alec replied, handing her the parchment. "I made many copies." Aleczander smiled to himself as he took his sister's arm and led her down the hall. Though told by many that he was handsome, compared to Ava, he felt rather plain.

Despite their rush, the two walked into the grand hall a little late.

"I told you we should have skipped practice today," Alec hissed through his teeth as everyone in the room cheered for a prince and princess of their kingdom. While Dominic would be high king one day, and the only one who could not marry into another kingdom, Tristan and Aleczander would be kings, and Ava a queen with many freedoms that their oldest brother would not realize. The position of high queen would be reserved for Dominic's wife, whenever he got around to choosing one; but there was no rush while King Henry was still on the throne.

"It's called being fashionably late; it's something normal princes and princesses do," she whispered as she smiled and waved to a particularly attractive noble's son.

Alec winced at his father's glare as he and Ava took seats on each side of their mother, as they always did during formal occasions. She nodded to them, smiling as if to greet them. However, her motherly demeanor did not fool the twins.

"The point of this affair is for your brothers to be cheered, not their younger siblings." Her voice was icy and meant to be harsh. Having dealt with this their whole lives, they knew what to do.

"I'm sure they will, mother," Alec started, "because the attire that you acquired in Cyrus for our brothers…"

"… is sure to leave all of the nobles in the hall in jealous admiration," Ava finished, not even bothering to look at her mom.

Alec and Ava had been finishing each other's sentences for years. This canny ability is one of the unusual traits that the goddess gave to the Artician twins. The queen found this trait charming in her youngest children and the pair used it to soften her mood whenever they found themselves in a tough spot, and the twins frequently found themselves in a tough spot.

Their mother sighed. Queen Angelica of Articia looked more like a mother than a queen as she straightened her son's cloak and pushed a lock of Ava's hair behind her ear. She smiled as she turned back to their father.

"Nice job on Alec's hair, Ava." The queen commented as the corners of Ava's mouth turned up slightly and Aleczander's face turned a slight shade of red.

Before Ava had a chance to tease him, the front doors flew open with a bang, and in walked Tristan and Dominic, clad in the magnificent gold and silver of the royal family. The only ones allowed to wear such brilliant colors on that day were Dominic, Tristan, and their mother and father. Ava and Aleczander would not normally include such extravagance in their wardrobes until they came of age at sixteen.

Dominic took a seat next to Ava and Tristan sat next to Alec. All of her children surrounded Queen Angelica. The king sat alone at a solitary table, according to a tradition that had begun a millennium ago when Articia consisted of mostly nomadic tribes and the leader of the tribe sat alone above the rest of the tribe. Later in the evening, Dominic would leave his mother's side at the table and sit at the right hand of the king. This would be the symbol of succession for the royal family. The King and his heir sit alone at their own table at all royal functions. Dom now sat at the table with the king as a symbol of the royal succession.

Of course, the funniest thing about the formal occasions was that they did not match the preferred life of the royals. The family usually took their meals at a table in the kitchens, a most informal setting. It was especially cozy in the winter when the cook fires warmed the area, making it the warmest and most comfortable location in Castle Articia. Though it was unusual for any royal family to eat in a kitchen, the king treated the entire castles workforce as part of his extended family. There is no one in his employ whose name and story he does not know. It is because of this that so many ordinary folk are devoted to the king. It is why they all take up arms to defend the king and country so readily whenever needed. He is noble and distant when he is required to be, but openly friendly to his subjects when not involved in matters of the state.

It was unusual that there was only a high king in Articia. It has always been a tradition and necessity to have large royal families to manage the significant amount of territory in the kingdom. A plague had afflicted Articia when King Henry was a young man and all of his siblings and his mother succumbed to its deadly effect. As a result, for a relatively brief time in Articia's long history, Articia had only one king. When Henry suddenly became king, his advisors quickly worked with him to return stability to the kingdom. The council set up baronies and a subordinate noble system to manage the growing needs of the plague-devastated kingdom of Articia. Most of the current barons in Articia are not directly related to the royal family. Now, the system was engrained and the current nobles wanted to maintain and even increase their power in the management of their territories and over the people who resided on their lands.

Their fear of losing their lands, authority, and status grew as the king's family grew. The animosity now heightened on Dominic's ascension; when a royal child reached such a rite of passage as the First Excursion, there would be talk of awarding him a territory and anointing him a king thereof. Speculation arose as to which pieces of whose territory might be reclaimed for this purpose.

Alec watched as Ava affectionately pushed a blonde curl back from Dominic's eyes. Alec and Ava had always been an oddity when it came to appearance. Their parents had blonde and light brown hair. The family was known for their deep blue eyes as well. But Alec and Ava had coal black hair and stormy gray eyes.

"How long do you think you will be gone, Dom?" Ava inquired.

Alec realized she was already worrying about the year in which princes who came of age traveled the kingdom to prove themselves worthy of the throne. Dom would not leave for a week at least; the feast was not even over yet and she was already worrying about him. Alec shook his head. Even as a toddler, Ava had fawned over her older brothers.

"I will be gone only for about six turns of the moon, Ava," Dom replied. "I couldn't stay away from my favorite sister for a full year."

"You mean your only sister," she said as she beamed at him.

The first course of the meal was collard greens, neither liked, nor consumed, by the royal children. Unfortunately, this lack of interest in the current course of sustenance usually left the royal children open to other activities. Tristan and Ava were using their inherent magic to annoy the royal chamberlain across the table with minor pyrotechnics.

The exasperated sigh from the chamberlain caught the attention of King Henry, who glared at the pair of siblings. The chamberlain suffered frequently from the antics of Tristan and Ava. Alec just smiled, knowing that Ava and Tristan's were just too mischievous to restrain themselves and their actions would be replayed many times tonight.

Alec often wondered about the blessing of magical capabilities. It seemed that the goddess bestowed the gift of cerebral arts completely randomly. The goddess had also bestowed a gift on his father and mother. Tris wondered why he and Dominic did not share their gift of sorcery. Though he sometimes thought he might enjoy the use of magical powers, he did not envy the free time his sister and brother lost to learning magical control.

As Alec was absentmindedly monitoring his sister, he looked across the room to admire Princess Kaitlin, who had traveled from the neighboring kingdom of Cyrus to participate in the annual Artician festival. When his glance swung back to Ava, Alec saw his sister's eyes turn from their normal gray to a light blue. "Ava, your eyes," he whispered.

She stopped and sighed as the color in her eyes slowly changed back. Ava was unique in both her appearance and her skills. Shortly after she had started to exhibit signs that she had magical talent; it became obvious that she had more power than most. Ava had other unique abilities that none who practiced the arts in the past had ever revealed. Most remarkable, and unique, was the change in the color of her eyes.

When Ava started her magical discipline training, they discovered that her eyes would change colors as she progressed through various difficulties of the arts she performed. When she executed rather simple acts of sorcery, her eyes would change from gray to light blue. The magical scholars tested every extreme of her magical capabilities and discovered that there was a progression, from light blue to light violet, light violet to green, green to light brown, light brown to dark violet, and dark violet to a blazing gold.

When Ava had reached the golden stage, all hell broke loose. She lost complete control and wild magic erupted from her body. Fortunately, the magical scholars were the ones to discover this about Ava and were able to contain her power; otherwise, she may have destroyed the entire castle and everyone in it. At that point, King Henry had put her into a strict magical training program so that she would learn to control her magical capabilities.

Despite a considerable amount of examination, the magical scholars could not determine what caused the change in Ava's eyes. It was clear only that it coincided with her use of her magical abilities.

As the guests in the hall finished the collard greens, the stewards removed the empty plates and started the next course, a breaded onion soup. This meal was one of the local favorites. The queen sighed relief, knowing that this was one of her children's favorites as well. She was confident that things would now settle down at the table.

Alec spooned his soup into his mouth and turned his attention back to Princess Kaitlin. Her brown hair waved down her back, with some of the strands tied and braided at the top. Her dress was a crimson color, though her cloak was green like his cape. However, the thing that caught Alec's attention the most was her eyes. They were a remarkable chocolate brown; to Alec, they were very warm and welcoming.

The third course of the meal was a cured beef that was a favorite of the royal family. The meal was specifically selected for this event because it was one of Dominic's preferred meals. Aleczander was beginning to grow bored after he had finished his serving. Then his father announced a break in the dining for a bit of dancing. Alec smiled as Ava slid down in her seat.

Several of the younger boys were so eager to ask her to dance that they had crashed into each other on the way to the table. This was causing a major problem for the other young nobles trying to reach Ava. Still, one lucky boy, at least three years younger, had managed to reach her.

"May I have this dance?" he squeaked.

Before Ava could answer, Tristan took his sister's arm. "I'm afraid you're going to have to wait, good sir, because I'm claiming my right as a prince of Articia for the first dance of the night with my sister." Tristan looked over his shoulder at the disappointed boy as he led Ava on to the dance floor.

Aleczander turned to look for his preferred partner for the night and caught her gazing at him. She looked down immediately, her cheeks growing pink and making her even more beautiful. Aleczander strode confidently, or at least hopefully, towards the princess from Cyrus.

"May I have this dance, Princess Kaitlin?" He bowed to her and kissed the tips of her fingers, very formally, even for him.

She smiled sweetly. "I will dance with you on one condition, Prince Aleczander." Her big brown eyes twinkled with mischief.

Realizing he was about to play into her hand, Alec straightened from his bow and gave her his arm as he spoke in a very silly and low voice, "I will do anything for such a fair princess."

Kaitlin raised her eyebrows and giggled, then said very seriously, "Please tell your sister and brother to stop shooting sparks across the table; their aim is horrific and I'm terrified they'll hit me." She grinned shyly.

Alec was a little surprised. *So, she had caught that*, he thought. Not only was she beautiful, but she had an eye for magical energies, even the more subtle magics that his brother and sister were performing tonight. It took a certain amount of talent or familiarity to see the magical activity. Alec was impressed.

As he took her arm, he replied, "Gladly. For you, Princess, it would be my pleasure. But do not expect them to listen to me."

She pretended to be puzzled. "Not even your twin? I would not know for sure, but I thought there was a special blood bond from being someone's double born."

Alec smiled a little as he thought of trying to control his sister. It would be going against the blood bond to suggest a change in behavior. Alec chuckled. "Regardless, I'd like to see anyone try telling my sister what to do. She can be quite stubborn, especially where I am involved."

Alec escorted Kaitlin onto the dance floor and twirled her around so he was facing the deep brown pools that were her eyes. They were happy, delighted even, intelligent, understanding, and welcoming; but underneath all that, they were somewhat sad, almost yearning. Before his eyes could inquire deeper into hers, she giggled, which brought him out of his daze. Alec stepped back and looked at her with confusion. She giggled again. "It's our third dance and almost every girl here is throwing daggers at me with her eyes."

He furrowed his brows as he turned to look. Sure enough, a group of the nobles' young daughters had caught him looking their way and hurriedly turned their eyes to the floor and the ceiling. They had clearly been glaring at Kaitlin.

Alec had not realized how long he had been gazing at her while they danced. When the song ended, he bowed to Kaitlin. "I'm afraid I must decline on the next dance, Princess." He kissed her hand, and as he made his way towards his sister, he whispered in Kaitlin's ear, "One more dance would have started more than just rumors; we'd have a brawl—you versus the rest of the over-enthusiastic young ladies in this hall." She giggled again, and then smiled as a much younger noble's son asked her to dance.

Alec shook his head and walked towards his sister, his curls bouncing. Ava was attempting to escape a young noble trying to ask her for a second dance. Alec smoothly intervened with an "I'm sorry," correctly interpreting the look of the young man he thought might be Cyran, one of Kaitlin's younger brothers. "But I must borrow my sister for a few dances." He whisked his sister away before the young man could protest.

"Thank you," she whispered.

Alec rolled his eyes. "Is it so bad just to dance with them?"

Ava glared at him. "All they want to talk about is themselves and the great things they have accomplished," Ava said with irritation. "Half of the remarkable deeds I am positive never happened at all. Most were remarkably outlandish and the remaining stories were highly questionable." Ava sighed as they crossed the dance floor. "Then there are those who find that all they want to talk about is me, which is far worse since they know nothing about me but think they do!"

Alec laughed at Ava's disgust as she continued her tirade, saying, "The worst was the one you chased away. I thought it was going to be all right to chat with him until he recited a poem he wrote *for me*."

Alec stopped dancing and had to laugh,

"Stop it! The poem was terrible, worse than the one you found." She paused. "All he talked about was his older brother anyway, who he seems to admire quite a bit."

"Sounds interesting," Alec, stated with a wink.

"At least the stories he told about his brother were believable," Ava responded. "I am most intrigued about him. But he is the only young gentleman in this room who hasn't tried to ask me to dance yet."

Alec chuckled silently at his sister's subdued but passionate outburst. "Where is this disgrace of a man who has not even asked you to dance yet?"

Ava rolled her eyes and pointed him out. "His young brother gestured to him so many times, he couldn't possibly have missed that we were talking about him. I think his face is burnt into my memory."

Alec examined the face of the young man for which Ava had inclined her head. "Hmm, I thought I knew every noble gentleman in court, but I do not recognize him."

The young man was maybe fourteen of average height. He looked lean but strong. He shifted in his seat and in the twist of cloth; Alec saw a glimpse of muscular arms. His chin was strong and sharp, his face angled. His hair was brownish-blonde and curled around his ears. It flipped up at the edges where it cut off at his forehead.

"He is quite handsome, Ava. Maybe you should ask him to dance," Alec quipped as he caught sight of the young man's brooding amber eyes. "He looks so ... bored."

I suppose this young man is sweet on the eyes to the young women in the hall, Alec thought, but he knew his sister rarely saw the world quite the same as any normal girl. Not only did she know how to use weapons, but she also dabbled in musical performance, not to mention the use of scholarly magic, something very few people could achieve. It put quite a twist on her character, making it difficult for her to relate to the other young women of Articia. No, she would have no interest in most of the boys here this evening. Somehow, this young noble was different. There was something about him.

"He seems all right to me, Ava. Not self-absorbed at least, Handsome, if you like pretty boys." The last part was just more of Alec's teasing, and she knew it, but did not rise to the bait. Instead, she made a curious noise and turned to the door.

"What is it, Ava?" Alec asked, concerned.

Looking up at him, she responded, "A messenger is about to come through that door, but I'm not sure what he's going to say."

She occasionally had these visions; he remembered overhearing a conversation between Brendan, the royal mage and Ava's tutor, and his father about his sister's ability to foresee things. They said that it was common for powerful practitioners of the magical arts. The fact that she could do it still made him uneasy.

They danced right into the next ballad as he waited in uneasy suspense. Sure enough, a few minutes later, the door flew open and outside in the courtyard a messenger dismounted his horse and ran through the door. After bowing to the king and delivering a roll of parchment, the messenger left as quickly as he had arrived. King Henry read the message quietly and then looked around the room.

The king seemed troubled as he addressed the guests. "I'm afraid I must postpone the rest of this lovely evening to deal with a matter that has come to my attention and that I must not ignore, so I must bid you all goodnight." The queen took the king by the arm as he turned for the door. "I hope you enjoyed the celebration and especially the collard greens."

Alec immediately looked up to his father. "Collard greens" was the prearranged code word for possible danger. Alec had always thought it was strange that before each public event, they would discuss a set of codes for different situations. Alec and his siblings were always amused that the word chosen was something that the royal children truly disliked, like collard greens or religious studies. He had not believed that they would ever use the code words.

Ava gave him a worried look and noticed that Dominic and Tristan were already moving toward the large tapestry along the back wall of the hall as the king and the queen left the chamber by the main doors. Alec and Ava did not wait for additional confirmation and walked casually towards the tapestry. Behind, it hid a door to the back corridor. When they entered, Dominic and Tristan were waiting with swords drawn. Dom looked to Alec and Ava and said, "We are not alone; I saw movement down the hall." His eldest brother was pointing to a bend in the passage that led to the family quarters.

Ava sighed, and without breaking stride, she reached under the folds of her dress and drew a hidden dagger. It had always been the tradition of the royal family to carry their weapons to any formal occasion. Henry's children had never heard of a need to use them before tonight. The four siblings continued down the hall cautiously with Dominic leading and Tristan providing a rear guard. It was not long before shadows started to close in on them.

"Dark magic," Dominic shouted, "Ava . . . !"

Before he could complete his sentence, a wave of power emitted from Ava's palm as her gray eyes progressed quickly to a light brown. This happened every time Ava was gathering her power. Alec braced himself for the explosion of magic that those light brown eyes indicated. Like the wave of a powerful hand, the force of Ava's magic felled the foreign men in the hallway and the sounds of their grunts and metal banging into walls filled the air. Alec drew his sword, Shadow Fang, and moved up beside Ava to wait for what was coming down the hall.

"Alec, cover the rear!" Tristan shouted as he moved past Alec to stand next to Dominic. With Shadow Fang in his raised arm, Alec stepped behind Ava and scanned the darkness behind his position.

"Ava, a little light please," Dominic requested. Ava made a motion with her hand and flames of light flew out in front of them; she turned and repeated it behind.

"How did they get behind us?" Ava shouted as she saw the threat past Alec. He watched as two armed men approached them cautiously from behind. Tristan smiled at his brother Dominic as the stunned men in front of them stood back up and collected their senses.

Dominic needed no prodding as they moved in quickly to engage the intruders before they could recover their weapons from the ground. Tristan was approaching his first target when he called out, *"Tartarus inferi"* and his sword glowed in a blue flame as he struck at the first man. Dominic moved in on a second. Alec waited for the two men who were behind them to engage before he struck, while Ava took the opportunity to pull a second dagger from a fold in her cloak.

Believing that he faced an inexperienced youth, the first attacker made a fatal mistake; as he raised his sword to strike, Alec drove in fast with Shadow Fang and his sword bit deep into the unfortunate warrior's flesh. The battle was on!

Ava saw her brother take down a man to her right, and immediately more men jumped out of the shadows. She tensed as she heard Tristan strike and kill another man-of-arms with his sword Silver Bane. Dom had already sunk his royal sword Ghost

Touch into many a foe. He pressed forward to engage another. How she wished to have the familiar handle of her sword, Last Kiss! Despite the fact that women were not allowed to train in the martial arts. Well she trained harder than most men train, and wished that she could defy tradition and had worn her sword as her brothers did. Without Last Kiss, she had to make do with her daggers and her magic.

Ava's training became a significant advantage for her in this skirmish with the first enemy she encountered. The ferociousness of her attack surprised the thug, who was not expecting a woman to be skilled in battle. Ava gripped her daggers and twirled quickly around her attacker, sinking one dagger into the stomach of that unfortunate soul. Blood now soaked his shirt as the man-at-arms started falling backwards.

Ava had to parry the thrust of another warrior because she tarried too long trying to retrieve her first dagger from the body of the unfortunate opponent. She grabbed the dying man's sword from his weakened hand and swung it under her arm to stop the progress of a man approaching from behind her. Her gown severely restricted her freedom of movement, a gown now covered with the blood of her unknown assailants.

They fought their way down the hall, "There are *a lot* of them!" Dominic called as he led them all into Ava and Aleczander's chambers. Tristan closed and locked the door and stood by while Alec and Dominic searched the room.

The sounds of the palace guard fighting the men-of-arms filled the hallways. After what seemed like an eternity, the noise subsided. The four children of Henry waited in the room for the all-clear signal so they could reunite with their mother and father. Dominic stood guard at the door while Tristan stood at the window that was open to the yard.

Dom heard the call of the captain of the guard at the door, who relayed the prearranged code. Dominic looked back at his siblings and nodded before he opened the door. Many men lay wounded or dead in the upper atrium as the guard addressed him.

"Sire, is all well with you, your brothers, and your sister?" the captain inquired.

"Yes, captain, we fared well. Is the enemy still in the castle?" Dominic asked as he stepped out the door into the atrium.

"Yes, but we have driven them to the concourse. Your father has joined the fight and sent me to see to you, your brothers, and sister," he replied.

"Tristan, it looks like things have settled down here. Let us go and help father clean up what remains." Dominic looked toward Alec, "Alec, lock the doors behind us and wait for our return. I believe this will be over soon."

Dominic and Tristan darted out of the room and turned down the hall toward the sounds of battle. Alec closed and locked the door and turned to Ava. "What the heck is going on here? We never actually had to fight before, though we have had plenty of drills. I never expected to have to use my skills for real!" Alec was clearly upset.

"Keep your voice down, Alec. We're alive, and together, and that's what matters." She turned and looked at the door. She knew that behind it was blood. There was lots of blood. She thought about the recent events and realized that it was not the actual blood or the battle that bothered her, but what the result of her actions meant, the real meaning. She thought about the loss and the lives that she and her siblings had extinguished. The men would have no second chance to change who they were and what they had done. They were condemned to the abyss, to the darkness. There would be no chance for redemption.

"The time will come when we will draw our first drink of blood, and that will be the day of sorrows. "

Ava recalled the words of Last Kiss and now understood their meaning. Her innocence was now lost, forever.

She had not realized how much it would bother her to take a life, but it was necessary in some situations, and this had been one of them. Dom and Tris would tease her and call her weak. To care for the lives of the enemy you took was not something you are supposed to allow yourself to feel.

As Alec looked at his sister, trying to understand her sudden silence, Ava jumped to her feet and grabbed Last Kiss. Sensing the danger from behind the tapestry on the wall, Alec jumped up with Shadow Fang and stood beside her.

Faster than they thought possible, a dark figure moved out from behind the tapestry and angled toward the pair. Ava, mostly on instinct, parried the lightning thrust, clearly aimed at her heart.

"An assassin, he came in through our training yard passage!" Ava yelled to Alec.

Alec was kicking himself mentally for not checking the passage when he and his brothers checked the room. He closed the distance with the assassin to help keep his sister safe. *This guy is good,* Alec thought, *not your standard man-at-arms. How is he managing to keep both of us from scoring a hit?* A dance of blades continued for what seemed an eternity before Alec allowed himself to become distracted. The assassin took quick advantage of this critical mistake and came in under Alec's thrust to score a vicious slash to his arm.

"Arrrrgh." The blow forced Alec to withdraw a few steps, clearly out of the fight for the moment.

Ava, seeing her brother's distress, stepped in front of her brother to keep the assassin from finishing the job. She could not contain the rage building inside her as she directed the power of her magic at the assassin.

Alec was holding his wound to staunch the bleeding. "Ava, no!" he shouted, as he watched his sister lose control. Her eyes were changing colors rapidly now.

As the assassin stepped in to what he thought was going to be an easy strike, the man looked into her blazing golden eyes. The assassin's eyes widened as a burst of wild energy exploded from her body. The burst of lightning and power blew him into the wall. Her magic immediately extinguished the life of assassin; Ava's power was too immense for him to survive the attack.

"Ava, regain control! You must regain control!" Alec yelled. Ava did not hear him as the energy continued to flow from her body, igniting the tapestry on the wall. Seeing the tapestry burst into flames and realizing his sister was lost in the power, Alec yelled a prayer, "Adara, help us!"

Alec covered his head, expecting the castle to collapse under the assault of Ava's uncontrolled magical power. As a soft light filled the room, Alec heard a whisper in his head just before he passed out, *all will be well, my son.*

...

Alec opened his eyes as he heard Ava speaking through the door: "Who wishes to speak to the willow?" Willow was actually one of Ava's chosen names; all of the royal family members had code names that described trees in the royal garden. The royal family never shared these names outside the family.

"Birch wishes it to be so." Ava smiled and opened the door for their father. The queen followed the king into the room and turned toward Alec with a look of concern. He now realized that he was lying in a pool of his own blood. Some of the elite guards were behind the pair and turned back to guard the door to the siblings' chambers.

Alec's mother saw the severity of the gash on his arm and started an incantation as she held her hand over the wound, "*Lumen sano!*" Alec's pain began to lessen. As she finished saying the phrase, the wound stopped bleeding and closed up.

"Well, Alec, it looks like you managed to get your first battle scar," Dominic said as he and Tristan entered the chamber.

The king and his aide moved across the room to examine the assassin. The aide reached down and pulled a brooch out of what remained of the assassin's cloak. He looked up toward the king and said, "Sire, this man was from the assassin's guild of the Mildanar tribes to the north."

"You are correct," Henry responded, "I recognize his affiliation from what remains of his garb." King Henry looked over at his wife and Alec, "Will our youngest son survive?" the king said sardonically for he knew that wound Alec received was not fatal.

"Of course, his wound was not so bad" Queen Angelica replied calmly. The queen stood up from tending Alec and walked toward the king. "It looks like we may have to commit more attention to our holdings in the northern territories."

The king nodded to his wife. She was always the politician and well aware of the pending danger a large royal family represents to the many duchies in the kingdom. "Well, gentleman, looks like you got your first taste of what we will face ahead. I would express how well you did protecting your sister but it appears that she managed to handle these things well enough on her own."

The king reached down to pick up Last Kiss. As he lifted the curved blade from the floor, sparks flew from it. King Henry quickly handed it to Ava. As he rubbed his hand, he commented, "It seems that your sword is not pleased that I handled it, Ava."

The royal swords had individual personalities and always selected their wielders; such was the way of the weapons' magic. Last Kiss was no exception. The soul of the sword would not allow a male to take hold of the blade.

In order for a sword to have power, it had to have a kind of intelligence, and generations of use by the royal family had added personality to each sword. When members of the royal family turned twelve, the royal family held a ceremony in to the chamber of the swords so each royal could be "selected."

Each sword has its own history and selects its new wielder based on that history. Alec's sword, Shadow Fang, one of the oldest of the royal swords, had been a gift to the eighth king of Articia, Heldar the Great, who aided the Silver Mountain dwarves in their war with the barbarian tribes of the east. Heldar united the tribes of the lower valley into what is Greater Articia today.

Tristan's sword, created in a time of strife and war, glimmered with flame against its silver blade. The dwarves of northern tribes had united with a group of outcast Silver Mountain dwarves in a revolt against the dwarven King Th'grem. It was the first time in history that the dwarves had fought each other. King Eric the Gold, of Articia, agreed to help the Silver Mountain dwarves defeat the dwarves of the northern tribes, and the weapon masters of Silver Mountain forged a sword for the great king that commemorated that occasion. It was the first sword the dwarves had ever created to kill another dwarf, thus its name of Silver Bane.

Ghost Touch, Dominic's sword, had an unusual history. It was the first dwarven sword given to a royal family member not forged specifically for royal use. One of the dwarven weapon masters named Garn had forged the sword as a way to commune with the dead. He had lost his beloved daughter in an accident in the silver mines and was so distraught that he neglected all else to forge the sword so he could speak to her again. He did not succeed in getting the magic to commune but managed to forge a sword that drew energy out of those it struck and transferred that energy back into the wielder, making him stronger. In his despair for his failure to forge a sword to commune with the dead, Garn neglected his other children. Because of this, his remaining children had to fend for themselves.

One early summer day one of those children, Grenden, encountered danger while returning from foraging in the forest. A mountain bear attacked this child of Garn and as he tried to flee the beast, he became trapped in a gorge. High Prince Hilgar, son of Eric the Gold, was out hunting and came upon the distressed dwarf. The prince fought the mountain bear off with his sword, rescued the son of Garn, and escorted the boy to his home. When Grenden returned, Garn was so troubled over the possibility of losing another child that he snapped out of his grief and recommitted himself to taking care of the remaining members of his family. To show gratitude, he gave Hilgar Ghost Touch as a gift.

Last Kiss was a special sword because it was the only sword forged for and specifically wielded by a warrior queen. In the northern reaches, beyond the kingdom of Mildanar was a band of nomads. They lived a hard life. In the nomadic society, women as well as men fought and trained out of necessity. Arianna was one of the strongest willed of the women of her tribe. In the winter of her fifteenth year, she had a vision dream from the goddess Adara that she was to journey east to the land of the dwarves to receive a gift. On this journey, she met and fell in love with Prince E'ward, son of King Telnard of the Articia territories. The two continued to the dwarven lands only to find the dwarves in battle with the goblins of Coal Mountain. Arianna could not resist participating in the battle and Prince E'ward joined the fray, not willing to let the remarkable warrior woman, of whom he had grown fond, fight alone.

In gratitude to this remarkable pair, the dwarves forged two swords. Last Kiss, the first sword forged specifically for a woman, and First Touch, the sword that King Henry now wields. When the pair returned to the territory of Articia, they raised quite the stir. Young girls and women came out of their dwellings to witness the sword-bearing warrior woman whose reputation had preceded her into the kingdom. Prince E'ward and Arianna were married soon after and none in court or in the entire kingdom dared to question her breaking the tradition against women carrying weapons. To this day, they do not know if the gift the goddess spoke to Arianna was the sword or Prince E'ward.

King Henry rubbed his hands, which were now a little numb from handling Last Kiss, and turned to his youngest children. Alec and Ava looked at each other with trepidation. "Um, I have been training with Alec for a couple of years now" Ava stated.

Dominic and Tristan broke into laughter as they saw the look on the faces of their younger brother and sister. The queen smiled at both of them and turned to the King "I will be heading down to the infirmary now to see if I can help the healers comfort and heal some of our brave warriors who were wounded in the fray."

The king nodded to his aide, who stood and called out to the elite guard to provide an escort for the queen. He then looked over at his younger children. "Why do you two look surprised? Did you really think anything would happen in my castle that I did not know about?"

Ava looked at her brother and started to smile. "So you are not mad that I broke tradition and that I am training in the martial arts?"

The king looked at her and said, "Since you were two years old, we all knew you would have it no other way. With your stubbornness and your athleticism, many of the court commented on how much you resembled your ancestor, Queen Arianna, in both spirit and attitude. But I knew you were destined to be a warrior princess when you, as a toddler, sneaked behind me into the sword chamber and Last Kiss lit up like faerie fire."

The king then turned to his aide. "We have to get back to our duty and secure the castle. We still have many frightened guests in the hall below that we need to attend. Arrange for escorts so they may all return to the safety of their quarters." As he headed to the door of Ava and Alec's rooms, the king stated, "I think under the current circumstances we should arrange for the nobles to return to their respective estates until we finish investigating the culprit of tonight's action."

The aide called out to the hallway to members of the elite guard, "Leave a small contingent to guard the royal quarters. The rest of you come with me to secure the rest of the castle and grounds."

The king turned back to the twins, "Later we will have a discussion about the carnage in this room." The king moved swiftly down the hall with his elite guard to the lower sections of the castle, as two stewards came in to remove the body of the assassin. Once the body was removed, the royal chambermaids arrived to clean the "carnage" that the twins had wrought in their residence.

"Ava, let's retire to our own rooms while this area is cleaned. Mother has ordered me to rest and recover from my wound. By the way, I really liked that tapestry you destroyed. I hope you plan to get me a new one on our birthday." He smiled back to her as he walked toward his room.

Ava entered her private bedroom and sat on her bed. She again reflected on the skirmish that had just occurred. She had not realized how much it would bother her to take a life, even though it was necessary in some situations, and this was one of them. The words of Last Kiss entered her thoughts again.

"The time will come when we will draw our first drink of blood, and that will be the day of sorrows."

Ava thought of the men she had sent to the abyss.

5
History Class

After one particularly tough training session with the weapon master, Alec was rather sore and did not envy that his sister still had to attend additional classes. After Ava cleaned up, she was going to be heading right up to Brendan's tower with Tristan to train in the magical arts. "Are you sure you have enough energy left to go to class today, Ava?" he asked.

"I am actually very excited about class today, Alec. We are not specifically learning anything about the magical arts today. We are talking about the history of magic and where it began," Ava exclaimed, "I can't wait to get started!"

"You are obsessed, Ava," Alec retorted. Ava just smiled shrugged she ran off to her room to clean up for class.

...

Dominic and Tristan ran into Ava at the bottom of the tower stairs. "Dom, are you coming to class today?" Ava asked.

"Yes, father *suggested* that it was important for the future king of Articia to understand its history," Dominic responded as he rolled his eyes, "especially after the events of this year's festival. Anyways, I have never been in Brendan's tower before and I am curious."

"Hey, wait for me!" Alec called. Ava looked back and smiled. "I thought you hated classes, Alec."

Alec caught his breath and responded, "Well, you made it sound so interesting, and with Dom and Tris here, I didn't have anything else to do for the next couple of hours."

They climbed up the tower stairs into the main chamber of Brendan's study. The round room had four windows facing out to the major Artician compass points. Brendan's tower was the largest of the castle's four towers. It measured thirty feet from the north to the south windows. A staircase, just offset from north window, circled up to another level that housed Brendan's private quarters. None of the royal children have ever visited or been invited to Brendan's private chambers.

Hanging from the stone supports, that held the up the staircase of the circular tower, were many tapestries, each depicting a part of the history of the kingdom of Articia. Brendan's desk was just beside the southern window and was piled high with parchments and books.

The center of the floor had soft baglike chairs for the students to sit in. Ava had asked once about the design of the chairs and Brendan had told her that he had read about them in the castle's archives. The documents described chairs filled with beans, though why someone would waste food to make furniture confused Ava. Brendan used the down of a many young fowl to fill his "bean" chairs and this made them very comfortable.

"Please take your seats and we will begin," Brendan announced. He waited for all of his students to be seated, and chuckled when he saw Dominic and Alec take two of the seats uncomfortably. It was the first time either had tried to sit in the soft chairs and both of them squirmed until they found just the right angle.

Brendan walked to the edge of his desk and started to speak. "I am going to start at the start of time. In the beginning, there was the void. The lands and the sky did not exist. Darkness ruled until the goddess Adara came into being with a burst of light."

"Adara did not always exist?" Ava questioned.

"No," Brendan replied. "Before her, there was only darkness. But the void could not persist on its own and Adara came into being to balance the overbearing darkness with the light," Brendan said as he walked over to a scale he used to weigh out his magical and scientific potions and powders.

"The balance is now the sole responsibility of Adara's consort, Aris. Aris came into being because of the need to balance the light and the darkness. The symbol of the god Aris is the scale." Brendan pointed to the device on the table. "It is the charge of Aris to maintain the balance of darkness and light. For without darkness, we would not fully appreciate the light."

Alec had not known that the goddess Adara and the god Aris did not always exist. He was starting to understand why Ava was so interested in history.

Brendan continued. "Soon after Adara brought light to the void, our land began to change. Plants and animals began to appear in response to the light. Eventually humankind came to the land that we now call Greater Articia."

"Did the land have a different name before it was Articia?" Alec asked.

"No, it was just the land," Brendan replied. "Humankind did not give the land a name until it stopped wandering. Let us continue. The first people were nomadic. They never settled in any region but lived off the land wherever they went. Adara did not interfere and only watched as the people developed into a civilized society." Brendan sat in the chair in the middle of the room.

"Then the darkness of the void revolted against Aris and disrupted the balance of darkness and light." Brendan paused here with a look of concern on his face. "The cataclysmic rift corrupted the land and some believe that this caused some of the beasts of the world to change. The old legends say that darkness corrupted humankind until they became goblins and demons. Those legends also state that some of the animals were corrupted as well and became the imps and the wolug."

As Brendan completed the word *wolug*, the hair on Ava's arm rose. She began to feel very uncomfortable. "Why did some of the humans become goblins and demons?"

"It was said that those who did not have innate magical ability before the enlightenment became goblins and those who did have innate magical ability became demons. We all know of the goblins, but few of us have ever seen a demon up close," Brendan said, "and let's hope none of you ever gets the chance." The mage sat back in the chair at his desk and turned to the students. "The imps act as servants to the sorcerers. They are attracted to the dark magic that the sorcerers perform. The imps can be rather nasty if you do not have the necessary magical skills to counter their innate spell-casting capability," Brendan warned.

"Recently, through our interactions with the elves of the Vale, we learned that all of these dark creatures were not specifically corrupted by the darkness but were thrown out of a mystical place in another world called Eden. We also learned that the darkness enticed the banished beasts to pass through the rift into our world. The worst of these creatures is the wolug."

"I have never heard of a wolug. Are they not common?" Alec asked.

Dominic and Tristan looked at Alec with surprise. They had not realized just how sheltered their younger siblings were from the dangers of the world.

"They are not common," Brendan replied, "and they represent the worst of the dark beasts. They look much like the wolves of the forest, but they are much larger than and as black as the night. They are fearful creatures with a poisonous bite. Some of you may have heard stories about them. They are more commonly known as the steeds of the goblin riders."

"The goblins ride the wolug!" Ava gasped.

"Yes, but not all of the goblin riders have wolug mounts. The goddess has blessed our world with balance so the wolug are very few in number. Most of the goblin riders ride on wild wolves," Brendan replied. "Only the worst of the goblin clans ride on the wolug, and even then only once."

"Why is that?" Alec asked.

"The wolug are so vicious in battle that they tend to kill as many of their riders as they do enemy men and their allies. Most of the goblin riders do not leave the battlefield alive," Brendan stated. "The dark beasts came into this world when the balance of light and darkness was disrupted. The goddess Adara intervened and rallied the dwarves of a world of magical metals to come to the aid of humans to counter the threat that the goblins presented. Many elves also journeyed here from Eden in their great hunt and pursuit of the demons." Brendan paused.

"The elves hunt the demons?" Ava asked.

"Yes, the elves are the sworn enemies of the demons. One of the books from the other world that we have stored in the archives describes the elves in detail and on that world; the native humans called them *angels*. But they have always had but one desire — to rid the domain of demonkind," Brendan explained.

"How does the goddess keep the wolug in check?" Ava asked.

Brendan smiled. Ava was his best student and she rarely missed the nuances of his instructions. She had surmised that the blessing of the goddess that kept the goblins in check was not just a special blessing.

"The goddess Adara knew that to defeat the wolug would require an alliance with a beast of significant power. She visited many worlds before she discovered the answer to Articia's woes. In a world where no humankind dwelled and the balance was shifted in favor of the more goodly beings was a special breed of stallion-like creature called by the name *destri*." At the sound of the name destri, Ava's heart soared. The mention of this creature touched her magical senses.

"The destri is the most noble and intelligent beast of its world and the goddess Adara was pleasing to them because of the goodness of her light." Brendan paused briefly. "They were honored to send some of the most courageous of their race to Articia to fight against the darkness. One thousand destri came on a pilgrimage to Articia during the early days of the first war against the darkness.

"When the forces of light had been assembled in Articia, the goddess came to humankind. The humans were an infant society and had no organized rulers or territories. They were almost completely nomadic like the ruffians of the northlands today. Adara spoke to them of the battle of the light and dark. The nomadic tribes were suspicious of the goddess for she had not made herself known to them prior to this gathering. Then, one single act of courage changed the hearts and minds of the nomads. A young girl stepped forward carrying a shield too large for her to effectively use and dragging a sword too heavy for her to lift."

"Heather!" Ava responded.

"Yes," Brendan replied. "The first warrior of Articia was Heather of the North. She was the first of the humans to take a stand against the rising darkness. The nomad warriors of the tribe all laughed at the young girl, but Adara smiled at her and looked toward the rest of the men. She foretold 'This young girl is the bravest of your tribe and will be favored in all she does. She will be a queen in Articia.'

"At hearing this, the rest of the nomadic warriors stood and committed to the fight because they were unwilling to be seen as less brave than a girl-child. Despite this initial stand, it took many years for the forces of good to organize into an army. Many skirmishes occurred across the land before humankind was organized into city-states." Brendan adjusted in his seat to stretch out his legs. "During that time the humans became more battle savvy and learned to work with the otherworldly races.

"The destri had never been ridden before and had no understanding of the man–mount relationship such as we have with the horses of our world. It took many years for humankind and destri to come to an 'understanding' in regards to mounted combat."

"Who was the first man to ride a destri?" Tristan asked.

"Ah, you make an interesting assumption, Prince. It was not a man or a woman who first rode a destri. It was a small child.

Though no one recorded whether it was a boy or girl," Brendan said, smiling.

"It was very early in the first war of power when the destri arrived on Articia. They came through the rift very close to a small village of equestrians. These villagers were comfortable with the wild horses that had always existed on Articia but none had seen a horse of such grandeur and size as the destri." Brendan put his hands on his knees as he leaned forward in his chair. "When the destri strode over to meet the villagers, the leader lowered its head and bowed to the villagers. A small child confused the greeting as an invitation to mount. So the child, excited for the opportunity to ride, scrambled up on the back of the huge horse."

The royal children laughed at this, but Brendan raised his hand to silence them. "Normally this would have been a great indignity for the noble horses, but their leader was amused and surprised by the innocent bravery of the young child. The destri stood as the child grabbed its mane and the mount took off to give the child the ride of its life.

"It took many years for humans and destri to forge a relationship where rider and horse were comfortable companions." Brendan sat back up straight. "When a human was selected by a destri to be its rider, they began a lifelong relationship. Only the most honorable warriors were selected by a destri."

"Did all of the kings of Articia ride destri?" Dom asked.

"No, my Prince, not all of the royal family are selected by a destri," Brendan replied, "In fact, very few have been selected."

"Why is that?" Ava asked.

"Because, Ava, the destri are independent and highly intelligent creatures. To be the mount of a king is to subjugate to the king. So, very few kings have ever had a destri as a mount."

"The cavaliers ride the destri. Are they cavaliers because they ride the destri or are the destri only selecting the cavaliers as riders?" Alec asked.

"Well, young Prince, there's the dilemma. That is almost as easy as answering the question, which comes first, the chicken, or the egg. Perhaps it is just easier to say, it depends." Brendan smiled.

"That's not an answer," Alec replied with a bit of a frown.

"No, my young Prince, it is not. But you have to get used to the fact that you will not always get the answer for which you are looking." Brendan said with a sigh. "Sometimes answers come as part of a journey."

Brendan stood and walked across the room to pull the curtain on the western window. The sun was now past peak and shining in his eyes, making it difficult to see his students. He turned back to his seat and continued his lesson. "The first war of power was long and arduous. Humankind had not yet learned the ways of magic or steel because the elves and the dwarves had not yet taught them those ways. So humans brought the best weapons they had at that time, mostly clubs and crude spears, and stood alongside the more experienced elven and dwarven warriors to face the hordes of the darkness. Many men, dwarves, elves, and destri were lost in the first war but they prevailed. From the fellowship of battle was born the symbiotic relationship we have today with the dwarves and the elves.

Articia's first hero and king was created by the first war of power, Calum the First, and as the goddess Adara had predicted, he chose as his queen the now grown Heather of the North."

Ava smiled at this, knowing that she would soon scour the castle library to find the historic tome that told that story.

"During that war the dwarven smiths forged many steel weapons for the humans to use in battle." Brendan pulled out a magical dagger that was clearly dwarven forged and passed it to the students to examine. "Humankind was very protective of their master weapon forgers and the dwarves yearned to forge better weapons for the human warriors, who truly appreciated the craft of the dwarves.

"The elves were more elusive and private. They interacted with only the most gifted humans. In the early days of the rift, it was discovered that some of the humans had innate magical abilities, with varying levels of power." Brendan thought back to the days of his schooling in the magical arts by the elves, and smiled. "The elves were more comfortable dealing with Artician's who the goddess blessed with magical abilities."

"What do you mean?" Dom asked.

"When one has innate magical abilities, one gives off a colorful aura. This aura tells much about the nature of a person's magical abilities and whether he or she is leaning to the light or the dark arts," Brendan replied. "The elves relied on this aura to measure our intent. They have a long history of being deceived by those with dark intentions, so they find it hard to trust beings they cannot easily read."

"I have never seen any auras around anyone," Tris commented.

"Not all of the magically gifted humans can, Tristan. Only Adara understands this mystery. Some of Articia's practitioners have this ability and some do not. We surely do not know why the goddess has bestowed her gifts in such a random fashion," Brendan replied. "For some reason, all of the elves are blessed with the ability to see auras. It was probably born of their eternal fight against the darkness.

"The elves' magical ability has always been innate. They do not need to use phrases or gestures to bring about their power." Brendan adjusted in his seat again. "The elves' ability is also common in the demons that came from the rift. It is thought that in the world, from which they came, demons and elves had similar power and it was carried with them to our world."

Brendan reached back to his desk and pulled out a book. "Humankind does not have this innate ability. In the early days of the first war of power, the elves brought many unknown things to Articia, including tomes written in the language of that world." Brendan put the book he had selected on his lap and continued. "Many were written in a language the other world called *Latin*. It took us many years to learn the nuances of that language, mostly because of its dangerous nature."

"It is dangerous because when you speak it aloud, it initiates magical ability," Ava responded. "Yes, Ava," Brendan confirmed. "But not for all, only for those blessed by the goddess with special power. Even then, not all Latin incantations work for all because innate color represents each magical art. The natural elements of air, water, fire, and earth represent each sect. Some practitioners have the additional ability related to what the elves call the natural forces of sight, sound, light, and power. Only the phrases of that ancient language that describe those elemental or physical effects create magic on our world."

We also discovered additional abilities associated with the healing arts." Brendan opened the book and looked out at the class. "But some of the most interesting books were not written in Latin but in a language they called *En-Glish*. Very few of these books made the journey through the rift with the elves, but one of their history books did and gave us great insight into the bravery of the people of the other world as well as the tragic nature of their life."

Brendan flipped through the pages of one of the books from his desk and again spoke to his students. "This book represents the history of the other world as recorded by William the Spear, from the land of Shakes." Brendan then started to read from a passage of the book called *King Henry V*.

> Once more unto the breach, dear friends, once more,
> or close the wall up with our En-Glish dead!
> In peace there's nothing so becomes a man
> As modest stillness and humility;
> But when the blast of war blows in our ears,
> Then imitate the action of the tiger;
> Stiffen the sinews, summon up the blood.

At the reading of the words, Ava's heart was soaring. It was a story of a pending battle engaged by great warriors. She was definitely going to have to learn the language of En-Glish so she could read all of this history.

"This passage is from the history of one of the other world's kings." Brendan paused. "His name was Henry." At the drop of that name, he had all of the young nobles' attention.

"Is my father named after the Henry from these books?" Alec asked.

"Many names that we use today have come from the history books of Eden, the world of the elves. There were many Henrys in the history of the other world. I was not near when your father was named by his parents, but it is possible he was named after one of the Henrys from the history of the elves."

"There was more than one Henry?" Tris asked.

"Yes, based on this recorded history, there were at least eight kings named Henry. Please, let us go on. We learned many other things about the people of Eden, but not all of their history translated well. At times they had points in their history that we would feel was rather nonsensical. Here, let me give you an example." Brendan flipped through the pages and read some more. "This is also recorded by William the Spear of the land of Shakes, in a story he called *Much Ado about Nothing.*"

> Love me! Why, it must be requited. I hear how I am censured: they say I will bear myself proudly, if I perceive the love come from her; they say too that she will rather die than give any sign of affection. I did never think to marry: I must not seem proud: happy are they that hear their detractions and can put them to mending.
>
> They say the lady is fair; 'tis a truth, I can bear them witness; and virtuous; 'tis so, I cannot reprove it; and wise, but for loving me; by my troth, it is no addition to her wit, nor no great argument of her folly, for I will be horribly in love with her. I may chance have some odd quirks and remnants of wit broken on

me, because I have railed so long against marriage:
but doth not the appetite alter?
A man loves the meat in his youth that he cannot
endure in his age. Shall quips and sentences and
these paper bullets of the brain awe a man from the
career of his humour? No, the world must be peopled!
When I said I would die a bachelor, I did not think I
should live till I were married. Here comes Beatrice.
By this day! She's a fair lady: I do spy some marks of
love in her.

Ava giggled at the end of the story, though her brothers were
a bit uncomfortable from the telling of it. It was clear to Ava
that this was a history describing the courting of a woman by a
man. Though she thought it odd to record such a history at all, it
must have been important to the other world to keep this kind of
record. Maybe it was the history of how a king and a queen met.

Brendan closed the book and put it back on his table. He
started to address the young nobles again. "Our knowledge of
this story and all of the things we have discussed today we have
because of the rift that we believe was created by the darkness.
Some things have been good for us, like the arrival of the elves
and these written works. It is unlikely that humankind would have
ever become the civilized society that we have today without the
battle of light and darkness. The trials and tribulations of those
days forced the nomadic groups to organize into nations.

Other effects of the opening of the rift have not been good
for the people of Articia. One of the deadliest things to come
from the rift is the birth of the plague in our lands. Before the rift
opened, humankind had never experienced illness that affected
such a large number of people. It was discovered early that the
plague only occurred when the rift was aligned to our world."

"The rift is not always opened?" Ava asked.

"No, Ava," Brendan replied. "The rift is always open; it is
just not always on our world."

"The rift moves?" Alec asked, somewhat perplexed.

"No, Alec, we do," Brendan responded.

At this, the children of the nobles were intrigued.

"How is that possible?" Dom asked.

"As we started to form as a nation and the dwarves and the elves interacted with us more frequently, many new mysteries were open to us. We discovered that the star that warms Articia is a fiery ball of flame. And the world that we now stand on circles around it."

"Well, everyone knows that!" Alec retorted.

"Well, my young Prince, everyone did not always know that," Brendan replied. "In fact we knew nothing about our world when we were nomadic. We understood the seasons and the hunt and we knew we lived and died. The people knew very little about the world around our heads. We knew nothing about the objects that moved above us in the sky. Nevertheless, we learned, and we discovered. Some of the mages studied the stars and learned that they too were fiery balls of flame very far from us that could have many worlds like ours. We made maps of the sky and matched the movement of the seasons. It was then that we realized that we moved, and the rift did not. As our world moves around the fiery ball, the rift stays in place and we move away from it. The rift is aligned with our planet for only a day, once a year."

"So our land is affected by the plague every year?" Ava asked.

"Thank the goddess, no, Ava," Brendan responded. "It is not fully understood why, but the mages believe that there are other worlds, not just at other stars but in other places. The elves call these other places the Endless Domain or the Ethos. Under the tutelage of the elves, the mages also came to understand that time may not pass equally on every world in every domain. This is why the rift does not always bring a plague; the plague returns only when our world is perfectly aligned to the world that it comes from."

"So how often does it align?" Alec asked. "The last plague occurred when my father was a boy."

Brendan raised his eyebrow at Alec's question. He had not expected that the young prince would be so interested or so insightful. Maybe he should suggest to the king that Alec attend more of these sessions. "You are right, Alec, it was recent. However, it is not a regular pattern, as your question suggests. The mages who study the stars discovered that we do not revolve around the star in a perfect circle. It has more of a shape like an egg from fowl. In addition, they believe this is true for the other worlds as well. The rift sometimes brings us to other worlds. One of these worlds is that of the destri."

"We can still visit the destri world?" Dom questioned.

"No, Dom, the destri have requested that we do not bring the darkness that afflicts us to their world," Brendan responded. "But they do occasionally move back and forth between the worlds. They somehow know when and where the rift will form and when it is close to their world. They do not share with us when it is going to happen. This is probably for the best since we would be tempted to visit. We are after all a very curious species."

"Does the rift touch worlds other than the world of the destri and the world of the dwarves and elves?" Ava asked.

"That is a great question, Ava, but unfortunately I cannot answer that. The rift does not always form in the same place. We have not been able to predict its pattern. Maybe after a thousand more years of study the answers will be found, but for now we try to estimate."

"So when have they estimated the next alignment to occur? When will we have another plague?" Dominic asked with some concern.

"They believe it will be sometime between now and ten summer seasons from now," Brendan replied.

"That's kind of vague," Tristan stated.

"Sorry, Prince, it is the best they can do with the information we have. The magical arts are not always precise." Brendan stood up and walked toward the door. "Well, our time is up for today. We can continue this subject area in a couple more turns of the sun." Brendan finished speaking and opened the door to the tower. "May a good day befall you all."

The royal children, clearly disappointed that they did not learn more of their land's history, left Brendan's chamber for the end-of-day meal.

6

The Harsh Price of Failure

"They were better prepared than we thought they would be, Baron," the master-of-arms reported. "The girl had power we did not expect."

"Enough," the baron responded. "I told you to take precautions when dealing with the royal whelps. Do you know what you have brought down on the barony?" As the baron finished his statement, he turned and looked wide-eyed as a demon grabbed his master-of-arms from behind and threw him out of the tower window. He could hear the soldier scream until he hit the ground in the courtyard.

"My kind takes it personal when promises are not kept, Baron. You do not understand with what you dabble," the demon said as he grabbed the baron by the shirt and dragged him toward the window.

"P-please, I am still committed to destroying the brood!" the baron screamed. The demon held the baron out the window over the courtyard. "You have already failed me, Baron. My kind does not give those who fail us second chances."

"P-p-please, I will do whatever you ask of me!" The baron was in total panic now.

"Anything Baron, what do you have that I could possibly need?" the demon responded.

"Anything, Tell me. I will give you anything!" the baron yelled.

The demon pulled the baron back into the room and looked the baron in the eyes. "Then I take your soul!" As he finished the statement, he reached into the baron's chest, pulled out his soul, and swallowed it whole.

The baron turned a ghostly white as he started to understand what had just happened. He was not dead, but it was a fate worse than death. He could feel the torment of his soul in the demon and his spirit was broken. "What is your wish, Master?" the baron asked.

"Now, Baron, let us discuss how we will eliminate our common threat to the darkness." The demon sat the baron down in a chair and started to pace the room.

...

"Master, while you were off to see the baron, a message from the citadel arrived from the dark sorcerers," the lesser demon reported.

"What was this message, then?" his master inquired.

"I would not presume to read a message that is directed to you, my Lord," the lesser demon said as he handed the scroll to his master and backed away. Before the lesser demon realized what was happening, the greater demon jumped across the room and struck the smaller demon so hard he flew into the wall.

"Do you really believe that you can hide any deception from me? I can see your lies before they leave your maw." The lesser demon slowly rose to a crouch and scuttered to the other side of the room. "My apologies, Master. Of course, you know all. I only read the scroll to ensure that your time would not be wasted in its reading."

The demon lord laughed as he opened the scroll. "Hmm, it seems that the dark master of the arts has an interesting idea. We may defeat the light yet. I will be leaving immediately for the citadel to converse with this dark practitioner."

"Yes, my Lord," the lesser demon responded, a slight curve of a snarl forming on its face.

7
Sunshine

Many weeks passed before the castle started to show some semblance of its normal routine. The elite guard had made many sweeps of the castle to ensure that there were no more internal threats to the royal family. The castle forces were still investigating the event to determine which of the northern nobles may have had a hand in the attempt to assassinate the twins. Under the current circumstances, the king had postponed until the spring Dominic's review of the kingdom. Of course did not please the young prince. It would probably be months before the castle returned to its normal daily routine.

It was still dark in the early morn, many days later when Ava slipped a green riding tunic from her brother's wardrobe over her head. She also pulled on breeches with a giggle. Most young women of the court would be aghast at the selection of male clothing that she sported, but Ava did not care.

She finished by buckling her sword belt and frog tight around her waist and sheathing Last Kiss. The hallway was very quiet in the early morning, with the exception of her chambermaid Bess, who had an uncanny way of knowing when Ava was leaving her room. Bess was there; ready to clean her room whenever she decided to sneak out early for a ride.

"Have a nice ride, Milady," Bess said as she entered Ava's room.

With the possible exception of Bess, it was easy to walk through the castle unseen so early in the morning. However, lately, because of the attempted assassination, the elite guard seemed to be everywhere. This morning the guard only gave her a passing glance. Her father had warned them not to restrict the movements of the royal children; it was not worth the trouble the twins would surely give his soldiers. Instead, he gave them instructions to be near to hand should they need assistance. Ava continued down through the courtyard to the stables.

At the very end of the royal stables was the pen where she kept her horse, Aurora. Aurora was very special to Ava. The foal, a remarkable colt, dropped from her mother on Ava's eleventh birthday. Aurora had jumped to her feet very quickly after birthing, born at night's midway, on an evening with very clear skies. It was then that Ava first looked into the pony's eyes; she saw the stars and the constellation named after the magical fire Aurora. Ava took as sign of the goddess to name the horse after the fire in the sky.

She slipped Aurora a carrot while she stroked her neck. Alec always chided her for spoiling her horse with treats and tenderness, but she knew this was the best way to handle Aurora. The horse was a free spirit, touched by Adara. Her magic was so subtle that no one but Ava realized that it existed. If not for an accidental fright the horse suffered when they crossed paths with a hill bear, she would have never known the special magic Aurora possessed.

"Shhh, girl, it is okay," Ava assured the skittish horse." Yes, we're going for a little ride." Ava put the bridle on and led Aurora out of her stall and toward the stable door. "I do not have lessons until sun high, so we have loads of time to train and graze and exercise!" She fed her an apple and another carrot. "Alec would nag me that I am spoiling you," she smiled. Aurora nosed her pockets for more but Ava backed away, cinching the horse's harness, blanket, and saddle. Ava connected the rounded spurs to her boots, mounted Aurora, and started toward the castle gate. When they were close, Ava whispered "Now, girl," and the horse and rider seemed to fade into a light mist.

Ava rode Aurora through the gate unnoticed by the castle guard and proceeded to gallop down the hill of the castle, which took Ava through parts of the city and eventually the village below the ramparts. She continued to move quietly down the road and through the outer gates of her home to the forest of Willnon.

The wind blew softly, moving the leaves only slightly so they made the softest patting sound, a sound like that of footsteps muffled by grass.

"Aurora, you do not need to hide any more, and your magic can be detected if you use it too long," Ava whispered into the horse's ear. As Aurora whinnied in reply, they reappeared on the trail.

The sudden appearance of a rider and horse startled many squirrels and birds as the noise near Ava and her steed increased significantly. Ava tied back her hair into a colt's tail. *Oh, how mother would have complained about her hairstyle not being appropriate for a princess of Articia*, she thought.

The tail of hair bounced on her back as she rode into the familiar clearing, where horse and rider normally practiced mounted fighting. However, today Ava decided she was going to work on her dismounted swordplay. She secured Aurora to a tree and let her graze, giggling when she neighed happily. Ava was always amazed how little it took to make horses happy; horses are so unlike most people, who seemed never to be pleased with their lot, especially a young princess yearning for adventure.

Many years of Ava's private training sessions had worn a circle of gravel in the center of the clearing. The hard scrabble had no grass or plants any more, due to her constant mashing of the ground. For the first time, she would be able to train here with her bonded sword. She drew Last Kiss and dropped her frog and belt to the side of the clearing.

Her martial-arts exercise started with sword technique and sword dances. The first style Ava practiced, taught to the royal family for generations, a simple moon cut dance. The only sound in the clearing was her quick breaths and the tiny tap of her short steps. The moon cut dance consisted of half-moon sweeps with precise foot placement for every sweep. Many minutes passed until she moved onto the sun setting and sun rising techniques.

The moon and sun techniques were primarily defensive moves that used the motion and force of the assailant to deflect the attack. The moon techniques were parrying techniques and the sun techniques, used for blocking.

Ava then moved on to more complicated attack sequences. First, the lion claw dance, a sequence of slashing attacks meant to draw the opponent's defensive moves farther and farther away from good form. The rushing waterfall sequence followed, used primarily to drive an opponent back and gain a better stance or position against the position of the adversary. She ended with a set that she had created and the weapon master called "one of the riskiest and trickiest moves I have ever seen." Ava called it the sleeping dragon stance.

Her brother Alec used to chide her that this move was cheating. She would start this move by pulling away from her opponent in an obvious position of weakness. When the opponent came in for the kill, she would use her magic to create force on the attacker's lead foot, causing him to lose his balance. This would usually cause her opponent to raise his sword arm to regain balance, which would be his fatal mistake because she would follow with an underarm sweep of her sword. Bryn called this a finishing move because it would put the person who used it in a remarkably bad position to follow through with any defensive counters. This particular strategy was the cause of many of Alec's bangs and bruises during weapon training.

Ava was breathing heavy at the end of her workout. Taking a moment to collect herself, she felt a slight tingle of danger. Her premonition had always been a remarkable gift. It had helped her get out of many unusual situations in the past.

Ava rolled into a somersault and moved her sword toward the perceived danger to face the presence she felt behind her. What she saw made her jaw drop. *He was so quiet; how did he get this close?* She thought to herself. A very familiar face stared back at her.

Ava had a sour look, caused by the smile on the face of young man sitting against her favorite tree. His blond-brown hair was wet as if he had been swimming in the river next to the ground that she chose to train. He was leaning against *her* tree eating an apple, smugly eating an apple. She looked him over and noticed he was comfortably dressed in a white cotton shirt and loose brown cotton trousers. Before Ava spoke, she noticed an amulet hanging from his neck marking him as a member of the royal family of Cyrus. Still somewhat in shock at how quietly he approached, Ava stared at him waiting for him to speak first.

"Oh, do please continue. I was learning some new techniques, Sunshine," The young trespasser said.

He chided her! Did he mean to insult her? Her initial shock passed, Ava rolled her eyes. "You should be careful about sneaking up on someone; you could have had an unfortunate accident."

He chuckled and moved from his spot against the tree and into the clearing. "You have quite the temper, Sunshine."

The nameless prince was really starting to irritate her. Ava turned from the interloper with annoyance. He finished off the last bits of his apple and tossed the core into the woods. Wiping his hands on the seat of his breeches, he looked over to her. "So," he said.

"So what," Ava replied looking over her shoulder at him, she would not give him anything to work with.

He just smiled. "You are an interesting one, a princess with a sword—rather unique." He looked into the woods as if communicating with some distant deity. Within a few seconds, Ava heard the gallop of a rather large horse. A white destri broke into the clearing and came over to the nameless prince. As she had learned in Brendan's class, a destri was a very rare creature indeed, hardened by its life in the mountains of the north, where the unique race of horses had settled in Articia.

Coveted for their aggressiveness in battle, destri were highly desired by young knights. The perfect warhorses, they were very intelligent and worked in harmony with their riders. *Was this young man already a cavalier?* She wondered. *Had this horse already picked him as a rider?*

Now that she was seeing one up close, she realized that these were truly remarkable beasts. Ava had read much about them after her first introduction in class a few weeks back, but seeing a destri up close was very different from reading descriptions in a book.

She had learned from her reading that they were almost magical, as if they had a sixth sense. Destri always seemed to be able to avoid tactics to knock them down or dismount their riders. The most notable cavalry, the renowned One Hundred, rode into Artician legend on destri, which were the only mounts that could take on wolug in battle. The unknown prince mounted the white horse as he looked back at Ava, "Until we meet again." He bowed slightly from his saddle and galloped in a direction away from the palace.

Why did this young man irritate her so much? She pondered irritably. Ava mounted Aurora, after giving her another apple, and set off at a dash towards the palace. She needed to make haste to get back to her room before her brother woke. She had let the unknown prince distract her; now there would be trouble for her if she did not hurry.

Aurora worked hard, raising her hooves faster than Ava thought possible. Her biggest fear was no longer of being back late but of waking the entire palace with the pounding of Aurora's feet against flattened grass. She reached the stables quickly and Ava gave the horse a baleful of hay for her hard work.

She handed the reins of Aurora to a stable hand; He would walk the steed so she could cool down. Turning from the stable's doors toward the castle, Ava heard a heated exchange between the gate warden and the captain of the guard. He was grilling the warden on how the princess managed to ride outside of the walls of the castle undetected. Ava was sure that she had gotten the poor man in trouble by not coming back to the castle with more care and stealth. The young unknown prince had left her truly shaken. Still distracted when she walked into her chamber, her brother caught her off guard for the second time today.

"Well, where have you been?" Alec said to her with a smirk.

Ava jumped and responded, "None of your business."

"Well, touched a soft spot," Alec retorted.

Ava smiled, remembering the lesson that day was not going to be like any previous trip to the training yard. Today she would train with Last Kiss.

Alec, who had clearly just dressed, walked to the basin to splash the sleep out of his eyes and tied back his curls. Ava was tying back her hair while she looked at the trousers and tunic on her bed. She had always had to use clothing that was too small for Aleczander, but today she could wear her own clothing.

Alec grabbed beat-up riding boots and pulled them on, and then grabbed his fencing gloves. He threw a pair of boots to Ava who had just entered the main chamber of their suite. She caught them and put them on. It was all part of their routine. Ava grabbed the fencing gloves she had made for herself, then stopped and looked at them and started to smile.

Alec had started to walk to the passage to the training grounds when he looked back to see Ava smiling. "Are you not ready to start yet?" he chided.

"Alec, we do not have to use the secret passage to go to the grounds anymore," a slight curl forming on her lips. Alec had forgotten that their father had officially approved Ava's training in response to the recent attack, though it would take some days yet for word to spread throughout the castle.

"Yeah, but Ava, it is fas ..." Alec started to smile, too, as he realized what his sister was saying and turned away from the hidden passage and to the door with his sister. The twins marched through the hall of the palace, as the chambermaids gasped. Ava was really relishing this; eventually the shock would wear off, but for now, she was thoroughly enjoying the reaction.

The twins walked onto the training grounds, where Dom and Tristan were talking with their father, as well as a foot soldier who was standing to the side and looking rather uncomfortable. The king regarded his daughter. She may not have realized it, but she looked menacing. In the tunic she now wore, she carried herself confidently on a muscled frame that showed superior strength for a young woman.

Not quite the sweet, gentle daughter of a king, Henry thought.

Ava strode confidently, more like a warrior than a princess did. Her chin was set; her eyes hard and determined. The king had never looked for a soldier in his daughter and had difficulty seeing his little girl as a warrior. The sword at her side he recognized as the one she had bonded with many years past, the one that had recently stung him with its power.

Ava put on her fencing gloves and stood at the ready. The king nodded approvingly. Ava knew none of what he was thinking, and because of this, she was nervous.

The king smiled and hugged her tightly. "I would spar with you myself, but tradition does not permit it. So this young man-at-arms has graciously offered to spar with you." The king waved the soldier over to the ring. "His orders are to only disarm you. Let's not overdo it for the first round."

Ava heard her brothers snicker behind her, and her father waved them off, wrongly guessing their intentions. For the king had not seen Ava fight, and despite her actions of late, still believed the weapon master's reports might well be inflated.

The bright sun shined in her eyes as she drew Last Kiss and turned to face the overconfident soldier. He moved quickly in to disarm her, but Ava stepped back and quickly to the side. It was too late for the surprised man-at-arms to react as Ava stepped in and tripped him. The poor soldier went down hard as Ava hilted the wrist of his sword arm, causing him to loosen his grip. Before he hit the ground, she worked his blade free. The soldier seemed quite surprised to see Last Kiss at his neck. Ava turned to her father. "Can I try another pass, father?"

"Clearly, the weapon master's reports are not exaggerated," the king mused while rubbing his brow.

"Maybe one of my brothers is in the mood to fight today," Ava wondered.

"Not me," responded Alec. "I already have my share of bruises, compliments of Ava."

The king looked over at her other brothers. "Well, which one of you is in the mood today?"

Dom and Tristan looked at each other, but Tristan responded, "Father, we have both sparred with Ava many times. She is quite adept and getting better with every engagement. In fact, the only reason I can still beat her is that I can see the subtle magic she uses in harmony with her sword movements." Tristan walked over to help the young soldier up from the ground as he finished with, "Dom is just a superior swordsman that she will probably never be able to master." Tristan looked over at her sister and smiled, "I am sure she would have no problem sparring today, but it would only confirm what we already know."

"Sire, I will take her on," a challenge came from across the yard. The nameless prince finished the apple he was eating while leaning on the gate of the yard.

"Prince William, I did not realize you had returned to court. Is your brother well?" the king queried the young prince.

"He is well, Sire, and has asked me to come and inquire as to what service the house of Cyrus can be to our lord in these trying times." William passed by Ava and gave her a wink as he approached the king and bowed. "He also asked me to deliver to you this letter describing our investigations to date on the recent incident."

Ava was a little stunned; she had not realized that her mysterious prince was in fact Prince William of Cyrus. There were many stories in court of his exploits. He was a remarkable swordsman and rider and had won many prizes in the Cyrus spring games. It was quite clear she would have to travel to more often.

The king read the message that Prince William had handed him. "As usual, your brother has provided valuable intelligence. Our steward will have a response for you to bring to your brother by the end of the evening. Please make yourself comfortable in my home while my advisors and I discuss this new information."

"Father, I believe I have an open challenge here," Ava interjected. "To let it lie would bring me dishonor."

"Yes, I believe you do." The king looked over to the handsome boy and nodded. Grinning, Prince William walked to stand across from her.

"Well, Sunshine, any time you are ready." William drew his sword.

Ava almost gasped, as his sword was very familiar to her. When she was a child, she had snuck into the sword chamber to look at the shiny swords. She recognized this one immediately. Ice Glade, the sword of ice, was one of the four most powerful swords of Articia! She wondered how and why Ice Glade had left her father's armory. Why did Prince William of Cyrus possess it? Although the swords chose their bearers according to history and personality, it was truly rare for one of the four most powerful swords in the kingdom to have chosen a prince outside of the king's immediate family. In fact, as far as she knew, it had never happened in history.

The dwarven smiths created Ice Glade during "The Time of Darkness." Brendan taught very little about this period of Artician history, and there is no information about it in the royal archives. All that Ava knew is that Ice Glade was second of the four blades forged in partnership by the elves of the Vale and the Silver Mountain dwarfs. Each of the swords forged with the power of the earthly elements, Fire Storm, Ice Glade, Rigid Water, and Silent Wind. The only sword known to be mysteriously missing from the armory was the sword of flame, Fire Storm.

Ava drew Last Kiss and dropped her frog and belt to the ground. The pair circled for what seemed like eternity, each watching for a break in the other's step or hesitation. Ava knew that he had seen her work out so she would not be able to use any of her normal routines against this prince. Their swords met with a clang, and Ava felt his strength as he pulled back and struck again. She blocked and countered fast, repeatedly, giving him no chance to recover. He was smart, though, and stepped back to try to make her over swing. She kept pace with him, stepping forward.

He smiled. "Quick there, aren't you, Sunshine?" He countered with another attack, which she sidestepped.

"You seem rather overconfident, Prince." She turned in order to free her left side and swung carefully at his feet, which he avoided with a jump and a laugh. *He is playing with me*, she thought as she swung at his side. He jumped back, flicking his wrist in an attempt to disarm her.

Ava held tight to Last Kiss and noticed a subtle aura of magic. It was very familiar, but she could not place it. The breeze quickened, but neither could move to gain an advantage because the other would react and disarm the opponent. She was not going to beat him, and he was not going to beat her. He was as good as she was; she was as good as he was.

"Well," the king commented. "It seems that we are not going to crown a winner of today's contest." Ava and William stopped their dual. Both were breathing heavily as William brought up Ice Glade into a salute and sheathed it. Ava bowed, and then picked up her frog and belt. Not sure about what just happened.

The king stepped up to both of the warriors. "I must now meet with my advisors. William, please have dinner with us and I will have the porters make up a room for you for the night. You can bring my response to your brother in the morning." The king smiled at Ava and left the training grounds.

Ava considered the prince and the relationship he already had with her father as she asked, "Prince William ..."

"Yes, Sunshine," he replied.

"Why did you not ask me to dance at the ball?"

"You didn't look too eager to be on the dance floor, so out of respect I did not try." He winked at Alec, who could no longer hold back his laughter at the entire spectacle. "Farewell for now for I must wash off the road and tour this wonderful city. The last time I was here, my excursions were interrupted by a bunch of interlopers." William smiled at her, bowed, and left the training grounds.

Ava stood and watched him for a moment, then sheathed her sword, suddenly wondering what it would be like to engage William in a mental contest with the game of chess; would that end up a draw as well? Ava turned to her brothers, who had stopped laughing at this point. She walked up to them, trying very hard not to smile, and almost succeeding.

As Ava walked by Tristan, she elbowed him in the side and said, "So, I will never beat Dominic in the spar; you just helped me decide what my next mission will be in my training."

Ava was starting to realize how hard it was to follow the path of a warrior. She thought of Queen Arianna, She thought of how hard it must have been to be a swordswoman in a swordsman's world. Ava then, deeply troubled by these thoughts, turned, and walked out of the training grounds.

8
The Summons of Darkness

"So you think you can call the dark minions of the other world?" the demon lord asked. "You presume much for a man thing."

"We believe it is possible. We just need to be at the rift when the alignment occurs," the dark scribe responded. He was very nervous being in the lair of the demon lord but the dark sorcerer had tasked him to deliver this message, and failure would lead to a dreadful fate. He finished, "Then my brothers and I can summon the dark hunters."

"If you are so confident that you can achieve this feat, why did you need to contact my kind?" the demon retorted.

"You know well that we have no means of predicting the time and place of the rift. Only your kind and the destri know of its passing," the dark scribe replied, "and the chargers of the light would not work with our guild."

"So you want my kind to tell you when the next rift will occur, but what is in this for me and my brothers?" the demon asked.

"We both serve the god of darkness; it would please him if we could destroy the gifted ones," the dark master answered.

"Yes, it would," the demon lord answered. "Well then, you better hurry because the rift of my home world will cross with Articia in three days, in the barren lands of the north, high on the side of a mountain pass." The demon turned to the sorcerer and challenged, "I hope you have some pretty powerful magic in your hat because even the best mounts of Articia would need a week to travel that distance."

The scribe responded with a smirk, "We have a method of travel that we discovered, shall we say, by accident. We can be there in fewer than four movements of the evening star."

The demon thought of the power the sorcerers achieved. They had discovered much since his arrival on this accursed world. Two days, and the riders would be moving toward the accursed city of the king. Then the balance will be broken and the world will become the domain of the demons. "Well, then, let us proceed. I am anxious to see my dark brothers again." The demon lord walked to the door of the hall and looked back. "It has been many millennia since the riders were summoned from the underworld."

9
The Goddess Orders

In the night, she comes to me,
She lights the darkness,
Balance broken.
Flee the wanderer.

Alec had not been sleeping well since the incident at the banquet. He dreamt frequently of that night, the image of the assassin's face playing repeatedly in his mind. He dreamed of the goddess Adara and her warm light on Articia. He dreamed of his sister Ava and he dreamed of the darkness.

Tonight his dreams were nightmares of destruction and waste. He dreamed of a pending evil and of sadness and loss. As he passed through a long, dark tunnel, he saw a young woman trapped by a dark lord. There was torture and pain, and as the demon turned its evil eyes on him, Alec was startled awake and found he was in a cold sweat.

"Adara, help me," he whispered. The two moons were still high in the sky but it was now the moment before dawn. He could sleep no more this morning so he dressed for the road and decided to take advantage of the early hour to go on a hunt.

...

Alec trotted Punisher out the door of the stable and toward the main gates of the castle; the warden confronted him as he approached. "Halt, young Prince, the hour is early and your father has put restrictions in place."

"Yes, Noah, I understand, but I intend to hunt this morning south of the castle. I know my father ordered you to discourage our passing, and I will assure him that you did. If it makes you more comfortable, you can send men to ride out after the rising light. If I have a successful hunt, they can help me to bring a stag back to the castle proper," Alec responded.

"As you wish, my Prince, I will open the gate." Noah turned the pulley wheel that allowed a single man to open the gates of the castle. It was quite an invention. Brendan said he had researched in the archives of the other world. Alec decided that he would spend more time with Brendan now that he knew that there were many interesting things to learn from him.

Alec reached the lower valley of the River Adara, and entered the clearing he visited often. He mostly visited the location when he was troubled, and would continue many times as an adult. From this place, he could see up three hundred hands to where a stream fell over an outcropping of rock. At the bottom of the small waterfall formed by the curves of the surrounding landscape, rushing water pooled into a small pond that filled and eventually flowed into the River Adara.

As a young boy, he had come here to play, to swim, and sometimes just to stare at the clouds passing across the sky. Now that he was older, he spent more time thinking than swimming. Recent events bothered Alec. Something felt very wrong about the assassin and Ava's reaction had scared him more than he was willing to admit, to her or to himself.

Alec unsaddled punisher and let him wander the clearing. He sat down taking in a deep breath of the fresh morning air and started to meditate. Bryn had taught him many things about the benefit of meditation. He would use it now to calm his soul. He also learned about balance in battle and in life. They talked about the never-ending conflict of light and darkness. He learned that true peace in could be achieved in Articia only when they were in perfect balance. Bryn also told him about how hard this would be to accomplish.

He remembered his first conversation about the subject with Bryn.

"How can the darkness ever stop fighting the light?" Alec had asked, as they were practicing archery,

"It will never stop fighting the light until it understands that it cannot exist without light, for how would you know the light if you did not know the dark? How would you understand the cold of the night without the warmth of the day?" Bryn had answered. During that conversation, the weapon master introduced Alec to the last of the known gods—Aris, the god of balance, who stands with his scale and a long sword, guarding the space between the darkness and the light. Now Alec wanted to shout to Aris for guidance. He needed, for just this moment, to forget Ava's eyes and the power she had wielded. Most of all, he just needed to think.

There were things that were still bothering him. Something about William seemed so familiar to him, but he could not put his finger on it. The duel between Ava and William yesterday had also disturbed him. It seemed that his father and brothers had barely noticed how similar the two of them were. None could have expected the outcome of that match. Nobody received better training in Articia than the royal family. Few people could have tied or beaten Ava in a duel, especially with the magic she wielded. Yet, Prince William of Cyrus had equaled her in a sword match. Something was wrong. Neither of the two could best the other in combat. He was sure that no matter how long they dueled, the outcome would not have changed, but he did not understand why he was so certain of this. It was like they were twins.

He pulled his silver charm out from under his shirt, a gift from Ava on his tenth birth-passing day. It had a crescent moon, the symbol of Adara with a long sword, one of the symbols of balance, which men have used to honor Aris. The sword crossed through the middle of the crescent moon, representing the bond between the goddess Adara and the god Aris. This paired symbol was recognition of an agreement between the light and balance to tolerate the darkness for the good of Articia. It represented an agreement that Adara would no longer work to push the darkness into oblivion. It was also the symbol of the unity and love between parent and child, husband and wife, sibling and sibling.

Alec pressed the necklace to his lips and gave a silent prayer to the god and goddess he had grown up worshiping and loving. Alec then stood up, untied his belt, and left it by his horse. He pulled off the leather armor, then the cotton shirt beneath it. He undid the strings on his breeches and slung them over his horse's back. He ran in only his loincloth to the pool and jumped into the cold water.

It was cool and crisp, just the temperature he preferred. His favorite time to swim was in the middle of harvest season, when the days were touching the edge of the bitter season; or days like today, in the spring, while snow still kissed the ground. That was the time that marked the end of the winter months. The trees, except the pines, were still bare and the air was still brisk in Articia.

Despite this, he swam to clear his mind. Swimming took just enough of his attention that he could not focus on anything else; soon the rhythm of his strokes eased him into an oddly peaceful state. As he floated on his back, he thought about the fact that he would catch a demon's wrath when his father learned he was out unescorted. Still, he yearned for his solitude enough to risk his anger.

Alec left the water and lay down in a batch of soft moss. He stared at the sky, thinking of the goddess and watching the stories that the clouds told across the sky. As he gazed from cloud to cloud, he noticed that the sun was rising above the eastern hills. "Damn, I have been here longer than I thought." Alec hurried to put on his clothes but something startled him. His senses told him he was not alone.

As he turned toward the rising sun, he saw a beautiful woman similar in frame to his mother, walking toward him. He cautiously put his hand on his sword in case there was going to be trouble; the thought of the assassin was still fresh in his mind.

"Stand, child." Alec heard in his head a voice that was musical and had a certain aspect of maturity. It had a remarkable effect on him, akin to the freshness of an early morning, though he knew that time had well past. His body started to feel soft and pliant, like it does when you have need of a first morning stretch. Alec was now worried that he had been snared in some kind of enchantment but there was nothing mortal about the figure that approached; he realized that he faced something divine.

Alec could barely focus on the image of the woman as tears came to his eyes. Nevertheless, he stood his ground and looked at the sunbeams that radiated and grew brighter as she approached. It was painful, but he dared to look straight into her eyes while resisting the urge to close his own against the light.

Adara smiled.

Alec could take the searing light no longer and lidded his eyes. In that instant, he realized he was facing the physical form of the goddess Adara. He fell to his knee and bowed his head.

"You are truly brave, young sentinel, though some would claim you ten times foolish for looking a goddess in the eye," Adara gently stated. "You are still quite young but already show some nerve to stare me down."

"My sister Ava tells me often that all men are born foolish and male warriors are even more foolish than the average man," Alec answered. "She has frequently declared me a doubly foolish warrior."

"Your sister is wise beyond her fourteen years, young Prince; you would do good to heed more of her warnings." The goddess looked down at him affectionately. "I have come to bear bad tidings for you and your sister."

Alec jumped to his feet. "Is Ava in danger?"

"Not yet, my Prince, but we have to act soon. You must evacuate to the countryside quickly; your life is in great danger from forces of which even I have no control. The dark god Arendeythl, my brother, pursues you and your siblings. He thirsts for your blood like a tired horse thirsts for water. In his yearning to have the darkness rule over all of Articia, he has decided that you and Ava are destined to stop him, so he must stop you. His minions have summoned monsters from another world and thrown off the balance. He intends to disrupt all that is good in Articia and rule over the light by eliminating you and your sister," the goddess finished.

Aleczander gathered his thoughts for a moment and attempted to take in all the new information. "So what must I do?"

Adara walked over to Punisher, the light not so strong now as it was when Alec first saw her in his grotto. Adara whispered in his ear and Punisher brayed, and ran off to the north.

"Where is he going? How will I travel without my horse?" Alec question Adara.

"Punisher is a brave steed; he has offered to create a diversion for the beasts that pursue you and others in the royal family. You need time to get well on your way," Adara responded. "A horse native of Articia will not be able to outrun those that are hunting you, my Prince." She saw the look of concern in Alec's eyes, "do not worry; it is not Punisher's time yet. He will find his way back to the stables after his task is done and enjoy a well-earned rest."

Adara closed her eyes as if concentrating on something distant. Within a breath's time, Alec heard the beat of hooves from the west. He turned in that direction and saw an entirely white, stately destri galloping to where they stood.

When the destri reached him, it reared into the air, waving his hooves as if walking on the line of the sky. It settled to the ground and inspected Alec. Alec understood the nobility of this horse from his classes with Brendan and proceeded to bow to show that he respected the station and reputation of the destri.

"Well met, Aleczander, I am Star Dancer. The queen of the light has asked that I assist you in your future deeds," said a voice in his head.

Aleczander stood startled by the interaction. He was surprised that the destri spoke directly into the mind.

"Where should I go from here?" he asked as he turned to the goddess, but she was already gone.

"Go east," he heard the fading voice of the goddess in his head. "Star Dancer knows the way." He looked over at Star Dancer, more confused now than ever.

"We must not delay, young Prince. The beasts are already in our realm and have caught your scent," Star Dancer communicated.

Alec reached over to recover Punisher's saddle and bridle, turned to the horse, and stopped. "I was told that a man does not choose a destri but that a destri chooses his rider. Have I been chosen?" Alec asked.

"We are to be companions, young Prince. It would be an honor to have you saddle and ride. Please, we must hurry" the large steed responded. Alec saddled and mounted Star Dancer and looked at the path that led into the forest, the path leading eastward.

...

Ava awoke with a fright, for she knew something was not normal. She jumped out of bed and ran over to Alec's room.

He was not there.

There was shouting from the courtyard of the castle and she went over to her window to see what the cause of the commotion was. She looked down and saw Alec's horse Punisher walking through the gate and into the courtyard, his saddle, and harness gone. Alec was nowhere in sight. She knew somehow that Alec was heading away from Castle Articia and knew he was facing great danger.

Ava ran from her room down to the main hall of the castle, with Bess chasing after her with her robe.

"Milady, Milady! You must not go out in such a state," the young chambermaid called behind her. Ava grabbed her robe and tied the sash about her waist. She stepped into the hall to see the gate warden responding to her father's angry rebuke.

"I thought I made it clear that none of my children were to leave the castle unattended," the king shouted angrily.

"Sire, you know we have no power to stop your children when they decide to do something they shouldn't. I alerted the weapon master immediately upon Prince Alec's departure and he seemed unconcerned," the warden explained respectfully.

When the king realized his daughter Ava had entered the room, he said with audible frustration. "Ava, this is not a good time."

"I know Alec is gone father," she replied. "It's not the gate warden's fault. It might not have been wise to disobey you and leave the castle but now that he has, I sense that he is being pursued and we ..."

"What have you seen, Ava?" the king asked

"I have seen nothing specific. It is just a feeling. I also know he has a powerful though unexpected ally," she replied. "I cannot see anything firm; I just know he is pursued by evil beings of great power."

The king looked at the gate warden and commanded, "Noah, get the weapon master. We have to organize a search party immediately!"

"Yes, Sire! I will also notify the captain of the guard to raise the alert," Noah replied.

"Ava, wake your mother, Dom, and Tris. We need to organize a rescue of your brother immediately!" The king left the room by the north door that led to the war room. Ava saw him walk to the table in the center and lean over the large map of Articia. She walked to the main staircase and up to the upper chambers of the castle.

...

Ava sat in the corner of the war room, listening to her father, Dom, and Tris talking strategy. Her mother smiled and came over to reassure her. "He'll be alright, Ava."

Ava looked up at her mother and said, "I know, mother. In fact, it is a mistake to send the men-at-arms out to find him. It will leave the castle undermanned and vulnerable." She got up, wandered over to the table, and spoke, "Father, we need to stop the search immediately. I sense that something else is in play."

"Ava, you do not have experience in these matters. You need to leave this to me and your brothers," the king responded.

"No, she is right," a voice from the door, answered in support.

"William, come in," the king answered. You look like you have been riding all night. How much do you know?"

"Bryn has told me that Alec has left the castle and has fled from some unknown danger." William passed the spot where Ava was sitting and whispered, "Ava, we need to speak. I have had a dream we must discuss."

William took off his riding gloves and put them down on the map table. "I have news from my brother's holdings that is not good. We have discovered that the goblins of Coal Mountain have started to amass." William pointed to an area on the map north of Lewisvel. "Based on our intelligence, they are wintering at the foot of the northern mountain pass of the Crystal Mountains" William pointed to a spot on the map before continuing "in preparation for action against us in the spring."

The king was stunned and looked over at Ava. "Do you know what numbers they now possess?"

"So far over ten thousand goblins have gathered. My brother believes that by spring they will be triple that number," William responded. "But that is not the worst of it. Our contact said they saw many wolug in the mass and that they have aligned with men of the north."

The king looked over at his wife and smiled. "Well at least now we know who was behind our little fracas in the castle. Has your brother started the assembly call of the cavaliers?"

William looked at Ava, then back at the king. "Yes, the call went out early this morning before the rise of the sun over the Crystal Mountains. He expects the One Hundred to ride in to the City of Articia well before spring's first evening," William answered. "He has also tasked the Cyran countryside to collect additional foodstuffs and rations to prepare for the coming siege."

The king looked at the section of the map that held the line of the Crystal Mountains, sometimes called the teeth of Articia because they curved around the eastern edge of the Artician border. This landform separated Articia from Cyrus to the east and curved up to the eastern edge of the northern wastes. It was the edge of the wastes that the king was most concerned. This is where the goblins would come. He thought of his old comrade at Lewisvel Keep. "It is time for another round my friend," the king thought as he let his mind wander.

At that moment, Bryn walked in with the captain of the guard to brief the king. "Sire, your son has headed to the east, though his tracks were hard to find. Alec has somehow acquired a destri mount since I saw him last."

"A what?" the king said in awe.

"I found it hard to believe, but I saw the tracks. Only a rider from the One Hundred could catch him," Bryn finished.

"I am afraid they are going to be otherwise occupied," the king answered. "William has brought dire news from his brother. It appears that the goblins have decided to make another run at us, and this time they have help from the ruffians from the north."

...

Alec had ridden hard for a day and a night before his new companion slowed to a stop.

"You may rest now, young Prince," Alec heard the now familiar voice of the noble steed in his head. He had many questions, but his fatigue was overpowering and he decided to rest while he could.

"When I am rested, I have many questions," Alec said as he laid out his horse blanket on the ground to rest.

"I am sure that you do, my young Prince," the destri replied.

...

Ava was unable to relax from the moment Alec went missing. Her father had accepted that Alec's leaving the castle was the will of the goddess, but Ava still felt utterly alone. She had not spent a day in her life without her brother Alec by her side. What scared her most was a sense of pending doom. An odd feeling of grief came over her that the simple life they once enjoyed was now gone forever. Ava was terrified that she would lose her brother Alec to some great darkness. Yesterday, Alec was here for her to talk about her feelings; today she stared at the ceiling, trying to drift off to sleep.

...

"Ava," she heard a whispered voice.

"Am I dreaming?" Ava queried.

"In a sense, for it is when you are between the real world and the dream world that I can speak plainly to you."

"Who are you?" Ava asked.

"I am the light that removes the darkness," the voice soothed.

"Adara" Ava questioned.

"You are always the wise one. Yes, it is I that lights the day," the goddess answered. "Tonight you also must flee the castle. While your brother heads east, you must head south."

"No, I must go help Alec!" Ava cried in her dream.

"He has all the help he will need, as will you," Adara whispered. "Your leaving will distract the dark one and he will have to split his forces. They are currently pursuing your brother and for him to survive their power must be reduced. The dark one does not understand that the power of those demons is only effective when they are together!"

"Demons, what will happen to Alec?" Ava asked. "Will he be safe if I do not go to aid him?"

"Only the Fates know for sure, but you must go south for his sake to distract the dark one." Adara's voice faded into the ether.

Ava woke with a start! She jumped out of bed and dressed for the road. She knew that she must not delay. She packed a satchel and ran down the secret passage to the training yard and across to the stables.

...

A throbbing from his head to his toes made Alec groan every time he rolled over. He had never slept so long on the hard ground of the forest. Dirt smudged his face and his clothes, both disheveled from the day of hard riding. Aleczander still did not know what he was doing, where he was going, much of why, or anything about his pursuers.

"Star Dancer, do you know who is pursuing us?" Alec asked.

"They are demons from another world," the destri answered. "It is said that when they were summoned to perform their deadly duty, all life on that world was extinguished."

Alec thought about this and asked, "How did they arrive in Articia?"

"My herd believes that they were summoned by a minion of the darkness." The destri looked off to the west. "My kin have also reported that the demons are in pursuit and are only hours behind us. We must continue on to the east."

"You can communicate with your kind at great distances?" Alec looked at the destri.

"We can communicate at great distance here in Articia," Star Dancer replied. "We believe it is part of the innate magic of your world. We did not have this capability on our home world."

...

Ava saddled Aurora and mounted. "Easy girl, we must be quiet. The gate warden will not let us out of the castle if we are detected."

Ava was present when King Henry had ordered the gate warden to inform him immediately should any of his other children attempted to leave the castle and to politely, but firmly remind them of his orders to stay put. Ava knew she would have to pass through the courtyard and out of the castle undetected if she was going to follow the goddess's orders. Aurora turned again into the mist that had shielded her previous escape from the castle. As she walked her steed into the yard, she noted that the gate is closed.

"This is an unexpected complication," Ava whispered. "We will have to wait here for someone to pass through the gate." Ava walked Aurora over to stand at the wall beside the gate and waited for someone to pass.

After what seemed like an eternity, a call from outside the gate caused the warden to turn the gate wheel to open for the requestor. Ava watched two equestrians enter through the inner gate opening. She almost gasped as she recognized cavaliers of the One Hundred. Ava gave Aurora a kick and slowly moved toward the opening of the gate. As she passed the cavaliers, one of the destri bowed in her direction and she heard the whisper of a magical voice. "Take care, young Princess, and may the road you travel be smooth."

For a second time that night, she almost gasped as she looked over at the cavalier. The rider turned and smiled. Clearly, they knew she was leaving the castle and did not stop her progress. When she cleared the gate and was well away from earshot, she put Aurora into a gallop that she would not stop until she reached her special clearing.

...

"Our pursuers have caught up to us; see there, across the river." Star Dancer turned in the direction of a sandy bank as

Alec looked toward the other side of the river. Here, for the first time, Alec saw the four horsemen. They were mounted on unusual mounts, the like of which he had never seen.

One dark knight, adorned in black appeared to be carrying a sword of dripping acid and a shield with a merchant's scale. The dark knight rode a black steed with devilish red eyes. Another of the demons, wearing red armor that covered the denizen from head to toe was on a red horse. The red knight wore a helmet that had no visor, no eyelets, and no vent of any kind to allow the knight to see out of his helm. This knight held a huge two-handed red sword. There was also a pale horse with a knight holding a sickle; unlike the other two horses, it was leaning on the large pole of the sickle, and where the pole touched the ground, all fauna instantly died. Finally, he saw a ghostly white knight on a white steed, holding a bow and wearing the crown of Articia!

The four fearsome knights grimly observed Alec from the other side of the river and did not react when he seemed to notice them. "Why do they not engage us?" Alec asked the destri.

"They dare not attack you during the day when the goddess Adara's power is at its prime," his mount replied.

"What evil created such knights with such foul horses?" Alex wondered. He knew they must leave now, for he would be no match for that deadly quartet. He urged Star Dancer into a gallop and continued toward the east.

...

As Ava rode toward her favorite clearing, she became aware that the wind that blew through in her hair was wrong for the early spring. There was something foul about it. Her steady breathing and the pounding of Aurora's hooves were the loudest sounds of the forest. She was riding through the clearing that brought her peace before she would have to make haste to the south. Aurora moved as if she had wings, and Ava stretched her arms out wide, letting go of the reigns, and felt like she was falling from the sky. She closed her eyes and let her thoughts drift into the abyss. It was a magnificent escape and made her feel much better about their dire situation.

Ava knew her brother was in grave danger. She could feel the evil that her brother faced. He would have to fight against conquest and death. She was not sure why she felt that both would be upon him. Ava dismounted Aurora and gave her a carrot.

She sat against her favorite tree, the one her nameless prince, who she now knew was William, had leaned against when he had managed to startle her as he appeared out of nowhere. Ava could not shake the feeling that he was important, that some part of her future depended on him. She thought about their meeting in the courtyard. She thought about the contest, how they would have fought for hours. Neither of them would have won. She also saw it in his eyes, the realization of the draw. Ava could beat almost anyone her age hastily, but not William. She had met a warrior who was her equal.

Something else puzzled her. She felt great sadness from him, as if he felt he belonged at Castle Articia. Ava thought of that and knew now it was going to be even worse when he was not around. Ava put her head in her hands and lost herself in her troubles and thoughts of the road ahead.

Then she wept.

10

The Command of Henry

"Sire," the cavalier captain bowed as he addressed the king. "Our unit is the first to arrive at your castle. The destri have taken the north woods to gather and will keep to that location until we need to ride. I expect my brothers to arrive at the castle well before we need to march to engage the horde."

"I am glad your unit responded so quickly. Have you been apprised of the situation?" the king asked.

"Yes, my Lord. We spoke to William when we arrived." The cavalier responded.

"Will William be joining your unit or will he be assigned to another?" the king questioned.

The cavalier looked at his lieutenant with a raised eyebrow and responded to the king, "I assumed that you sent him off to keep watch on your daughter."

The king looked at the cavaliers with confusion. "What are you talking about? Why would he …" The king went to the window and saw William riding fast through the gate on his destri with a fully loaded pack. The king turned to the cavalier. "You saw my daughter leave the castle? Did the gate warden not try to stop her?"

"The gate warden would not have seen her; we only knew of her passing when our destri informed us that she was riding by us and out of the castle," the knight responded. Ava's invisibility did not surprise the king; nothing about Ava's magical abilities surprised him anymore.

"And you did not think that odd enough to question?" the king inquired a bit sarcastically.

"We hesitate to question a princess but we do not question the will of Adara, the cavalier replied. Our mounts told us that she was sent on a quest by the goddess."

The king looked over at the map and wondered what was at play. He then called to his steward, "Inform the queen that we need to speak." He then turned and looked over at the cavaliers. "Something dark has come to our land. Somehow, the youngest of the royal children are directly involved. The goddess does not share her plans or opinions with us, so we must rely on your relationship with the destri to learn her will. Keep me informed of anything unusual that happens."

The knight bowed, "We are yours to command, Sire."

"My steward will show you where you will be housed until we are ready to engage the forces of the darkness. The king nodded to the steward, who motioned for the knights to follow. The cavaliers bowed as they passed the queen entering the room.

"So, what are these whisperings of grave news I hear from the maids?" the queen asked.

"Ava has left the castle, apparently on orders of the goddess," the king informed her. "Our deity has been rather busy lately with the youngest of our children," the king finished.

"Do you would think she might consider asking for permission once in a while?" the queen mused playfully as she moved to put a hand on Henry's shoulder.

"I wish I knew more about 'what was in play,' as Ava put it." The king said as he turned toward his queen.

"I am sure that Ava will be fine," the queen assured her husband. "She has proven herself capable and that she has the power to handle most of what she will face." Yet she was worried about the prophecy and concerned by the price her family would have to pay. "I am more worried about Alec," the queen said.

"Is there any word from our contacts in the east?" the king asked Queen Angelica.

"No, I have reached out to my brother in Cyrus to warn him of Alec's approach, but he has not yet responded," she replied. The queens brother and twin, Sir Genost, was one of the nobles of Cyrus, married to one of the king's cousins, he was now the weapon master of Cyrus. Angelica was always able to project her thoughts to her brother, even at large distances. This provided a significant strategic advantage for the king because they could put out a call for arms without having to send a rider. The queens bond saved many days of travel. "Though he can hear my call, he relies on the pigeons to send messages back to me. It will be a couple of hours before a pigeon could arrive from my brother's estate to acknowledge my warning."

"We will have to trust the Fates." Henry rubbed his chin, as he looked south. "William has headed out after Ava; she will have some help in whatever the goddess has in store for her."

The queen raised her eyebrow at that news. "Do you think she knows?"

The king smiled back at her. "I suspect that she does by her reaction the last time they interacted."

"We have kept the twins in the dark for so long. They were bound to find out soon on their own." The queen put her arm around Henry's waist. "Do you think they can bring balance and peace to Articia?"

"Only time will tell" The king closed his eyes. "If the promise is kept, only time will tell. For now, we must focus on the problem at hand. Spring is but two fortnights away and the goblins will march as soon as the dark pass is open to them." The king moved back to the map and called to his aid to get Bryn and the captain of the army.

11

Distraction

"The horsemen are in full pursuit of the whelp, my Lord," the imp told his master.

"Good," the dark master thought aloud. "They will make short work of this. The prince should be finished soon; the horseman's power will be too great for him."

The imp chuckled and asked, "When they have finished with him, should we send them for his sister?"

"His sister is still in the castle and out of our reach for the moment," The dark master replied.

"No, Master, she is riding south now as we speak," the imp said.

"What!" the sorcerer grabbed the imp by the neck and drew him close "I told you to tell me right away if she did anything unusual!"

"I ..., *cough, cough*, I just found out just now!" the imp tried to respond despite being choked by his master.

"Do you know why she is heading south?" The master threw the imp onto the table as he walked across the room to look at the map.

"We do not know. No one knows what that young sorceress is about," the imp snarled while it rubbed its neck.

"We cannot miss a perfect opportunity to eliminate her." The dark master looked over at the imp. "Get to the horsemen immediately. We need to split their forces to pursue the young princess." The dark master walked over toward the imp "NOW!"

12

Letum Vir Equus

Knowing that they were under the protection of the goddess, they rested during the day. Aleczander glanced at Star Dancer as he stood calmly watching the path. It was difficult to think about what could happen if the demons caught up to him. He knew he would not have a chance against the fearsome knights.

Despite his concerns about the current situation, Alec let his thoughts wander to the castle. He had thought his life was full of excitement, but compared to the current situation, it was mediocre. The daily routine had made it possible for him live his days half-asleep. He had not realized what it meant to be truly alert and awake until he was on the run from the demons that pursued him as he headed to the east.

Alec reminisced about the simpler times and found himself missing the exquisite feel of his mandolin strings on his fingers, of the comforting grasp of his sword in the practice yard. Alec found that he was missing Ava the most. He had not noticed he was finally drifting off into a deep enchanted sleep. His rest came as a release of total exhaustion as he finally fell into a troubled, dreamful slumber.

...

Ava drifted deep into a meditative state and reached inside herself for the place where her magic flows freely. Once there, she established the energy of a dark green pool that allowed her to form the chain of magic that connected her heart and soul to her brother Alec. It was the first time she tried to perform this kind of magic, but she had read many times, about how the destri could mentally reach for family members with their innate psychic capability.

She felt the warmth of his being, which meant he was still well or least still alive. Ava had never revealed to her brother that he had some magical energy because it was so small, he would never be able to form spells and she did not want him to be disappointed when he could not do even the most simple incantations

Alec was a stubborn, just like Ava, neither of them would be willing to accept that they could not expand any part of their natural capabilities. It would drive him to insanity that he had magical abilities that he could not use effectively. However, it had changed, grown. She could feel real power in him now. She would have to investigate this further when she reunited with Alec.

Ava used a part of the training she received from Brendan, a magical sensory trick that allowed her to share the senses of another being. Once she reached out and tapped the senses of a hawk that was flying outside of her window. It was a wonderful feeling to fly. She used this ability now to see through Alec's eyes. It appeared to be dark except for the remnants of a dream. Alec was asleep before the sun descended! How lazy her brother could be at times.

...

"Wake up, fool!" Something arid reached Alec's nostrils and made him cough painfully. He was pushed into a sitting position and water poured down his throat. His sight slowly came back as he realized that he had slept too long.

It was now into dark time as the sun had retreated to the west. It took him a few moments to register how terrible that one revelation was and how serious his situation had become. What had happened? Why had he slept so long?

"Quickly, mount your steed or they will be upon us!" A boy, whom Alec did not recognize, called to him as he jumped onto the back of a black horse. In the dark, he could only make out that the cloaked boy was perhaps a bit younger than he was. He had a bow on his back and a sword at his side. Who was this young man?

The young man looked down the trail and realized a pair of the dark horsemen would be on them soon. "You sleep into the night with the *Letum vir equus* tailing you! Are you mad?!" The sound of unknown boy called but his head, still filled with cobwebs. "Come on then, mount!"

Alec climbed onto Star Dancer. As the destri galloped after the strange boy, he almost unseated the half-asleep Aleczander. "Why did you not wake me?" His thought aimed at Star Dancer, as they closed in behind the other boy's steed.

"I tried. I did everything I could, except light you on fire; you appeared to be under some kind of enchantment." The destri looked back down the trail as it ran. "As hard as I tried to wake you, you slept on. I felt a presence near us earlier, probably some corrupt magical effect by some unseen force."

Alec could hear the pounding hooves of the demons' horses. He turned back and saw they were too close for comfort. Star Dancer sped up. "Had this young traveler not come upon us with a forest sense and wisdom, I would have had to stand against the riders without you. I am afraid the result would have been disastrous," Star Dancer whinnied as if to further his point. He saw the young boy falling back a little bit and the four horsemen not far behind.

"The boy cannot keep up with us; the horsemen will overtake him soon. We should turn back to aid him," Alec shouted.

"It is your decision to make, for I am only here to make sure that you have the support you need for your quest. But the path you take must be your own," the destri replied.

Alec looked back again, and his eyes widened. The horses were barely sixty yards behind the young boy of the forest. Even more alarming, only the pale and white horses were in sight; the black and red horse had disappeared. Alec pulled Star Dancer around and pulled Shadow Fang from its hilt. He called out to the young rider, "Form up close on me. We will try to split their attack down the middle," he yelled to the boy.

"Bumpkins, you fool! ride on; I will distract them as long as I can. Go! Follow the trail; I will catch up with you during the daylight. The young man turned and drew his sword.

"I'll fight!" Alec yelled, stopping Star Dancer.

"No you won't!" the boy yelled back. "The only way you can defeat the riders is by running faster, go now!" Alec saw the boy turn and charge the demon on the white horse. He turned Star Dancer around and, despite his bruised pride and honor, dashed away from the battle as ordered by this rather overconfident young forester.

Alec continued to hear the clang of swords and the pounding of horses' hooves on the ground. The noise of the battle diminished behind him as the sound of his escape finally overcame the sound of the remaining horsemen.

. . .

What Ava saw next through Alec's eyes startled her. He was finally waking up; she did not see anything but blurry images. She started to sense that Alec had risen to his feet. Ava saw something she did not expect out of Alec's eyes. "A boy, who is he?" she thought. However, what she saw next disturbed her greatly—two horsemen, one pale and one white. She lost control of the magic and lost the shared vision with her brother. She would not be able to reestablish it for quite some time.

. . .

Alec turned back and saw that the pale horseman was still in hot pursuit. "The white horsemen must have engaged the young boy", he thought. Alec looked back and realized that the pale rider was too close. He would not be able to outrun this demon. At least there was only one of the foul beasts to face.

Alec decided to turn and fight! Star Dancer turned in response to his thoughts as he raised Shadow Fang and they charged at the dark rider.

"So this is it, is it?" the destri asked.

Aleczander answered aloud. "Not if I have something to say about it."

The pale rider raised the sickle to strike at him as it passed. Alec deflected the attack but the deadly staff raked across his chest and burned though his light armor. It seared his skin and caused excruciating pain. He nearly blacked out and almost fell from the destri.

The pain was immense but his adrenalin was now flowing and Alec pulled Shadow Fang into a back swing off the deflection and caught the pale rider on the back. It screamed in pain and anger, a terrifying and ghostly sound. Alec had never heard anything like it.

The pale demon pulled its horse to a stop and turned to face Alec again as it readied for another charge. Fire was shooting from the pale horse's nostrils as the rider started into a gallop to make another run at him. Alec, better prepared for this pass, knew that this battle would only end in disaster.

As he thought of the pending charge, Star Dancer called to his mind, "A rider without a horse will not be able to pursue us. This rider may be undefeatable, but his horse may not be indestructible!"

Alec smiled, for he understood the instruction well. Dismounting a rider had been part of his regular training. He felt like an idiot for forgetting the basics that Bryn had taught. In battle, you should first try to remove the mount of an opponent to gain an advantage over its rider. Alec was about to execute a very risky strategy. Bryn had instructed him to use the tactic only as a last act of desperation. "Well," Alec thought, "this is a desperate situation."

You had to make sure that the rider you charge does not realize that you are going to lean down for a strike. Alec edged forward on the saddle readying for another charge from the foul beast. Alec knew he had to approach the strong side of the pale rider before he and Star Dancer would pull to his opponent's weak side at the last moment. Alec hoped the pale rider would not be able to bring that deadly sickle down for an attack. Star Dancer put down his head and charged at the pale rider as he acknowledged Alec's tactic. As they closed in on the pale rider, Alec glimpsed the rider's face through the helmet visor. It was a fiery white skull!

The pale rider raised the sickle to strike, but at the instant before contact, Star Dancer turned quickly to the weak side of the pale rider's mount. Alec lowered his body to the side of the destri and swept the front legs of the pale horse with his sword. The pale rider's mount fell heavily to the ground, ending its charge with a deathly scream. Star Dancer was right. The horse was mortal and could not get up from the blow that Alec had dealt.

Alec turned and headed again to the east. He soon realized how badly injured his joust with the pale rider had left him. The lethal staff had left a burn across his left shoulder and chest. Now that he was coming down from the excitement of the engagement, the pain had returned. Alec leaned over the neck of Star Dancer and passed out.

The destri knew that Alec had lost consciousness but kept up the full gallop to put many leagues between him and the stranded horseman. The last thing the destri heard as they rode off into the distance was the frustrated scream of the pale rider.

13
William and Danny

Alec opened his eyes to see the canopy of a tree with an expanse of blue sky just beyond. For some time he lay there; he was in no pain, and he thought *I should be in pain.*

Alec surmised that he must be dead. He really saw no urgency, then, to get up and face anything now other than his own thoughts. An odd feeling it was, to be dead. It was as if you were feeling … nothing at all. He sat up and looked around him before slowly rising to his feet.

Where was he? It was grassland as far as he could see in front of him and a forest to his back. He was wearing soft, cotton trousers and a plain, white, cotton shirt. He had no armor, no sword, not even shoes as he wiggled his toes in the grass. *Well I can feel that*, he thought.

Alec ran his fingers through his black curls—clean, he realized—he had been quite the sight caused by the hard ride before his battle with … He couldn't remember. The curls fell across his forehead as he released them and marched forward. He was not sure where he was going, so he stopped to decide on a course of action. What was he supposed to do in the land of the dead?

"Going somewhere?" Alec heard behind him. He turned, not exactly startled, though he should have been. Behind him was a beautiful, no, *stunning* young woman where he had been lying. She was wearing a midnight blue dress. Her wavy, auburn hair was loose down her back. When she smiled, Alec saw the dimples on both of her cheeks. Her eyes were an odd, enchanting, bright violet. It was nothing like the color that his sister Ava's eyes turned. Alec did not even blink.

"I'm not sure, Milady. Would you be able to help me with that?" He smiled at her, flashing his own dimples. "Am I dead?"

The young woman laughed. "No, you are not dead. At least you are not dead yet."

Alec absentmindedly put his hands in the pockets of his trousers and examined the endless grasslands once again. It was too peaceful here. It was so quiet, and he thought he would go crazy if he were required to spend an eternity in such a boring place with so little chance for adventure.

"Where do you want to go?" the young woman asked.

He thought about that question as he walked back toward the remarkable young woman. He didn't want to be here … So where did he want to go? "Home," he whispered.

The girl smiled and walked toward him. "Good choice." Her fingers touched his temples and dark blue magic swirled around him. *Home*, he thought. *I want to go home.*

…

Ava abruptly withdrew from her trance. What she saw shook her to the core. She had been meditating for some time and it took her a minute to refocus her eyes. Sitting in front of her was William, gazing at her with a slightly worried expression.

"Your eyes were changing colors," William commented. "Is this a normal thing for you?"

Ava smiled a little, probably for the first time in days. "It's normal; there is no need to panic." She stood up and looked at him, quite irritated. "Why are you following me?"

"Remember when I last saw you in this clearing, Sunshine? I just keep running into you by coincidence," William lied. "But at that time, we had not been formally introduced. I have been rude; please let me correct what has been poorly done until now." William stood up, bowed, and said, "I am William, Prince of Cyrus, brother to Prince Ericson and Lady Kaitlin of Cyrus. You have also met my younger brother; he attempted to recite a poem to you. He means well but is just a bit witless and, I have to admit, a terrible poet."

Despite her irritation, Ava laughed at the memory of the silly verse the young gangly noble had recited, with its terribly rhymed lines and the squeaky voice in which he recited it. Prince William smiled at her, and turned to look at her horse, grazing in the plain. Ava suddenly thought of her brother and decided to change the subject.

"William?"

"Yes?" he responded.

She pondered for a moment how to phrase her question, and then asked, "In Cyrus, are there any myths or stories about pale- and white-horsed warriors? Their horses have red eyes and their riders carry unusual weapons."

William looked at her with a note of concern. "I might have."

She looked at him somewhat surprised, "Please tell me about them."

"A traveler came to our palace some time ago," William began. "We invited him to stay for the winter with my family. He insisted on paying for his lodging by telling us stories of odd lands far away from Greater Articia. One story that he told us," William paused, "was about a religion in a place not much different from Articia. They worshiped one god, and his army of angels fought against a major demon whose name I cannot remember." William sat back down in the grass and crossed his legs as he looked at Ava. "He said that the four horsemen signaled the start of a tremendous cataclysm that brought about the end of that world."

"Go on," Ava prodded.

"These horsemen had many names, such as the death horsemen and the four horsemen of the apocalypse, which is another name for cataclysm." William looked Ava in the eyes. "The old man said that the horsemen are from such an ancient time on that world that they had a name in the special language of Latin, the *letum vir equus*. There is a pale horse, death; a white horse, pestilence; a red horse, war; and a black horse, famine."

"So the pale horse and the white horse may have been part of this troupe," Ava said.

"The pale and white horses... What is amiss, Princess?" William asked as Ava turned her head away, searching for something to change the subject to, but he leaned under her gaze, which forced her look at him. "I think you are trying to hide something. I hope you're not getting involved with something dangerous," William pleaded.

She looked at his concerned face oddly; he was acting just like Aleczander. He had that same irritating look on his face that was warning her not to try anything funny, and it felt comforting, as it always did with her brother Alec. "I'm not hiding anything, if it concerns you so, *Prince*. I am not *involved* in anything I cannot control," she retorted.

He looked at her a moment, to see if she was serious, then released his gentle hold on her chin and looked at the sky through the canopy of trees. "Well, if you don't mind the company, I would like to journey with you for a while," William stated

"What makes you think I am off on a journey?" Ava asked.

"The pack on your horse is rather heavy for a short ride. I have traveled once or twice and I am quite good at recognizing someone who is on the run," he replied.

Ava looked back at Aurora and smiled. "I guess I could use the company. I am heading south but have not yet decided on my destination."

William stood and walked over to his mount. "The only thing of interest to the south is the Great Library," William offered.

"Then maybe a stop at the Great Library will be one destination on my journey. How far is it?" she asked.

"The only time I traveled there, it took about a fortnight. It was quite the journey from Cyrus but from here, I believe it is just a few days," William responded. "There are many villages and boroughs on the way where we can stop for provisions and to rest. When would you like to leave?"

"There is no time like the present," Ava responded, as she got to her feet and mounted Aurora. Together they rode off to the south.

...

His eyes flew open and he took in a forest scene. Alec blinked slowly, thinking he was still half-asleep. However, when he opened his eyes, instead of the blue walls of his room, he saw the forest canopy. He tried to sit up and look around, which he immediately regretted as pain shot through his chest and arm.

Dizzying memories of the pale horseman flooded his mind. He grunted as the pain ebbed and then adjusted his body so he could sit up slowly and lean against a tree. His chest and his left arm were bandaged with clean, white linen and he noted quite a few scratches and cuts on his legs. He was breathing heavily from his effort to sit up as he looked around the small clearing.

Star Dancer was eating hay and oats, as was the black stallion he had seen the stranger riding last night, if it had been last night. Alec looked up and saw the sun high in the sky. It was now midday. He was immediately alarmed and tried to get up until he remembered maiming the horse of one of his pursuers. Had the boy taken care of the other? A figure with a black, hooded cloak came into the clearing from behind the horses. Under the hood, Alec saw the eyes of the boy as their gazes locked.

"Who are you?" Alec inquired slowly, trying unsuccessfully to study the boy underneath his cloak.

"I am Danny," the boy answered, brushing the back of the stallion that he had ridden earlier.

"Daniel?" Alec wondered aloud.

"Actually," Danny corrected as she pulled off her hood to reveal the hair of greyish waves and violet eyes similar to the girl from his dream, "it is Danielle." The young girl looked at him strangely, and then smiled. "You must have hit your head harder than I thought you did when you fell from your mount.

Earlier, I rode past the area where you downed the pale one. You may have bought us some time and saved yourself in that moment of genius. You killed its mount." Danny turned to kick dirt onto a smoldering fire. "We need to move from here as soon as possible. You'll have to get on your horse somehow," Danny commanded

"*Horse*" the destri retorted!

Danny stopped short in her tracks and turned to the destri.

"*I am not one of the silent beasts, young warrior,*" Star Dancer communicated to her. Alec smiled when he realized that Star Dancer was talking to her. Then he realized he did not hear him doing it.

"*Yes, Prince, I can control who hears my thoughts. I do need my privacy once in a while.*" Star Dancer continued to eat, clearly famished from a hard day of running.

"Get dressed. We cannot linger long here. You are still being pursued by the white horseman," Danny instructed.

Alec stood up painfully and pulled on the white shirt. He was wearing the brown trousers he had set out in, and they had rips in the cloth of the legs. He would have to live with it for now. He bent down slowly, picked up the sword belt, and buckled it. Walking was easier because he did not really have to move his stomach or chest muscles.

As he tried to mount Star Dancer, he doubled over in renewed pain. Star Dancer had bowed down to try to make it easier for Alec to mount, but it did not help him in his current condition. Star dancer rubbed his snout to Alec's face and helped him stand straight. "*Steady, Prince.*"

"Turn around," Danny commanded. Alec slowly turned toward Danny, still wincing in pain from the wound from the pale rider's sickle-staff. He was standing before her looking pitiful. Danny put her hand over his burn and whispered, "*Lumen sano maximus.*" A red glow flowed from her hands and washed over the wound on his chest, which took away most of the pain.

"Better?" she asked.

Alec realized that he *did* feel better. Having two siblings with magic, though, he knew how powerful she had to be to have exhibited a form of the healing magic.

"You have significant magical power. You could have fully healed me already!" he said accusingly. Danny looked over at Alec and smiled as she realized the insight this young man just displayed.

"Usually it is better to let wounds such as this to heal naturally if you are healthy. It makes the muscles and skin stronger and gives a warrior valuable experience," she replied. "But in this case, I did not fully heal it because this wound is unnatural from an unnatural being. It would take powers much greater than mine to completely heal that wound."

"I remember the rider's sickle-staff. I saw it touch the ground, and everything around the staff died," Alec told her.

"A powerful weapon indeed," Danny replied. "You need to get on your horse now so we can go. It is many miles to our destination. There we can rest undisturbed by the demon beasts."

Alec nodded, a little overcome from the magic she had used. He thought of Ava, and wondered what she might be doing now. Alec felt a bit unnerved, knowing the white horseman was still after him and he had left the castle without any armor. He was unprepared to battle the foe he was sure to have to face again. Aleczander pulled his cloak over his shoulders. Mounting Star Dancer only caused a little pain now, so they settled in to follow the girl, who was now riding ahead of them on her black stallion.

The young women had tied her hair back. Clearly, she was dressed in the same forest garb he had seen worn by many of Articia's woodsmen. Her dark blue shirt was barely visible beneath her black cloak. Danny broke into a gallop and headed east. Alec pushed the destri into a gallop and pulled up beside the girl.

"You never answered my question. Who are you?" Alec asked.

Danny looked at him and sighed. "No one you would know, for sure, unless you keep track of every orphan peasant in your kingdom."

She sounded bitter, and Alec looked down. "I'm sorry," he whispered. Alec, though not meaning too, had touched a nerve.

She shook her head. "Don't be. It is not your fault that I have no parents. Before my mother and father died, they taught me much about the royal children of Articia. I had seen many images of you and your sister and have only recently learned that you are far from the spoiled children I had thought you to be. You are rather privileged but not spoiled."

Danny smiled a little, and Alec realized something in a few moments that he should have confronted her about earlier. "You can speak to Star Dancer."

She nodded. "Now that I know he's a destri. I heard him because he has chosen for me to hear."

Alec and Danny did not speak for a bit while Star Dancer filled him in on what had happened while he lay wounded. It had taken a few hours for Danny to track them. They had run from the battle in such haste that that they were easy to track by one who had knowledge of the forest. Before Danny had arrived, his mount had chased off a wolf that had been out hunting. They were lucky that the white rider had not immediately pursued them because it had turned back to aid the pale one.

Alec fell asleep early and missed the sunset. He slept through the night and into most of the next day. When he finally awakened, Danny did her best to get him to eat a soup that she had made from plants in the forest. She smiled at some of the faces Alec made as he consumed the bitter soup. She had also fed the destri and her mount from her food supplies.

"This is truly disgusting concoction!" Alec said as his stomach growled. Danny outright laughed. She had a beautiful laugh, the kind that just made you smile.

"Here, have some." She pulled out two strips of meat that had been cooked, jerked, and salted to preserve it and handed them to him. Alec ate them quickly as they resumed their travel down the wooded path.

Alec looked in awe at an oak they passed that was taller than any tree he had ever seen near the city of Articia. The wind played games with his hair and the sun that dappled through the leaves of the forest shined into his eyes. Surprised by his exhaustion; the day he had already slept had not helped to rebuild his stamina. Despite his fatigue, they rode on for the rest of the light.

Alec still wondered about the encounter that had occurred just a day ago. He decided to press Danny further on the subject. He thought for a moment about how to state his question and asked Danny, "You called those ... things," he started, unable to call them people but he didn't know what they were otherwise, "*letum vir equus.*" What does that mean?"

"*Letum vir equus* is death horseman in the language from another world. Where they are from, the people called them the four horsemen of the apocalypse. Their arrival signaled the end of that ancient world. In my studies, I learned a lot about them. They were a very negative society, always inventing ways that they could ultimately destroy themselves. From what I was taught, it is believed that they succeeded," she answered.

"How did you learn all of this?" Alex asked, somewhat confused how a girl of the forest would have any opportunity to study.

"My parents and my master taught me much about the other world and the magic and the beasts that existed in that place. They had many books, some that they had asked me to exchange at the Great Library on occasion," she responded.

"I have never heard of the Great Library," Alec admitted.

Danny raised an eyebrow at this. "The Great Library is quite famous. I thought everyone knew about it."

Alec turned to her and said, "Well, *I* have not heard of it."

"I am surprised. How could such a thing be unknown in the city of Articia? I would have thought the royal family would have known that a place like the library existed in their kingdom," she commented.

Alec thought about this for a moment and decided to change the subject. "I managed a strike on the pale rider. Did I critically wound him?"

"I do not think so." Danny seemed a bit uncomfortable at that moment. "I am actually surprised that you wounded him at all. My parents fought them and, despite striking them many times, did no damage to them at all. They did not survive the encounter."

This new information caught Alec of guard. "When did your parents die?"

"A fortnight back, on a road north of here. We were returning from a pilgrimage to the Temple of Adara when we came across those deadly riders coming from the east," she answered.

"You escaped?" Alec asked.

"No, the goddess intervened. She said it was not yet my time and that I had a destiny to fulfill," she answered. "I thought I had died at the hand of the pale rider but when I awoke, I found my parents lying beside me, dead on the ground, but I was still alive."

"I am sorry," Alec offered.

"Thank you," Danny replied looking away from Alec so he could not see the tears welling up in her eyes.

They rode quietly for about an hour before Alec spoke again. "Where are we heading? I was supposed to travel east, but I cannot tell in the forest here which way the sun is going."

"We are still traveling east, we will stop at my master's house," Danny answered.

"Tell me about your master."

"When my parents discovered that I had magical abilities, they arranged for me to train with a local practitioner," Danny responded. "When we get to the master's house, we'll be fine, though. If you …" she cut off suddenly and looked at a tree directly in front of them.

Danny drew her sword, and with a sudden motion, hopped from her horse to the first branch and disappeared in the leaves. Alec was surprised by how quickly and quietly she moved. There was a rustle of leaves and Alec heard a grunt as two figures fell from the tree and hit the ground hard. Danny jumped down gracefully. Alec thought he saw subtle magic easing her descent, but he was not sure.

The two boys got up and brushed themselves off, both wearing goofy grins. Danny looked at them disgusted. "You followed me, didn't you? I told you both to go home." Danny sheathed her sword as she continued lecturing the pair. "I could have mistaken you as one of our pursuers. You are lucky that I did not just kill you both!"

Alec saw two young boys step up as they continued to brush off the dirt and leaves acquired on their trip to the ground. Both still had the foolish grins on their faces as Alec turned to Danny and asked, "So you know these guys?"

"The big bloke with the girly brown hair is Jamal. You can yell in his ear and the echo will resonate out the other ear. He is as strong, and sometimes as stupid, as a mule." The young boy she had just described stepped forward and smiled as he flipped his brown hair to the side. It was about shoulder length and curly. He was wearing a white mohair top and brown trouser.

The boy named Jamal had what appeared to be a makeshift war hammer in one dirty hand. His face was equally dirty and the pack at his back showed its age, items stored inside hung from the holes of the worn satchel. The young man slung his hammer into a handmade holder on his backpack, and then he shoved his hands in his pockets and winked at Danny. "Well that's kind-a rough, doncha think, Danny?" He looked down, still smiling. Alec noticed that his speech was every bit of an uneducated farm boy.

Danny rolled her eyes in disgust. "The one with the mop of blonde hair and big dopey-looking blue eyes is Dustin." Alec looked over at the other boy, who was decently muscled and had bright blue eyes. His blonde curly hair fell in his face and he had a bow on his back. In his hand, he carried a scroll. This one was clearly the smarter, and cleaner, of the two young men.

It was clear that Dustin had been around nobles at some point in his life as Danny introduced him, he bowed to Alec. Dustin was not the typical farm boy one would expect.

"I met these two *heroes* on an errand I was running for my master," Danny explained. "On the return trip, I passed through their town and found that it was being raided by a small group of goblins." Danny looked over toward the pair. "With a lot of my help and a little of their luck, we managed to slay the four invaders," Danny said with an air of annoyance. "They have been *helping* me ever since."

"So they are battle hardened then," Alec replied as he winked at the pair.

"I would not give them that much credit," she replied. "But they now believe they are worth something in a skirmish."

Alec suddenly realized that Danny did not have a peasant's accent, as it was quite different from the accent of the local boys. "I say we should order these dim-witted, bright-eyed *warriors* home, but it's your call, Alec." Danny's eyes looked at him pleading.

Alec looked from one boy to the other.

"*They would be a good distraction you know*" the destri communicated to him.

Alec thought back, "*I know. But we could be put at quite a disadvantage if we have to nursemaid that pair.*"

"*You mistake my meaning. I was suggesting they might be a distraction to our pursuers,*" the destri answered.

"*You would sacrifice them?*" Alec responded, rather shocked at the destri's suggestion.

"*No*," Star Dancer replied. "*I believe they can hold their own if they are tested in a real battle. You should never underestimate the capabilities of the simple folk. They are a hardy people who have deep feelings of honor and family. They can be very*

protective of their friends and quite the terror to their enemies.
This pair would be worthy allies".

Alec thought to himself. Honor is a thing you learn, not a thing for which you are born. Maybe this pair is part of his destiny. "So, Dustin, tell me about that scroll of yours?" Alec asked the young boy.

Dustin looked from one to the other, Alec and Danny, fearfully. He obviously already respected Danny, and he was not sure about Alec, who he did not know well. "I-It's my magic incantations sc-scroll." He looked nervous, very nervous.

"Oh!" Danny acted excited, and he looked a bit more relaxed. "How powerful are you?" She was waiting with her hand on her hip now.

Dustin smiled in a bragging way. "My dad says I must be the most powerful wizard in the world because I can throw fire!"

Danny smirked. "Really, let me see. Throw one at me."

The boy was so excited that he missed Danny's sarcasm. He was going to show them his powerful magic. Jamal sat on the side looking irritated. "I really don't think I should. I might hurt you," Dustin said nervously.

"Don't worry. I have a little magic of my own. If I feel that I am in danger, I will dispel the fire," Danny assured him, never thinking him powerful enough to put her in any danger.

Dustin did not wait for Danny to ask twice, he quickly started an incantation to show off his ability with magic. He started to form the fireball in his hand. The difference between a wizard and a sorcerer, like his sister, was that wizards used incantations and they did not have innate magic. Dustin spoke an incantation that he read from the paper. When he released his fireball, it was barely the size of his fist. Though Alec had not had much experience with wizards, he recognized a weak fire missile when he saw one.

Danny caught it easily and sent it back at him, bored almost. Then she sent out a string of power-force magic that caused Dustin to stumble backward. She reached out with her magic and flipped him upside down, then lifted him in the air. Danny smirked as she moved him to the left a little and dropped him on top of the other boy.

"You two will need some additional training," Alec said as he laughed at the comical pair. "But I think your company is welcome."

Danny looked at Alec in surprise. She sighed with disgust and turned her horse to walk away from the motley crew.

"Will you walk the whole way with us? How will you keep up?" Alec asked

"We have a warhorse!" Dustin beamed as he called into the woods. After a few minutes, and a few more calls, a shaggy mule bumbled into the clearing. "We will catch up. We can track well." Alec rolled his eyes and rode to catch up with Danny.

As the day wore on, Alec was feeling much better. Danny's magic had hastened his healing and the wound he had received from the pale rider's sickle-staff was now just a nuisance. They finally stopped for the night when there was no light left above the horizon. They unpacked their bundles and spread them in a small grove by a slow-moving river.

"I should redress your chest wound," Danny said as she came over to him. He nodded in agreement and pulled his shirt off. Danny bent down, untied the knot to release the bandage, and gently pulled it off his chest. She examined the wound and then let out a startled gasp.

"What's wrong?" Alec looked down at the burn on his chest. A thin layer of skin had already starting to cover the scar. Alec did not understand what was bothering her.

"You should not have healed that fast. Have you had training in the magical healing arts?" she asked.

Though he always healed faster than his brothers did, he assumed that the magic she had used earlier was the reason he had improved so quickly. "No, I have no magical abilities but I have always been a quick healer," Alec replied.

Danny looked puzzled at this new development. Nevertheless, she cleaned the major wound and then bandaged it with fresh linen. When she was finished, she examined his other minor injuries. When Danny realized the minor cuts that had been there in the morning were gone, she looked at him and asked, "Can I try something?"

Alec wondered what she was thinking. "Exactly what do you want to try?" Alec asked, thinking that she was intending to get intimate with him, which made him uncomfortable for some reason. As Danny leaned into him, he picked up her natural aroma. Yes, he was definitely feeling uncomfortable now.

Danny reached out and put her palms on his temples. *Just like the woman in my dream*, he thought. He found himself drifting into *something*, a state of mind that he had never previously visited. There was Danny, standing beside a pool of water that was a vibrant shade of red.

"What is that?" he asked her.

She looked up at him. "It's your magic. We are in your being, your magical sense."

He looked at the huge pool of water. "I don't have magic. I asked my sister Ava to test me and she said there was nothing of substance."

"Does your sister always tell you the truth?" Danny smiled a little. "Maybe she thought you might have too little magic, which would allow you to do little more than light candles or cast the simplest spells."

"That would have been helpful, here and there," Alec muttered.

"A little is never enough," Danny replied. "Your sister probably knew that and did not want you to chase the unattainable."

"Shouldn't that have been my decision to make?" Alec said annoyed.

"Don't blame her," Danny replied. "She may not have even been able to see that you had magic of any substance at all. From what my master told me of your sister Ava, she is a powerful practitioner. Your magic is actually present and trainable, but it must have looked insubstantial from her perspective."

"Her perspective," Alec sputtered.

"Do not take it to heart. It is only because I am not as powerful as she is that I can perceive it at all," Danny said. "Think of the insects that fly around us. You are not aware of them because they are not important. In the same way, Ava's sphere of magic is so large that minor magical capabilities make no impression on her."

"What is the nature of my magical abilities?" Alec asked.

"Your magic can be described as a red aura magic. This is healing magic," Danny explained.

"Like my mother?" he asked.

"And like mine, though I have some other minor magical skills as well. The red magic is the most common form of magic that practitioners can perform, and you probably did inherit this capability from your mother," Danny responded. "But from what my mother told me, I suspect that your mother has significant power. You should not have been able to attain such strong healing strength without additional training."

"How can I be healing myself without knowing?" Alec asked.

"I think" Danny surmised, "Your ability is unique. Your natural magical ability has had to practice subconsciously on *you*. But you would have had to suffer injuries constantly for it to reach the level I have seen."

"You have not witnessed the regular beatings that my sister Ava has dealt me on the training yards," Alec said as he started to smile. They both laughed at this as Danny and Alec slipped out of the meditation.

Danny pulled back her hands and smiled. "Did your sister explain the significance of the pool?"

"No, we never really talked about magic and I only recently found interest in the classes she was taking," Alec replied.

"Your magical stamina is represented by a pool of colorful water," Danny instructed. "I knew you had healing magic based on the color of the pool you have. As you get stronger, your pool gets larger. With a larger pool to draw upon, your magical stamina increases."

"So I have a pool of magic?" Alec asked.

"Yes. Apparently your sister was helping you with those regular beatings," she smiled. "Since your innate magical ability was focused on keeping you healthy, it grew over the years."

"So how powerful am I?" Alec asked with curiosity.

"With some good training, you could heal almost any wound," Danny answered. "My magical pool is the equivalent of a pond and I am no slouch. Your pool looked as large as a lake. I was quite shocked when I saw it."

Alec tried to take all of this new information in at once and realized he truly did not understand the significance of the pool. Rubbing his forehead, he looked back at her. "How big is Ava's pool?"

"I have not seen it, but my master saw it when Ava was a toddler," Danny responded. "He and his companions were quite shocked to find that at such a young age your sister's pool was much like the oceans on the eastern or western shores of Articia."

"What, how could that be?" Alec asked.

"My master believes that it was a gift of the goddess," she responded.

...

About an hour after Danny and Alec arrived and settled the campsite, the two boys galloped, if that is what you can call what their shaggy "warhorse" did, into the clearing. They quietly set their cloaks on the ground and, as instructed by Danny, went to get wood for the fire. When they were gone, Danny turned to Alec.

"I think it is important that you have some basic magical training. Based on the occurrences of the last few days, you may find being able to tap that power beneficial," Danny suggested.

"All right, though I am still a bit stunned at the news that I have any magical power at all," Alec responded.

"And since you have invited them to go with us, I want you to train those two simpletons to fight as a disciplined unit," Danny commanded, "for the safety of all us."

Alec groaned and turned to look at the two boys. Having been snooping on the conversation Alec and Danny had been having, they both acted eager as soon as he looked over. He remembered when he had first started training in swordsmanship. Alec recognized those eager looks, and he sighed. They deserved a chance to learn.

"*You mature more each day, my young Prince. This road may yet help you to become a man,*" the destri communicated to him.

"So you heard?" Alec asked.

"*I already knew,*" the steed answered

"Why didn't you tell me?" Alec questioned.

"*It is not our way.*"

...

"An unexpected event has occurred," the imp informed his master.

"What event?" the dark master questioned.

"The um ... whelp escaped the pale rider!" the imp replied.

"WHAT!" The dark master turned to the imp angrily. "How is that possible? He does not have the power to best that rider!"

The imp backed away from the angered conjurer. "He only wounded the rider; he bested his horse." As he spoke, he inched farther away from his master.

"He bested his horse!" The dark sorcerer thought about this for a moment. "What of the white horseman? Why did he not attack the young prince?"

"He was distracted, my Lord," the imp replied.

"Distracted by what?" the mage shouted.

The imp cowered lower into the alcove he was planning to escape from if the sorcerer's violence escalated to a dangerous level. "A young boy came to the aid of the prince."

The sorcerer laughed at this news. "How is it a young boy managed to distract the white horseman?" The sorcerer loomed over the imp.

"It would appear that the boy has some power," the imp replied.

"Power, tell me what you know." The sorcerer reached over and grabbed the imp by the neck as he pulled him out of the alcove.

"My ally used sorcery on the royal prince so that he would not wake to run from the horsemen. The boy arrived just before the horsemen and dispelled the sorcery." The imp struggled in the dark lord's grip. "He distracted the riders, which allowed the prince to mount and run."

"Go on," the sorcerer demanded.

"The boy used some sorcery to hold the white rider in place, so only the pale rider pursued the young prince," the imp continued. "The prince then did something unexpected. As the pale rider charged, the prince maimed his horse."

"So where is the prince and this boy now?" the dark lord demanded.

"We do not know," the imp replied.

"What!" The sorcerer angrily threw the imp against the wall. The imp bounced off a wall and rolled under the desk to hide from the dark lord's wrath.

"My ally was detected by the boy and had to withdraw. The boy had too much power for him to remain hidden." The imp shouted with its hands over its head as it cowered under the desk.

The dark lord went over to the map on his wall. "Where did they last see the prince?" he asked.

"At the edge of the forest," the imp replied, looking for the nearest exit.

"Which forest?" The sorcerer turned to the imp, who was still cowering under the desk in fear of the mage's anger.

"The Valemore Forest," the imp said sheepishly.

The dark sorcerer's anger reached its peak as he shouted, "*Flamma dexterous manus.*" A fire burst from his hand to engulf the imp. When the fire dispersed, all that remained of the imp was a small pile of ashes.

The sorcerer walked back over to the map and muttered, "We will not be able to touch you there, young Prince, but you cannot stay there forever." He slammed the door on his way out of the room.

In the alcove, the imp reappeared and looked at the pile of ash. "These humans are so witless."

...

William and Ava rode for a day before they approached the hamlet of Lorden. William broke the silence. "I am known here, but we should keep your identity hidden for now. It is not clear who is our friend and who is our enemy."

"Do you think I will be put in danger in this hamlet?" Ava asked.

"No, the people here are very friendly, though a bit reserved. Over the last couple of ages, their village has been a frequent stomping ground for armies traveling from the southeast. They suffered at the hands of every army that passed through the hamlet on the way to invade the city of Articia. That long history has made them very cautious," William answered, "For now, you are my cousin Astra. They know of her but have never seen nor met her, so you should be able to get away with the deception."

"What a beautiful name. You must tell me about her some time," Ava commented.

"Unfortunately, her name does not match her appearance or disposition. She is a rather horrid person," William replied. "But her reputation is not known this far west."

Ava looked at William with a raised eyebrow. "So your cousin Astra was the best fit for my personality and appearance?"

William stopped his mount abruptly, "Oh, um … that was not my intention. Astra is the cousin that I see most often. I meant no offense."

Ava laughed as she galloped past William into the hamlet of Lorden.

…

They had been traveling for a day into the Valemore Forest on no obvious trail. Ahead of Alec, Danny pulled into a clearing and dismounted. "We will camp here for the night. We are well into the Valemore Forest now and the dark riders will not follow us here." She pulled the saddle off her black mount.

"We are near the Vale?" Alec asked surprised. "When did we enter the land of the elves?"

"About three miles back as we entered the edge of this forest that they call Valemore," she answered. "We are now under the protection of the elves that live here. I am sure they are already watching our approach."

Alec removed Star Dancer's saddle and blanket as he asked, "Your master lives among the elves?" Alec asked.

"Well, sort of," Danny replied.

"Well, sort of what?" Alec asked again.

"He has a cottage in the center of the Vale, on the edge of the citadel. Though there are many other elves that live near him," she replied.

"Other elv … your master is an elf?" Alec inquired rather surprised.

At that moment, Jamal and Dustin lumbered into the clearing on their shaggy warhorse, shouting to Danny and Alec. "Did you know we are in the land of the elves?!" Dustin said excitedly.

"They scared the cow dung right out me," Jamal included.

"You saw the elves?" Alec asked.

At this time both of the boys dismounted, or more like fell off their shaggy beast. They were tripping over each other to get to Alec, each trying to tell the story first. "Wait; wait, one at a time. Dustin, tell me what you saw," Alec asked.

Dustin stuck out his tongue at Jamal before he spoke. "We were following your tracks and then three of the tallest beings we have ever seen were all of a sudden in front of us."

"They jiss appeared out the air," Jamal interjected to Dustin's annoyance.

"They asked us why we were tracking the chosen ones, but we did not know who they were talking about. We told them we were a warrior and a wizard and we were catching up to our charge," Dustin added.

"How did they respond to that?" Danny said with contempt.

"They smiled and told us to be on our way and may the goddess be with us on our important mission," Dustin replied. Danny made a sound of disgust and walked over to her horse to pull off the blanket and pack.

Alec pondered this for a moment and walked over to talk to Danny. "What do you think the elves meant by 'the chosen ones'?"

Danny stopped for a moment to think about Alec's question. The chosen ones, the boys had said that. If she had not been so annoyed, she would have caught that, too. Maybe she would have to stop being so hard on the pair. "I don't know. In a couple of days we will be in the heart of Valemore and into the Vale and we can ask my master," Danny replied.

...

William led Ava to a small hovel at the far end of the village. Many of the villagers looked at the pair suspiciously, as they passed by, but their expressions changed as soon the residents recognized William. After that, they offered friendly greetings, which William returned.

When they reached the small hovel, he dismounted his destri and knocked on the wood planks. They were the best effort of the occupant of the shelter to add a door to the small structure.

"One moment, do not get your knickers in a twist!" a crackly old voice came from inside the dwelling.

"Come on, old man, would you pass up some free labor and a visit for dinner?" William responded.

The door opened with a burst and an older man, not what Ava expected, came out and embraced William. "You young stag, what brings you to my village so early in the season? You know I have not yet planted the vegetables. There is nothing for you to help me harvest this time of year."

"Nicholas, you old dog, just because I eat you out of house and home when I visit does not mean I only come for the food. Your tall tales of war and conquest would draw many a young man to this shack you call home," William joked.

"And who is this ravishing young woman …?" Nicholas's eyes went wide when he realized who was accompanying William. "My Lady, I am sorry I did not immediately recognize you. Welcome to this humble abode. I am at your service."

"I am honored by your invitation, but please no pomp and circumstance while we stay here. I am traveling incognito and need to remain that way," Ava responded graciously. "Please call me by my alias, Astra."

Nicholas raised an eyebrow at that name. "Astra," Nicholas looked at the young prince with a question in his eyes.. "I am sure the name is for disguise only and is no reflection on your personality."

Ava looked over at William, who had stiffened at Nicholas's response. "I see you have heard of William's famous cousin. Perhaps his choice was not the best for my disguise."

"No worries. Prin-, um …, Astra. This old man" Nicholas said referring to himself, "gets around a lot more than the average villager does. No one else in this small place will know of his cousin's dubious distinction. Please lead your mounts to the back of this humble home. There is hay and grain. Then come on in for some food and tale trading," Nicholas finished as he turned to lead them into his small home.

...

Danny led the troupe through the thick forest. Alec realized that if he had tried to find his way through this maze of a forest on his own, he would never have found his way. Danny did not seem hindered by the lack of trail.

The two boys had no trouble keeping up with them now since the thickness of the forest had slowed him and Danny down considerably. Though the shaggy horse did not fare well in the thicket, its fur was now quite full of branches and thorns. Alec, amused by the actions of the shaggy beast, watched, as the beast try to scratch is shaggy back at every tree it passed. At every attempt, it almost knocked the two boys to the ground.

Alec looked around at the forest that they were passing through. The distance between the trees was so tight that the trail was almost not passable. His trek through this forest helped him to understand the reason why a foreign army had never invaded the Vale. With no specific trails or roads, it would be hard for any force to move through the forest that surrounded the Vale. He wondered if this was a natural condition of the forest or if the elves had somehow ensorcelled it to keep out intruders.

On the first day in the forest, they stopped in a clearing to camp and rest. Alec, as promised, worked with Jamal and Dustin to improve their fighting skills.

"Dustin, you must learn to defend yourself!" Alec chided the young man when he knocked him down for the third time. The boy would not plant his feet on the ground to deflect Alec's attack.

"I will use my powerful magic to defend myself," Dustin pouted. "I do not need to learn the ways of the warrior."

Alec thought about this for a bit and then responded to Dustin. "Dustin, my sister Ava is one of the most powerful sorcerers I have ever had the privilege to know. Most of the practitioners of Castle Articia are even afraid of the power she could wield. Despite the fact that she could easily defeat any opponent with her magic, she is one of the most talented swordsmen—sorry, *swordspersons*—I know."

"Why would she need to practice the warrior arts if she had that much power?" Dustin asked.

"The magical arts cannot be used in all situations. And no practitioner has unlimited power," *though he was not sure about Ava.* "There will come a time, like there has for my sister Ava, where you will need to defend yourself with your physical skills," Alec instructed.

"Well, if a princess of Articia is willing to learn the warrior arts, despite having magical abilities, then so will I," Dustin stated. The young warrior-to-be lifted up his staff and beckoned Alec to attack again. He still lost the joust, but this time he was trying much harder to defend himself. Dustin planted his feet much firmer on the ground when Alec attacked.

Danny watched this whole exchange from a distance and was impressed with how well Alec worked with the boys. Despite the inferior skills of the two young men, as Alec trained the boys, they showed remarkable improvement. Maybe there was hope for them yet.

Alec enjoyed working with Jamal. Even though he did not always make the best decisions, he possessed a remarkable amount of dumb luck. Alec felt that the goddess truly favored this young man. Jamal was truly strong, even for such a small boy. Alec soon discovered that in a match of pure strength, Jamal could easily beat him.

Alec had never sparred with someone wielding a war hammer, or at least something close to a war hammer. He got his first lesson in strength when Jamal tripped through one of his assaults, missing his frontal objective, and caught Alec in the back of his thigh with his hammer.

Wow that hurt more than I expected it would, Alec thought as Jamal jumped to his feet, clearly pleased with himself at the success of the accidental strike. He would have to be more careful to avoid that hammer now that he knew the full force that Jamal could deliver.

"We need to work on your balance and the delivery of your hammer blows. What you are doing right now is what martial tutors call *diving in*. When you do that, you overcommit your attack, and a smart warrior will just side step your advance and trip you or let you pass. You are then vulnerable to a strike from behind. Let's try it again, but slowly, and I will show you your mistake."

Alec set up for Jamal's next attack, "Remember … *slowly*," he said as the young boy started forward in a much exaggerated slow-motion attack.

Jamal even gave a slow-motion version of battle cry. "Arrrrr … gggggggg …."

Danny was barely able to suppress a giggle at the amusing show that Jamal was providing.

"Now as you close in on me, swing the hammer overhead slowly. I will step aside from the attack." Alec moved slightly to the left. Jamal did an exaggerated head turn toward Alec, making a badly acted surprised look.

Alec smiled as he said, "As you pass, a good warrior will strike out with his foot to your knee, like this, and swing in with his weapon to your unprotected back, like this." As Jamal was moving past, Alec gave a slight kick against Jamal's knee with his foot and hit the flat of his sword on Jamal's back. Jamal had turned too far back to see what Alec was doing and lost his balance. He took two wobbling steps and went head first into a tree.

"Jamal, are you all right?" Alec asked with concern.

Jamal backed up from the tree, clearly annoyed that it had gotten in his way. He put his head down and rammed into it again.

Alec just shook his head and started to walk away. "That's enough for today, Jamal."

Danny could not contain it any longer and started to howl with laughter from the other side of the camp. Alec, Dustin, and Jamal looked her way, then at each other and started to laugh as well.

...

"So how do you know who I am?" Ava asked the old man.

"I have been to the castle many times to visit one of my closest comrades, Bryn, though the last time I was there you were but nine. I watched you train from a window above the courtyard," Nicholas said.

"I do not remember your being at the castle," Ava commented.

"Many people came and went from the castle while you were growing into a young woman. Can you name every merchant or carpenter, every man-at-arms? No, you actually saw this old man pass through the hallway many times, for I am quite plain. I am only truly visible when I practice my craft," Nicholas returned. William was enjoying the interchange. He had known Nicholas for years and had trained under him in Cyrus before Nicholas decided to retire to this small village.

"So what was your craft?" Ava asked, sipping the herbal tea that Nicholas had brewed for her and William.

"My craft was to train young William here in the warrior arts," Nicholas replied. "It was my new profession after I decided to settle down from fighting back the goblin horde with Bryn."

"You are Nick!" Ava said with excited recognition. "You trained Bryn in the warrior arts. He talked often about you and the adventures you both had. When winter was at its worst and the snow was too deep to train, Alec and I would listen to the stories for hours."

"I am sure that my legend far exceeds the truth of my actions," Nicholas said as he laughed. "But Bryn and I go way back." Nicholas crossed to the far wall of the one-room shelter and reached for a long pipe resting on a shelf that was acting like a mantle over a small brick and mud fireplace. "I was in the Artician army as a junior officer when Bryn joined the brigade and our leaders immediately took a shine to his attitude. He had a remarkable succeed-despite-it-all demeanor and we became fast friends. It wasn't long before his intelligence and attitude impressed your father and Bryn soon became my commander!" Nicholas lit the pipe and took a puff. "What an upstart he was, but he was the best warrior I had ever met. He soon exceeded even my capability."

"I had assumed that you were dead," Ava stated. "In order to be a master and be able to have trained Bryn, you have to be over seventy summers."

"More like ninety-two summers, my young Princess," Nicholas responded. "And thank you for the compliment."

Ava was shocked at Nicholas's revelation. Over ninety summers! No one lived that long. At least no one she had ever met.

Nicholas took another long puff on his pipe. "William, what news do you have from the east? It has been a long time since someone has ventured through this small village."

"I am afraid it is not good news. The goblins are massing in the winter pass of Coal Mountain. We expect them to move on the capital soon after the spring melt," William answered.

"Goblins are generally not so organized. Who is behind the sudden incursion?" Nicholas asked.

"We are not sure, but we believe that there is demon interference. There are a large number of wolug riders in the mix," William answered.

Nicholas raised an eyebrow at that unusual news. "This is not the first time we have faced the beasts. Have the One Hundred been assembled?"

"Yes, they are gathering at Castle Articia as we speak," William answered.

"But you are here," the old weapon master observed.

"The goddess has given me a different charge." He looked over at Ava as he spoke.

Nicholas looked oat Ava and smiled. "This is still nothing to get overexcited about."

"There is more," William offered. "The ruffians from the north have added their power to the goblins."

"That is an unexpected turn," Nicholas responded. "Has your uncle started the inscription to build his forces?"

"Yes, and many have come to volunteer from the countryside. The farmers know well the damage the goblins would do if the horde were to run free. They all want to put a quick end to this," William answered. "He expects to have a pike force of about two thousand and an equal number of archers well before the goblins march."

Nicholas banged the pipe on his hand to discharge the spent tobacco. "How many has the king mustered?" Nicholas asked.

"Other than the One Hundred, I do not know. We left the castle a day ago and I did not participate in the planning," William stated.

Ava listened to the conversation between the two generations of warrior and felt she needed to add the information she had been keeping to herself. She knew she could trust old Nicholas with the knowledge of the demon riders. "There is more."

Nicholas and William stopped conversing as Ava spoke. William looked at her with concern. She knew that he knew something or suspected something that he had not yet discussed with her.

"Demon horsemen have been riding the countryside in pursuit of my brother and me," Ava said.

William jumped to his feet, "They are after you, too! Describe the horsemen that pursue you."

Ava almost backed away from the emotion of William's reaction but continued to provide the details that she now felt was important to reveal. "There are a black rider and a red rider."

William rubbed the stubble that was forming on his face. "That would make four horsemen." He looked over to Nicholas, who had stopped puffing on his pipe and lowered it to his waist.

"The horsemen are here. This is dire news," he said. "Does your father know of the horsemen's arrival?"

"I do not know, Aurora and I road from the castle when the goddess came in a dream and told me to ride south to act as a distraction. I did not stop to tell my father this because he would have discouraged my departure," Ava said.

William realized it was time to tell Ava why he had wanted to journey with her. "The goddess came to me in a dream as well. She told me that you were to be my charge and that I was not to leave your side."

Ava looked toward William and smiled at this revelation. She was glad that she would not have to continue on the road alone. She had assumed that William was traveling with her because Nicholas's house was his destination.

Nicholas interceded with a panicked look on his face. "If you are being pursued by these dark demons, then they will pursue you here!"

Ava realized the impact of that statement. "I would not have this village suffer under the presence of those dark riders. William, we must leave immediately and continue south."

William nodded. "I will gather the horses. We can leave in a few minutes."

"Ava, stay behind. We must briefly talk before you go," Nicholas stated as William left the small one room house.

"I hope we have not brought disaster to this village," Ava told the old weapon master.

"Do not distract yourself by such things. I assume you are heading to the Great Library," Nicholas asked.

"That is our destination; it is the only thing of significance in that direction. It must be the place that the goddess is directing me to visit," Ava responded.

"You will be protected there. It was originally built by the elves to hold the vast library of knowledge that they brought from the other world," Nicholas told her. "The horsemen will not enter the library grounds because of the aura that the elves put on it. So they will only pursue you until you enter the gates of the library grounds."

"I wish you would come with us," Ava pleaded.

"I must travel to your father's castle. They must know that they face more than the goblin horde," Nicholas said. "Go now. You must make haste for the library. When you get there, you will meet Mr. Tipple, the librarian and a scholar."

Ava headed for the door and met William and the horses outside. He was already mounted and ready to run. "Ava, one more piece of information that I think you need to know," Nicholas called to her as they started to ride off to the south.

"Yes?" Ava asked as she turned back to look at the old man.

"You are not a twin," he yelled as William was pulling her horse away. "You are a quad!"

"William abruptly stopped his horse and looked back at the old man. " Are you sure it was wise to tell her about that?"

"Now more than ever you need to discover the meaning of this truth, William. It would have become clear at the library anyway. Help her to understand. Now run!" Nicolas reached into a storage bin in the front of his house and pulled out a travel pack. He picked up his staff and waved to the pair as he headed up the north road.

Ava sat stunned at the words that Nicholas had said and looked over to William. "What did the old man mean by me being a quad?"

"It is a long story that would be best told by Mr. Tipple at the Great Library. We must go now before the riders catch our scent," he urged and started to gallop down the road.

As she kicked Aurora into a gallop after William, Ava wondered, *a quad. What could he mean by that?*

...

After riding for almost another full day, Alec, Danny, and the boys passed out of the forest into a large clearing. They had reached the center of the forest surrounding the Vale.

Alec pulled Star Dancer to a halt. He had heard stories of the city in the center of Valemore Forest, but none of them gave justice to what he was seeing in front of him. The Vale was a valley, with a city in its center. There were many farms surrounding the city, which itself was surrounded by a twenty-foot high translucent alabaster wall. He had never seen anything like it.

Alec could see many buildings and the shape of people, or rather elves, moving about through the wall, as if it was a window. The city had hundreds—no thousands!—of buildings in a circular formation. In the center of all of the buildings stood the largest building, he had ever seen. The two towers of the structure looked like they touched the clouds in the sky.

The remarkable building had more than just the two large towers in front of it. A large door between them stood as high as the walls of Castle Articia. He knew it must be an optical illusion, but that central building looked like it was at least four times larger than the castle Alec called home.

The silence was broken when Dustin and Jamal broke out of the woods and stopped short. "Wow!" they said almost in unison.

Danny looked back at the trio, "Come on, gentlemen. It is still a long ride to my master's house and I want to get there before the evening meal."

They traveled down a road of marble tiles, each step of the horses resonating around them. The elves that were tending the farmland looked over at them with a nod. Their farms were abundant with crops and fruit. Alec realized that it was far too early in the season for these farms to look so close to a harvest time. Yet everywhere he looked, the plants were mature and the fruit and vegetables appeared to be prize quality and ready to harvest.

When they reached the gate, they saw two elven warriors standing guard. They were wearing armor that looked like it was fashioned out of the whitest feathers of a dove, though it appeared harder than any material Alec had ever seen. Each stood with a long white spear tipped with a golden multipoint blade. The elves carried shields of white with a symbol that Alec had never seen. They were also wearing helms that covered most of their heads except for slits running down from openings for their eyes to their chins. The pair stood tall enough to almost look Alec in the eyes as he passed between them mounted on Star Dancer, who bowed to the gate guardians as he passed. The two warriors returned his greeting by putting their hands over their hearts as they lowered their heads.

"Have you been here before?" Alec whispered to the destri.

"*I have not personally been here, but we are familiar to each other,*" the destri responded. "*Both of our races are from worlds other than Articia.*"

Alec thought about this and remembered the one class he had attended with Ava. *So they did come from another world,* Alec pondered. "Star Dancer, what happened on the world of the elves? Why are they here now?"

"*That is a long story, but in summary, the people of that world destroyed themselves. The elves were immune to the disaster but could not stay on that world in service of its deity any longer. The demons had already left the barren place after having a large part in causing its demise,*" Star Dancer told him. "*The elves followed the demons to make sure that they could not destroy another world.*"

"The demons want to destroy our world?" Alec asked surprised.

"What?" Danny questioned.

"Nothing, are we almost to your master's house?" Alec changed the subject.

"Yes. We have arrived," Danny said in response. "Boys, stable the horses and then lead the destri to the grass behind this house. You will sleep in the stable with the horses," Danny told them as they started to pull the shaggy beast toward the barn. Alec looked at her with a question in his eyes.

"It is nothing personal. There is only one guest room with two cots in the master's house. They will be more comfortable on the hay than on the floor," Danny assured him. "Come, I am sure my master is already expecting us. We must not keep him waiting."

...

"What is the dark magician planning?" the demon lord asked the imp.

"He is planning to add his magical army to the goblin army in the offensive against the king," the imp replied. "He has committed four powerful sorcerers to the battle."

"Four? What is the significance of that?" the demon lord asked.

"One for each of the elements—earth, air, water, and fire," the imp instructed.

It is a formidable force, the demon thought and said aloud, "And we can arrange for an unfortunate accident for these sorcerers when the battle is near end."

The imp, confused by this revelation, questioned the greater demon. "Why do we want to eliminate these practitioners?"

"Since we have come to this world, I have noticed that our original powers have been greatly diminished. In order to maintain control, we cannot let the dark sorcerers gain too much power or else they will be controlling us," the demon explained.

"Removing those practitioners will tilt the balance back in our favor."

"Why not just send me and my brethren to poison them in the night?" the imp asked.

"Because we do not want them to know that it was us meddling with the balance of power," the demon responded. "What is the situation with the pale rider?"

"We tried to reanimate his horse, but it did not have the power to carry him anymore. The decay had proceeded too far by the time we arrived," the imp relayed to its demon master. "The pale rider was rather frustrated by this and one of my brethren paid dearly as the butt of its wrath," the imp conveyed sullenly.

"We must find the pale rider a new mount," the demon lord stated.

"No mortal horse could carry that rider." The Imp replied.

"I was not thinking of a mortal horse for that one." The demon lord laughed.

14

Preparation for War

"The goblins have massed at the summer pass of the Coal Mountains. They now number just over thirty thousand strong," Prince Ericson reported.

"Your intelligence, as always, has given us an opportunity," King Henry responded. "I believe that the horde will take the north road once they cross into our territory. The south road will put them too close to the Vale. And we both know they would never pass through the Valemore Forest even if they were whipped."

"We should not take any chances," Dominic interceded. "They have not been predictable in the past and if we leave the south road unprotected, they might decide to turn east to Cyrus. It could lead to disaster."

"We could set up a diversion or some trickery," Brendan offered. "If the leaders of that force thought we were massing troops to the south, they might turn northwest toward the capital."

"It is still early in the growing season," Tristan stepped in to add some insight. "I do not believe a lengthy siege will be good for the kingdom. The eastern farms and orchards would be devastated by the invading force and it could take years for them to recover."

"I do not intend to let them get that far, Tris", the king responded. "I intend to catch them here at the three choke points of the Crystal Mountains. At this point the goblin army should be fairly fatigued after traveling eighty leagues to the foothills." The king walked to the map of Articia and put a finger down on the point on a gap in the mountains. "These three points in the eastern foothills have a great advantage. Moreover, there are many trails through the pass. Any army that passes will not be able to reach the trails from the lowest road. And if that army is intent on attacking the capital would have to traverse through this pass. Our archers could fire unhindered from the heights and drive the invading force deeper into the trap. Then our forces could strike the heart of the invading army at this point here, while we move a flanking force south and around from the road to Cyrus to trap the goblin force and gain a strategic advantage."

Bryn interceded. "The plan is sound but has risks, my King. If the invading goblins turn south to avoid the pass, they will run into our flanking force here. It would force us to come through the pass from the north. It would also take our archers many hours to come down from the mountain trails to support our forces."

"We need to ensure that the goblin force takes the path we intend," the king commanded. "Bryn, come up with some strategies so that we can react to any action the dark forces take. It is critical that we get the army of goblins to take the pass."

"Tris and I will work on additional plans in case the goblins do not cooperate and do something unexpected," Dominic offered. "I will go over them with Bryn when we have some firm alternatives."

The king smiled and nodded to Dominic and Tristan. He was happy to see his eldest sons take the initiative.

As the king's mind flashed on what Ava and Alec might be encountering, an old man entered the war planning room escorted by one of the palace guards.

"My King, I have some critical information," Nicholas reported as he hurried into the room.

Bryn's face lit up as he saw his old mentor and friend. The king went over to Nicholas and greeted him. "We welcome the wisdom of your experience in this planning session. Apparently, the goblins have decided that the beating we gave them at the Battle of the Bandit Hills was not enough; they have returned for another grab at our kingdom."

"I see," said the old man. "I have just come from an enchanting tea with your daughter."

"You have seen Ava? How does she fare?" the king asked.

"Quite well, actually," the old man answered, "though she has chosen to parade around in a rather bad disguise."

"What disguise?" the king asked.

"She has taken the name of William's cousin, Astra," Nicholas replied in a neutral tone. At this revelation, the people in the room burst into a round of laughter. All those present knew of Astra and her dismal disposition.

When the laughter died down, the old man spoke again. "I am afraid that is the only amusing news I bear, for your wayward children are being pursued by the four horsemen."

...

"I hope you will be more helpful than your kin," the dark sorcerer warned the imp. He was annoyed that he had had to summon another of their kind, but they tended to be very useful servants.

Only the imps could travel great distances instantly with their innate magic. They were also one of few creatures of Articia that could converse with the demons with little to no fear of becoming a meal. The sorcerer grimaced at the memory of the foul reaction of the demons that had tried to make a meal of one the horrid creatures.

"I only wish to serve, my Lord," the Imp replied.

"I must know what the king is up to," the sorcerer instructed the imp. "Is there any way your kin can enter the castle to see what they are planning?"

"While the king's sorcerer is within its walls, we cannot enter. His power is significant and we cannot hide from him," the imp replied, knowing that the mage Brendan would detect them any time they tried to enter the region around Castle Articia.

"We must find out what they plan. It is critical to our success," the dark mage insisted. "Have your kin keep watch on the roads from the capital perchance they find a traveler with a loose tongue."

The imp bowed and left the chamber.

As the imp disappeared from the room, the sorcerer's scribe entered. "We need to muster the rest of our forces," the sorcerer commanded. "Has the baron arrived yet?"

"Yes, my Lord, he is waiting to see you" the scribe replied.

"Send him in," the dark master commanded as he went over to the wall to review the map of Articia.

As Baron Gerund entered the room, he addressed the dark master of the arts "My Lord, I have news from the front. The goblin horde is now fifty thousand strong and we have been able to assemble two hundred wolug riders."

"Good. What of the ruffians from the north?"

"We believe they have traveled undetected. They have split their forces; a number of them joined the second goblin force that will act as a diversion at the northern pass. The main body of the ruffians' stands at around ten thousand men and is now camped with the main goblin army north of our objective in the woods. They are well west of Lewisvel Keep," the baron responded.

"Excellent. If they remain undetected, then we will surprise King Henry's forces on the other side of the Crystal Mountains pass."

"Do you think that the demons will commit the four horsemen?" the baron asked.

"I do not know," the dark master answered. "The demons seemed to be fixated on Henry's offspring."

"Is it wise for the demons to divert the resources of our army at this time?" the baron asked. "Surely those dark horsemen would erase any advantage the king would have on the field of battle."

"The demons believe that the children are a threat to the current order," the dark sorcerer responded.

"Will they be a threat to our operation?" the baron asked

The dark sorcerer laughed at this. "They are just children of barely fourteen winters. There is no chance that they will escape the fate that those dark riders have in store for them."

"Let's hope so," the baron said with worry. "We have committed a significant force to this endeavor. If we fail, it will be the end of my barony and you know the king will then be fixated on your order."

"We will not fail," the sorcerer replied.

That pronouncement amused the invisible imp on the shelf. *These humans are so overconfident.*

...

"How fares the pale rider's new mount?" the demon asked.

"He seemed quite pleased with it," the underling answered. "It was the first time I ever saw one of those beasts cower. Those demons have significant power."

15
The Prophecy

One will leave, in darkness, reprieve.
One will fight, to seal the light.
One will rule, with death will duel.
One will die, but live within the sky.

"Master, we have arrived. I have brought Alec, as you instructed," Danny said.

"Welcome to my home, young Prince." The large regal elf smiled as he said, "I am glad that you made it safely to our domain."

"I am overwhelmed by your city and your home. It is an honor to be here," Alec said with a bow.

The elf smiled at Alec's formality. "Our gates are open to all those who have good intentions; this has always been our way. Most, however, never have the proper heart to find their way here. Only the purest of spirit or intention succeed in making their way through the forest to the Vale without a guide like Danny."

"It was a hard journey; I had not expected the forest to be so dense," Alec replied.

The elf put his hand on Alec's shoulder. "Be at peace. I am Raphael."

Alec had a feeling of peace. He forgot his worries and no longer felt overwhelmed by his foreign surroundings and deep uncertainties.

"Why am I here?" Alec asked, realizing that was all he could think to say.

"A journey to the Vale is a journey of knowledge. Sometimes the answers to your questions come as part of that journey," Raphael instructed.

Alec had not realized he was on a journey. *Why am I here? Why are those fearsome horsemen pursuing me? What am I supposed do now? What does Adara want from me?*

"How is my sister?" he thought to ask when he remembered he was worried about her.

"Your sisters are fine," the elf responded.

Sisters! "You must be mistaken, sir. I have one sister and two brothers," Alec respectfully corrected the elf.

"My young Prince, I am never mistaken. You have three birth mates as well as your two older brothers," the elf responded as he reached for a teapot on a shelf.

Alec, shocked by this revelation, did not know what to think. This could not be true. His parents had never—no; no one had ever—told him that he had more siblings. "How can this be? Why has no one ever revealed the fact that I have more siblings?" Alec asked.

"Just because something is not told does not mean it is not the truth. Come now, young Prince, have you never heard of such a thing as a secret?" the elf cajoled.

"If it was a secret, why have you told me?" Alec asked.

"Secrets are not meant to be kept forever," the elf replied. "Sometimes, information is not immediately given for the safety or well-being of an individual. Many wise people felt that this knowledge would be dangerous for you to have. However, things are now in motion that will require you and your siblings to become involved."

Alec wondered if the reason that the goddess sent him east was to have this information revealed.

"Alec, why are you here?" Raphael asked.

Alec was curious why the elf would ask him the question he had just posed to the elf. "Because Danny brought me here to see you," Alec responded.

"Alec," the elf paused this time. "Why are you here?"

Alec was starting to get frustrated. The elf was now doing what his mother used to do whenever he did not give her the answer she was looking for; she would keep asking him the same question until he exhausted all avenues to get to the answer she wanted to hear.

"Because the goddess came to me in a dream and told me to journey east," Alec responded.

"Ah, so you are on a mission from the goddess. Adara has sent many of the royal children on missions over the centuries, and some do come by to see us here in the Vale once in a while," Raphael commented.

Over the centuries, just how old are the elves? Alec thought. "Am I here to train with you?" Alec asked.

"Maybe, it is one of the roles we are expected to fulfill," Raphael replied. "It seems natural since one of your siblings has already trained with me."

"How could Ava, Tristan, or Dom have trained with you? They have never left the capital." Alec said somewhat confused by the direction the conversation had taken.

"I have not trained Ava, Tris, or Dom," the elf replied. Danny, who had been listening to the interchange between Alec and Raphael, suddenly turned pale as the meaning of Raphael's words hit her.

Danny had not known until this moment her true relationship to Alec. It now became clear to her why her master had sent her to find him. As far as she knew, the parents she had lived with her whole life were her natural parents. With Raphael's revelation, she fully understood what Alec was a little slow to understand.

Alec noticed that Danny seemed upset by the elf's disclosure.

"Master, you must explain. If I understand you correctly, I am not an only child," Danny asked with her eyes tearing up. Her whole life she lived in a cabin in the woods on the edge of the Vale. Her parents had never told her that royal blood flowed through her veins. "You tell me that I am no longer an orphan, or for that matter, was never one."

Alec looked at her and as soon as the realization hit him, he was stunned. He did not know what to think but he could see that

Danny was very upset by this news. "Please, sir, how can this be true? Why would my parents have sent one of my siblings away from the family?" Alec paused before speaking again. "They would never have done anything like that."

"Many years ago there was a prophet in the hills of Lirkon who had many visions of the future. One of these visions foretold a birth of four siblings who would rise to great power," Raphael told the pair. "Your father's advisors read and interpreted these visions to mean there was great danger to your father and the kingdom of Articia if a quartet of heirs was ever born to a royal family.

"When you and your siblings were finally born, they all panicked. Your father argued long and hard with them, but they finally convinced the king not to take the chance. He agreed to separate you and your siblings, but he put his foot down and convinced them there would be no danger if two of the quads stayed in the castle. Reluctantly, his advisors agreed."

"How did they choose which children would stay and which would go?" Danny asked. Alec remained quiet as Danny struggled to understand.

"The parents did not decide. The healer who attended their birth instantly fell in love with the first daughter born. She asked to raise that child as her own. The king reluctantly agreed as long as she gave the king and queen reports of the daughter they might never be able to claim," Raphael responded. "Meriab Coralm and her husband, your mother and father, loved you very much, Danny, and our people mourn for your loss."

Tears were streaming down Danny's face. She had been holding in her grief for many days, working to keep them all alive as they fled the dark riders. She collapsed to her knees, bent down, and put her head in her hands as she wept.

Alec started to move toward her but Raphael put his hand on his shoulder. "Tears are the silent language of grief," Raphael whispered, almost as if he were speaking to a spirit, "and we must give sorrow expression, for the grief that does not speak burdens the o'er-fraught heart and bids it break."

Raphael led Alec to the garden outside. "We must speak some, young Prince, for the hour is near when the nobles of Articia will yet again be tested."

The garden was remarkable for the sheer number of flowering plants, and all were perfectly pruned and blooming. The aroma of each blossom was delightful. "I have known Danny for many years," the elf said. "Her foster mother brought her here to train in the magical arts when she was just a toddler."

Raphael bent to smell one of the flowers before he spoke again. "They discovered early that she had a feeling for the healing arts because she kept running around and healing the woodland creatures near her modest home at the edge of the Vale."

"But Danny is also a warrior," Alec pointed out.

"That was a requirement of her foster parents. They wanted to ensure that Danny would be able to take care of things alone when they were gone from this world." Raphael replied. "Did you train Danny in the martial arts?" Alec asked.

"No, my brother Michael was her instructor in the ways of a warrior," Raphael responded.

"Is Michael a great warrior?" Alec asked.

"Michael is our greatest warrior. He has led our army triumphantly over the ages," Raphael stated. "But that is not important now. A pivotal battle is coming that your family needs to be prepared to fight. Your sister Ava is on her own quest of knowledge, but time is running short."

"What is the urgency?" Alec asked

"The dark forces have amassed in the Coal Mountains and will be marching after the spring melt for the capital of Articia," Raphael informed him.

"What! Does my father know of the peril?" Alec responded in shock.

"He has mobilized his forces and the One Hundred have been mustered."

"I must return to the capital at once. This is no time for a prince of Articia to be wandering," Alec said with apprehension.

"There is plenty of time before you will be needed, young Prince."

"But the melt has already started. The pass will be clear through the Coal Mountains by week's end!" Alec countered impatiently.

"Ah, but I do not think the weather will cooperate this year, my young Prince. For a late snow has already started falling in the mountains. It will be at least two more fortnights before that pass will be clear enough for any army to cross." Raphael smiled as he answered. "And you have much to learn before you can be of any assistance to your family. Nevertheless, come, it is late and we must consider an evening meal. I believe you have two companions napping with the horses as we speak," Raphael said as he pointed to the stable. "They are sure to want to share our meal. Please, go wake them and meet us back in my house. I must now provide some comfort for Danny."

Alec was a little in shock at the whole affair and started toward the stable as Raphael walked to the house. *Why do I always feel like a pawn in one of Ava's chess games?*

...

Danny had calmed down quite a bit since Alec's earlier encounter with the young warrior.

"Danny, um, Danielle," he said as he looked at her eyes still swollen from the tears she had shed.

"Just Danny, it is the name I prefer," Danny responded and added, "it is the name my mother always called me."

Alec noticed that she struggled with those last words. "We will soon have to visit the capital. I think my … our parents will be very pleased that you could come home."

"Home," Danny snorted in irritation. "That has never been my home."

"I guess you're right. Nevertheless, I am sure everyone would still be very happy to have you stay. Ava will be ecstatic to learn that she has a sister," Alec said as he sat down beside Danny. "I had to stand in many times to fill that role when she wanted to play when we were younger. She tortured me regularly by making me wear a smock for pretend tea."

Danny showed him the hint of a smile. "Now that would have been a sight to see." At that moment, Jamal and Dustin busted through the door in a hurry for dinner.

"Stop, you will both go down to the stream and get yourselves cleaned up for dinner. You look like you have been a month on the road!" Danny expressed loudly to the boys. "Do not come back until you are presentable. You will not sit at my master's table looking the way you do."

"Aw, Danny," Dustin cajoled.

"We're starvin'," Jamal finished.

"NOW!" Danny yelled as the boys fell over each other back out the door and down to the brook that ran through a canal in the center of the city.

...

"The riders are frustrated, Master; they cannot enter the forest of the light to reach the Vale," the imp informed the demon.

"Then we need to find a way to tempt the young prince out of that accursed place," the demon stated. "What of that young boy that came to his rescue? Is he still in the Vale?"

"I believe that the young man is still there, my Lord."

"Maybe we can use the young man to draw the prince out of the vale. Do you think there is any attachment between the pair?" the demon asked.

"There appears to be and I believe that youngster resides in a house on the edge of Valemore Forest. We could send some minions to lie in wait there in case the young man returns to the house, perhaps with the prince," the imp said.

"Perfect. Let's set a trap then," the demon plotted. "Then the young prince would be compelled to rescue that one out of honor."

"As you wish," the imp replied and then he left the chamber and scooted down the hall.

"Why did you not tell him of his error?" a voice in the corridor asked.

"You will learn that we are not really here to help the humans or our brother demons. What fun would that be?" the imp snickered.

"Do you believe the young girl will return to her home in the woods?" the voice asked.

"We shall see."

...

Raphael came into the dining hall of his house and sat at the head of the table. Elves that Alec had not seen before carried trays of food from a preparation room and laid them on the tabletop. He was amazed at how fair the elves appeared. They seemed perfect; none showed any blemish or flaw.

"There is no pomp and circumstance at my table. Please, eat and enjoy," Raphael invited.

Jamal and Dustin wasted no time. Both of the boys overfilled their plates and started eating as if they had not eaten in a week. Danny rolled her eyes and started eating with a bit more decorum.

Alec thought of the conversation they had previously with Raphael and was troubled. "Sir, earlier today you said that I had three birth mates. I know of Ava and now Danny, but who is the third?"

Danny stopped eating and turned to Raphael as she thought, *first in the forest and now this I must pay better attention. Alec noticed something I did not in the words someone was speaking.*

"There is another sibling, but that is Ava's journey of discovery. In due time, the four of you will journey together.

Now finish eating. You have some long days ahead and need to recover your strength."

...

Ava and William moved south at a quickened pace. They were still a day and a morning from the edge of the territory that brought them to the entrance of the Great Library.

"*Our pursuers' are close at hand,*" William's comrade and mount Comet communicated to him.

"How do you know?" William questioned the mount

"*The birds above are fleeing to the east and west, which means we are being pursued from the north,* " Comet replied.

"How do I know what?" Ava asked.

"Sorry, Princess, I forget sometimes that people do not always hear the voice of the destri," William told her. "Comet has told me that he believes the dark riders are closing on us from the north. He has been observing that the fowl have been fleeing east and west as we have proceeded to the south."

Ava looked off to the east. She thought of Alec then. "You know that is the first time that you told me that your horse's name is Comet?"

"We have really not had time to chat," William said. "Once we are on the grounds of the Great Library, we will have some time to get to know each other."

They pair proceeded hastily to the south and toward the Great Library. However, William realized that they were on the verge of crossing through a small hamlet in the fief of Count Riddyl. "There is a small village a short ride down the road," William informed her. "If we go through it without stopping, the villagers would be very suspicious."

"It might also bring the riders down on those villagers," Ava responded. "I do not want to put them at risk."

"Our choices are to turn to the southwest, which brings us through a very populated area, or to head southeast through the thickest part of the Artician forest," William stated. "The southeasterly route puts fewer people at risk but will slow us down considerably." He looked back to the north briefly. "The riders are sure to catch us if we take that route."

"Despite the risk, we need to go southeast. I could not live with myself if innocent people got hurt because of me," Ava stated.

"Southeast it is, then" William answered. "It will add almost a day to our ride."

"Then we will be a day late getting to the library," Ava commented as she turned Aurora to the southeast off the main road.

...

After dinner, the boys retired to the stable to sleep. Over the last couple of days Alec had discovered that he admired the free lifestyle of the simple folk like Jamal and Dustin Even though they have difficulties and challenges, have to work to feed themselves, struggle to survive and they don't have the comfort of a castle Articia with servants and other pleasantries as he. They live life with no other worries, no real responsibility, just their regular daily adventures or misadventures. Alec smiled as he walked back into the common room of Raphael's house. Danny and Raphael were sitting by the fireplace, which now had a fire burning in it. Alec had not realized that the evening had gotten cooler until he felt the warmth.

"Come in and sit, young Prince. This is my favorite time of the evening, when we all sit around and tell stories of our adventures," Raphael beckoned.

Alec went over to a chair and sat. He noticed that Danny was staring blankly into the fire. "You said that winter was going to last longer and more snow would block the pass for more fortnights. How do you know this will occur?" he asked Raphael.

"Because we made it happen," Raphael answered.

"You can make changes to the weather?" Alec said with curiosity. "How is that possible?"

"We cannot really control the weather, but we can adjust it a bit," Raphael responded. "But my people will pay a high price for that interference."

"What kind of price?" Danny was becoming more interested in the conversation.

"Many things are possible with the innate magics of this world," Raphael commented. "But every action has a consequence. In order to maintain balance, nature reacts to any tampering."

"How does nature react?" Danny questioned.

"The natural things of Articia cannot tolerate imbalance. For every wetland, there is a desert, for every forest, a plain. When those who have the power to tamper with the natural balance use it, nature pushes back. The elves will pay a high price for the tampering this year," Raphael provided. "We will likely see winter for many seasons in our valley," Raphael responded.

"The winter season is not that bad," Alec said. "It is part of the natural order of things."

"Yes, but it has never come to the Vale," Danny responded with concern. "Was it necessary to take that risk in this situation?"

"We have taken many risks over time," Raphael admitted. "Not all have produced the results that we had hoped for; such is the randomness of life. My people felt that more time was needed for things to be balanced in this situation."

Danny seemed upset by this. Alec started to notice more and more that whenever they discussed anything about his family or the kingdom, Danny was annoyed or angry.

"I am sure that the people of Articia will be grateful that you gave them more time to respond to this threat," Alec said. "The common people are too often devastated by the actions of the goblins. This will give them time to strengthen their defenses or get out of harm's way."

Danny looked somewhat confused. "I was not aware that the royal family cared much about the common folk."

Alec was a little annoyed at Danny's accusation. "My family cares very much about the people of Articia. It is our charge and responsibility."

"Then why do so many go hungry and homeless and have little hope of a better life?" Danny demanded with anger.

"We do all we can to help. Just because we are royal does not mean we do not care. We walk the pilgrimage to Adara's temple on our feet like everyone else. My mother constantly travels from village to village, healing the sick and comforting those who can no longer be healed," Alec defended. "My father spends a remarkable amount of time and fortune distributing any food surplus from the farms we control to villages that could not grow enough food for themselves."

Danny was going to speak but stopped.

"When the winter came early four winters past, it destroyed the crops of the northern farms. Our father used money from the royal treasury to buy food and feed from the southern baronies to help the northern farmers and villagers make it through the winter. We even housed four remote farm families on our estate because they were caught off guard by the early storms and could not gather enough wood for their fires," Alec said.

"My family rationed food in the castle that winter for all— soldiers, servants, princess and princes, king and queen—so that the food would go farther for the villagers in the north. It was a hard year for the castle, but we all did our part," Alec finished.

Danny stared at Alec with surprise. "This is not what I had been told about your life."

"What have you been told and by whom?" Alec asked, still stewing with anger at what Danny believed his family was like.

"Duke Marquin stopped at our house two seasons ago," she responded. "He came to see my parents … I mean my foster parents," Danny said as she was flooded with memories of the loving people who had raised her. "He told us about the royal family and how they had grown selfish and proud, that they rode on the backs of the commoners who supported Castle Articia. He spoke of crushing taxes and harsh laws that had the villages and towns of Articia near ruin."

Alec knew his parents did not like the duke and no longer tolerated him in court. "You will have to spend time with us then to see that the information that the duke has given you is false."

Raphael sat in his chair, taking a long puff on an ornate pipe. White smoke drifted into the air as he blew it out of his mouth. "My young child," Raphael said toward Danny. "You have lived a wonderful but sheltered life with parents who loved you very much. You have a much longer road to walk before you discover the truth about whom and what you and your siblings are to each other and to Articia."

"Why would the duke have lied about such things?" Danny inquired.

"My father, our father, the king, and the duke are not on friendly terms," Alec replied. "He would probably not speak kindly of my family in any forum."

"For two passing of the summers I have hated the royal family for their uncaring rule, over a lie?" Danny responded. "I was not happy to hear that I was one of their children. I felt abandoned and thought it typical of their behavior based on a lie. Alec, I am so sorry, I thought the worst of you."

"You cannot be faulted for believing in a deception, my dear" Raphael provided. "It is the deceiver who is to blame for your misguided emotions."

"Then what I was told is really not true?" Danny asked Raphael for assurance that Alec was telling the truth.

"Truth is a funny thing. From one man's perspective, the world has a definite view; from another's, it is completely different. If you only see the world through eyes of hatred, then all you can see is hate. If you watch the world through eyes filled with light, then you shall see light," Raphael instructed. "You must measure the world through your own eyes, Danny."

Danny thought about this for some time as the trio stared at the fire.

"Raphael, if you only tampered with winter in the mountains, why will winter come for many seasons to the Vale to balance that action?" Alec asked.

"It is caused from our interfering with the natural order of things," Raphael responded. "My people have learned much about maintaining the natural balance here in Articia. We have learned that the more we interfere with that order, the stronger the reaction that occurs. For every push, there is a pull and with our people. Elves act as a focusing lens; much like the glass that the guilds use to light fires, our guilt makes it worse."

"I am not sure I understand," Alec said.

"Think of a child swinging on a rope." Raphael said. "When he controls his own motion, he can make the rope swing as much as his own momentum and courage will take him. When someone gives him a push, he is no longer in control of the swinging of the rope; he is no longer in charge of his own action. Because of the action of pushing the swing, the child no longer experiences the consequences of his own actions. He is now living with the consequences of someone else's actions."

"But don't we already live with the consequences of others' decisions anyways?" Danny asked.

Alec knew that she was talking about the decision to split up the quadruplets at birth. *What is it like to find out your whole life has not been what you thought?* Alec wondered.

"It is one thing when someone from this world has an impact on the natural order of things," Raphael suggested. "It is a completely different matter when an entity that is not part of this place interferes. This world is alive with its own rules and the natural order does not like when its rules are tampered with by a foreign being."

"How is Adara part of this balance?" Alec asked.

Raphael pondered Alec's question carefully, surprised by the insight of this young one, he withheld the true answer to his question. "That domain and its relationships are information for a future quest, Alec. For now, we must focus on the problems of today."

"Are the demons a natural part of this world?" Danny asked. The only demons that she had ever seen were the riders, but she felt in her heart that they could not be a natural part of this world.

"The demons fled to this world after they had destroyed the one where they were created. They are not natural inhabitants of Articia," Raphael answered. "They did not realize that when they brought about the destruction of that world, my people would be free to pursue them for justice. The rules of the world where the demons lived were permanently broken, so they fled to Articia hoping to escape from my people."

"So they only came here to escape from the elves?" Alec asked.

"No, they came to destroy. It is the only thing that brings them satisfaction," Raphael responded. "We followed to help maintain the balance that my people did not understand was so important on the world from which we came."

"So the world you came from was destroyed because you didn't understand the rules?" Danny asked.

"No," Raphael responded with sadness. "It was destroyed because we did not follow the rules. Our war with the demons escalated and until each side, the dark and the light, could no longer tolerate each other. The people of our home world were so corrupted by our and the demons' interference with the natural order that they eventually destroyed themselves and their world."

Alec looked over at Danny who was also shocked by this revelation. He had thought the elves perfect and without flaw, but now he saw that even they could make mistakes and feel regret for fatal ones."

"So we are ruled by Articia and its natural order," Alec noted aloud.

"Somewhat," Raphael responded. "The people of Articia are a part of its order. It is when the supernatural interferes with the natural that the balance wavers."

"Then it's all about balance," Danny commented. "To maintain balance, you only interfere when the demons do something against that natural order, right?" It was Alec's turn to show amazement because of Danny's insight.

"Yes, young one," Raphael responded. "We no longer relentlessly pursue the destruction of darkness. My people have learned the lesson that without out the dark, you cannot truly appreciate the light."

The trio was quiet for a time before Raphael spoke again. "Now it is your turn to tell stories. I would love to hear about your journey here, and I think it would be good for Danny to hear tales of life behind the castle walls."

They spoke for a couple hours more with Danny telling Raphael about their encounter with the pale and white riders. It was the first time that Alec had heard of how Danny had made a feint attack at the white rider, who angrily pursued her into the brush. She had circled the rider into thicker and thicker underbrush until the rider could no longer move. Danny laughed as she wondered how many hours it would take the rider to find his way out of the maze that she had led it.

Alec spoke of growing up in Castle Articia, of the hard training and many beatings his sister Ava had given him. Danny smiled as Alec told of the many martial lessons he received from his sister Ava. As Alec saw her smile, he started to feel that Danny and Ava would get along very well. He continued to tell stories of life in the castle and court until the fire was just embers.

"Well," Raphael commented. "It is late and we should soon retire. Tomorrow will be a long day since we will have to help with the harvest to ensure that we have enough food for the pending winter in the Vale."

Alec stretched his arms and retired to the antechamber where the sleeping cots were.

"Master," Danny asked.

"Yes, Danny," Raphael responded.

"I will be leaving early in the morn because I want to ride out to my cottage to collect some of my personal items. The house that once was the home of my foster parents will no longer be the home where I live. I do not want to lose the things that are special to me when the forest reclaims our small farm," Danny commented.

"Yes, indeed," Raphael replied. "I hope your path will be uneventful until your hasty return to our city."

As Danny walked off to the sleeping chamber, Raphael frowned and thought of the struggle to come. *We fight in honorable fashion for the good of humanity. Fearless of the future, unheeding of our individual fates, with unflinching hearts and undimmed eyes, we stand at Armageddon, and we battle for the Lord.*

Raphael leaned back in his chair by the dying fire, took a puff from his pipe, and blew smoke into the air in front of him. *"To sleep, perchance to dream."* How many millennia has it been since he had slept? As he thought of the destruction of his home world, a single tear rolled down his cheek and dropped onto the hand that held his pipe.

...

William and Ava had slowed the horses to a walk. The forest was too thick to continue at such a fast pace. "I think the forest will slow our pursuers down enough for us to relax a little," William stated.

"Yes, I agree" Ava responded. "Maybe now you can tell me more about yourself."

He told her about his homeland and the adventures he and his cousin had shared. William also told her about life at court in

Cyrus. It was very different from Articia. "The people of Cyrus are far less tolerant of the possibility of women in positions of power than those in the city of Articia."

"It seems to me that your people are a little narrow minded," Ava responded to his description of the social order.

"Yes, they can be, and stubborn as well," William admitted. "My cousins learned to read because the prince regent of Cyrus insisted that no royal family member would be a dolt."

"That's practical," Ava said, somewhat annoyed at the possibility that women in Cyrus could not read.

Ava had heard of the decree of the forward-thinking prince regent of Cyrus.

"The decree required all citizens be required to learn to read. However, in Cyrus, The only people recognized as citizens were men and landowners. Regardless, most of the people did not believe that reading was necessary to their survival and did not follow the rule of the prince," William paused to give Ava time to absorb what he had said before he continued. "It became a fight against the traditions of the principality, the people revolted. This angered the prince. He then expanded the decree and required all children to be taught to read as well."

"It was quite the scandal when the prince declared that every child in the city was to be educated. A large number of people, mostly the men who had controlled society by maintaining a level of ignorance, were near revolt as a result of my uncle's proclamation."

"So how was the revolt avoided?" Ava asked.

"Well, it seems that the wives and sisters of the male revolutionaries were not pleased with the actions and did a far better job dispersing them with rolling pins than our soldiers could have ever done," William stated.

Ava stopped her horse on the wooded path and looked at William, who was smiling rather funny. She burst out laughing and continued her ride to the southwest.

Ava told William about her brother Alec and life at Castle Articia. She told him about the day that Alec insisted she learn the skills of a warrior, and how stubborn they were as a pair. She tried to describe her brother's character to William but could not quite catch who and what he was with words. William, being a young man of royal of blood himself, understood what she was trying to relay.

The sky started to darken and it became difficult for them to proceed on the narrow path. "We need to risk stopping until the first light of morn," William said. "The trail is far too dangerous to pass without the light of the moon, which is not getting through the thick canopy of these trees."

"Can we risk staying in one place with what is pursuing us?" Ava asked. "I could produce a magical light to guide us through the thicket."

"I believe that if you use magic it will be like a beacon to our pursuers. We have no choice; we can pass no farther this evening. Please make yourself comfortable and try to get some sleep," William advised her. "I will watch for the riders."

"I can take a watch while you sleep as well," Ava stated.

"No, Princess, it is part of my training to go many days without sleep. It will be no bother for me," William assured her.

"What training?" Ava asked.

"I have been training to be a member of the One Hundred. Part of our training is to ride hard for days and remain fresh for a fight," William said.

"You are one of the One Hundred, the suicide squad!" Ava gasped.

"It is not a good description of what we do. Though we are prepared to die for a cause, our goal is to survive to fight another day," William clarified.

"But the One Hundred never retreat. They fight until there are no more enemies on the field or there are no more cavaliers," Ava said with dismay. "Someday you will charge with those who will not return."

"It is a possibility," William said.

"But you have seen only fourteen winters!" Ava protested. "You are too young to make that kind of a commitment."

"The One Hundred are not born cavaliers; they are trained for many years," William explained. "I am still training to be a cavalier. It will be many years before I will be asked to ride into battle with the One Hundred."

"I don't understand. You said you are one of the One Hundred, but you are not yet a cavalier?" Ava asked, somewhat confused.

"You are correct. There are three generations of the One Hundred. In the first generation are the oldest riders, the Knights. They are the ones who have survived their years of service," William said, "including the few who returned from battle. They are the ones who train the men chosen to become the One Hundred." Ava thought about this as William continued. "Bryn and Nicholas are Knights of the One Hundred who have survived some of the fiercest battles in Articia," William said.

Ava gasped at this news. "I did not know that Bryn was one of the One Hundred! He never said anything."

"Bryn and Nicholas are with us today because their destri fell in battle and they could no longer participate in the charge without their mounts. They both returned to the regular army because they only had one desire, to continue fighting for Articia."

"So if a rider's mount is killed, they no longer ride with the One Hundred?" Ava questioned.

"That is true. No Artician-born mount can face the wolug in battle, so the One Hundred must have destri steeds and no other if they are to confront the beasts in the charge. When they no longer have a destri, they can no longer be effective against the riders of the dark beasts," William answered.

"That seems so unreasonable. Why could they not just find another destri mount to carry them?"

"The bond between a warrior of the One Hundred and his mount is so pronounced that neither a rider nor his mount can bond with any other," William answered.

"That's tragic," Ava responded. "So Bryn's and Nicholas's mounts were both killed and they are no longer active warriors." Ava thought for moment and asked, "What happens to destri that lose their riders?"

"They no longer have the heart to stay in Articia. They return to their home world and we do not know what transpires after that event."

William continued, "The active generation of riders is the Cavaliers. They are the warriors called upon when Articia needs them the most. They are the only force that can stand against the mounted wolug."

"The third generation is the riders in training. I am a Tyro," William finished.

"That is a comfort," Ava said sarcastically. "You will not go off on your suicide run until the next war."

William looked at Ava's pleading eyes. Has she discovered the big secret? "Ava," William sighed. "We all have our special destiny. I believe I am on the path the goddess has chosen for me, including the path we are on at this moment."

"I am worried for you," Ava admitted. "I fear that with the honor you have shown me, if you participate in the charge, you will not come back." A tear was rolling down Ava's face as she lowered her head.

William walked over to her and put his hand on her shoulder. "I always do what honors my family. I will always do what is necessary to honor the goddess. I will always regret not getting to know my sisters and brothers better."

Ava looked up at William and smiled, "How long have you known that I discovered the secret?"

"I knew after our duel you were suspicious that there was a relationship between us. When it ended in a draw, your eyes gave away your confusion." William said. "And then when Nicholas told you that you are a quad, I thought for sure that you would confront me immediately about our relationship. I am actually surprised that you have not said anything to me about it until now."

"During the duel I realized that you had disguised your appearance. I could not see through the illusion but I knew it was there," Ava revealed. "Since I did not know why you had needed the elaborate disguised, I felt if best to not reveal what I had discovered until I knew more," Ava responded. "So I believe that now would be a good time to tell me your whole story, *brother*."

"When we were born, the practitioners predicted that we would bring about the end of Articia, that we had been demon touched," William started the story. "The barons argued with the king that we had to be split up so that we could not unite in power and harm Articia under the demon's influence." William sat on a rock on the edge of the fire to finish his tale.

"Duke Marquin wanted even more than that. He said that the king should have us all destroyed. Our father refused his request and dismissed the duke from the castle in anger. However, the other Nobles insisted that the king split up newly born heirs and send them to faraway lands so that they would never re-unite.

"Father reluctantly agreed to let me and another be sent away, for he did not have enough power to take a stand against the barons and the Duke. He had only enough support to maintain the stalemate that is in place today. But the king insisted that you and Alec, the last two born, stay in the castle."

"I have not met Duke Marquin," Ava said. "He is no longer allowed in court."

"He would be executed if he ever showed his face in Castle Articia," William stated adamantly.

"Why?" Ava asked.

"When we were born, and he could not convince everyone that we should be killed, he tried to kidnap us from the castle," William revealed. "But his aide was a loyal subject and alerted King Henry to the plan. Unfortunately, the duke was already far from the castle before the king mustered a force to arrest him."

"So why then were we split up after the duke's attempted treachery?" Ava asked.

"The barons still insisted that at least the king split us up. Our father reluctantly agreed, but now it would be on his terms. That is why I was sent to stay with his cousin, the prince regent of Cyrus. The city-state had become part of Greater Articia through a political marriage so it was a safe place to send a child of the king. You and Alec, being the last born, stayed with our parents," William told her. "I do not know where our oldest sister was sent."

Ava looked up, surprised at this statement. "I have a sister?"

"Yes, that is what Nicholas meant by the phrase 'you are a quad.'"

"Once things are back to normal, I want to find her," Ava promised.

"Rest now, we will have a full day of riding tomorrow to get to the protection of the library," William said.

Ava nodded; lay down on Aurora's horse blanket, and with many thoughts spinning in her head she closed her eyes to rest.

…

"Ava, wake up!" William whispered. "We have company."

Ava blinked open her eyes. The forest was no longer quiet. "What do you see?" Ava asked William. "I see nothing. It is too dark."

"The woodland beasts are panicking and fleeing to the south. They never move under the darkness," William stated.

Ava looked into the distance and saw through the trees the red glowing eyes of the dark riders, who were approaching at a gallop. As they bore down on the pair, William drew his sword and instructed Ava, "Prepare yourself, they are mounted and will come in swinging."

Ava reached down and drew Last Kiss as she raised her hand and formed the spell for a wave of power she intended to use on the riders. She yelled to William as she ran by him. "William, stand ground. I have an idea."

William, caught off guard by Ava's aggressive move, was too late to stop her charge. When she was far enough ahead of William, she threw a wave of power from her hand that brought both of the riders to an immediate stop. The foul horses reared back, knocking the unsuspecting riders out of their saddles.

Ava then concentrated hard as she yelled, "*Terra lacuna!*" The earth started to shake below the demons' feet. As William watched, a hole opened in the earth below the riders. It grew larger as they started to tumble into the sinkhole formed by Ava's magic.

"William, you must mount Comet and run now!" Ava said as she turned and ran back toward William. She jumped up onto Aurora's back, leaving behind her pack and blanket. "I do not know how big this will get!"

As the hole widened, Comet galloped over to William, who jumped onto the destri and galloped off after Ava. The last thing he heard as he leaned down to grab Ava's pack was the scream of frustration coming from the dark riders as they plummeted into the deepening sinkhole. He caught up with Ava and looked back to see that the dark riders had disappeared into the ground.

William saw the look of concern on Ava's face but he could not help but laugh. Ava looked at him in surprise and then started laughing as well. He looked back down the road one more time and stated, "We should probably just keep riding until we reach the library."

"I think that is a good idea. I am not sure if the dark beasts that were pursuing us will be contained by the trap I sprang on them."

"I agree. The sun will be up soon anyway. Let us keep heading to the south. When we clear the forest, we will make a run for the library," William replied. He looked back at the large hole that had now stopped growing and asked "So where did you learn a spell like that?"

"About four winters ago I attended a funeral with my teacher Brendan. The ground, frozen solid, had created a problem for the gravediggers. They could not dig a hole to bury the poor man. As I watched, Brendan used a similar spell to loosen the ground enough so that they could dig the grave. I think it was important to him that one of his long-time friends was buried properly with honor and dignity." She smiled as she looked at him. "I have always been curious if I could modify the spell to make a bigger hole. Now I know it is possible."

William looked at her and just shook his head.

...

Danny quietly led her horse out of the barn so that she would not wake the boys. She wanted to be on her way as soon as the light was rising in the east. She needed to get an early start so she could reach her house at the edge of the forest before nightfall. She wanted to recover many things from her old life before the forest swallowed the place where she had once lived. Danny knew that Alec would be mad that she traveled without him, but she wanted some time alone to think about the all of the recent changes in her life. As she crested the hill where they had stood when they first arrived, she looked back once at the city of the Vale then turned and rode off to the west and back into the forest.

...

Ava and William reached the southern edge of the Artician forest and rejoined the road to the Great Library. As they started down the field, Ava looked back toward the trees. She had a feeling that something, someone was watching them, but she saw nothing.

"She is a powerful one," the imp said to its cohort. "She almost detected us."

"Yes, she has a surprising amount of power. More than I would expect from a typical Artician," the imp replied.

"It is as if there has been some supernatural influence with these children. Come, we must free the dark riders. They are sure to be rather perturbed right now and I would like to avoid losing any more of our brothers to their wrath."

...

Alec slowly rose from his slumber, sore from the days of riding. He looked across the room to see Danny's cot was empty. *Hmm, she must have gotten up early.* He thought that she must be an early riser because of the daily demands of her life on the farm at the edge of Valemore Forest.

Alec dressed and entered the main room of Raphael's cottage to see him staring dreamily into the fireplace. "Good morning," Alec said cheerily.

Raphael turned toward him. "Good morning, young Prince. Did you sleep well?"

"Yes, thank you," Alec responded. "Best sleep I have had in a couple of days. Is Danny about?"

"She has gone on a brief errand. She should return in a couple of days," Raphael responded. "Danny has asked me to spend some time with you to teach you something of the healing art. She told me that you have some innate talent that could be useful in future encounters."

"Yes, I learned I have healing powers like my mother," Alec responded. "But I have not been formally trained."

"Well, we have a few days before Danielle returns. So let's make good use of the time," Raphael said. "Why don't you sit down and we'll go over the basics before breakfast. It may still be an hour or so before the boys in the stable wake."

...

"What! She did what!" the demon yelled at the imp, who was shaking his head as he explained how Ava had delayed the horsemen so she and William could elude them.

"We will need two new mounts for the red and the black horsemen. Their steeds did not survive being buried in the sinkhole she created," the imp replied.

"This young woman is certainly creative," the demon lord said. "We might as well replace the white horseman's mount as well. At least they will all share the same kind of beast when they ride against King Henry."

"So have you decided to recall the riders to prepare for battle? Are we ready to march yet?" the imp asked.

"No, an unexpected problem has occurred. A late snow has fallen in the mountains that have delayed the melt for at least another fortnight."

"Will that cause an issue?" the imp asked.

"It is still too early to tell. The longer the army is delayed, the greater the risk that the ruffians will be discovered in the northern forests," the demon said. "We will have to wait and watch."

...

"Tristan and I have come up with some strategies for the battle ahead," Dominic said to the war council. "There is one approach that the opposing army can take that could disrupt our plans."

King Henry was pleased with the young princes' initiatives but he knew it would be unwise for him to give the princes complete control over such an important aspect of the battle ahead. The pair have no battle experience with the four horseman on the loose, everything is as stake. Henry thought back to his first battle. He was about the same age as Dominic. The King did not have a father to consult with, his father before him had succumb to the plague.

Still, the experience they have the opportunity to gain will serve Dom well when he rules over Articia. The king felt that he needed to give Dom the chance to gain the experience that he so dearly lacked when he took the throne. The King thought of a task his oldest sons could take that would not present a significant risk to his heir.

"We can send some of our scouts to ensure that the goblins are not using an alternate strategy," the king replied. He would send some of the One Hundred with them to make sure they did not get in any serious trouble. "The keep at Lewisvel has no Cavaliers or their Destri. Once your unit finishes scouting the edge of the northern forest, I would like your unit to go to Lewisvel Keep and work with its weapon master to secure the crystal mountain pass.

"A good strategy my king," Bryn stated as he realized he was giving the young princes a chance to participate in the battle from the protection of Lewisvel keep.

Lewisvel Keep, constructed almost two hundred winters past, was on a narrow river run that split the Crystal Mountains. Prior to the existence of the keep, the pass was open and allowed the goblin hordes access to attack the Artician lowlands at will. It builders selected the narrowest part of the pass, where it would block the march of goblin attacks. Most of its strength is on the eastern walls, the western walls had lighter fortifications since its builders were sure that no goblin attack would ever come from that direction.

"If any army gains a foothold in the western valley of Lewisvel Keep, Lewisvel will no longer be a hindrance to any that passes the region. The Artician army could be outmaneuvered," Dominic finished.

At that moment, a messenger rushed into the room "Sire! I have an urgent message from the Lewisvel watch."

The king read the note and smiled. "It looks like the goddess has blessed us in our endeavor. It is snowing heavily in the northern mountain passes. It will be a least a fortnight before it is clear enough for the goblin horde to march."

"That is fortunate," said Bryn. "It gives us more time to prepare for the siege."

"Dom and Tris, take a unit of riders and head north and quietly check the northern forest to see if anything is amiss. Then I want you to visit with Viscount Traner at Lewisvel," the king commanded. "Ensure that his defenses are sound."

The King spoke to the captain of the One Hundred next. "Send two Tyros from the One Hundred with them as well. Having destri in the field will allow us to communicate with them should anything *unusual* occur."

"It will be done my king," the captain responded.

16
The Great Library

Ava and William crested the hill at the edge of the garden that surrounded the Great Library. Ava had never seen any building like the one that stood in the center of this meadow. It was perfectly square from the front and many hundreds of hands high.

"It's something else, isn't it," William said to Ava.

"I had never imagined such a large building in Articia. How is it that this has remained hidden for so long?" Ava asked.

"I believe it is part of the elven magic. Those who are meant to return remember the place; those who are not, do not," William responded. "It is still a couple of hours of riding before we get to the main entrance, but from here on, the land is protected. The riders will no longer be able to pursue us."

William and Ava rode off down the road toward the Great Library as a hidden danger watched them from a hill to the east.

. . .

"The demon lord will not be pleased," the imp said to its companion. "If she finds the scroll, she will know all."

"Our lord should have destroyed this accursed place long ago," the second imp said.

"I do not believe he has the power to do that on this world. There are far too many restrictions on what we can get away with in this domain."

. . .

Alec spent the next two turns of a day working with Raphael, learning the healing arts. Though he struggled with some of the language of healing, it was familiar to him. In his youth, he had watched his mother practice it many times.

"Remember, the combination of the healing phrase and the old language decides the power of the healing effort," Raphael instructed Alec. "Try again with the plant here."

"*Lumen sano*," Alec said as he held his hands over the plant, and a light reddish glow engulfed the plant. After a few moments, the plant started to look healthier.

"That is the form of light healing. It is used for most superficial wounds," Raphael instructed. "You have to be careful to not over heal your patient. The goddess of this realm has specifically restricted us to let life in this place heal as naturally as possible. It is through this natural healing that we grow stronger as beings."

"Why is that important?" Alec asked. "It would seem to me that if we could heal everyone, there would be no suffering in the world."

"It is all about balance and the natural order of things," Raphael reminded him. "If we heal every weak elk beast, how would the wolf then do its part of thinning the herd? What purpose would the wolf have in our world?" Raphael paused for Alec to ponder this and then said, "When all elk are healthy, then there are not enough grazing areas to support them." Raphael then thought *and who would lament at the fall of a hero if no hero ever fell?*

"So you are saying that even though we can heal everyone, everything, it doesn't mean that we should," Alec responded.

"As a healer, you must always consider the balance. There is only enough space and food in the world for a fixed number of inhabitants," Raphael said. "If nothing or no one ever died, then the balance would be disrupted. The hardest part of the healing arts is the knowledge of when not to heal."

"How do you know when to heal and when to let nature take its course?" Alec asked his instructor.

"You must depend on your instincts to make that judgment," Raphael answered.

...

Danny rode into the farmstead and noticed that the forest was already working to swallow the only home she had ever known. She had only been away from it for a short time, but the brambles had blocked the path to the front gate.

Danny tied her horse to the rail in front of the house and walked to check the garden. Of course, she would not be around to harvest it, but it was something she had loved to tend. Danny absentmindedly pulled some of the weeds and scrub from the ground as she looked at the house. How lonely it seemed now that her parents were gone. She brushed off her hands and walked to the front door. Her house had changed little since she last saw it last, except the flowers in the vase hanging from the door. They were dead from lack of watering.

As she opened the door, Danny heard the same familiar squeak. The house smelled musty, stale, as she entered the main room. She reached up to take the small doll that was still on the mantle. Her mother had given it to her when she was very young and it was one of her most treasured possessions. She sat holding the doll in a chair beside the fireplace as she stroked its hair. Danny stared into the wood box by the unlit fireplace and started to weep.

...

Ava and William reached the front gate of the garden of the Great Library. Ava was surprised that it was open and that there were no guards posted at its entrance. Even in times of peace, there were wandering dangers that could bring damage to the library. William led them to what appeared to be a watering spot for the horses. There was no stable here, but Ava felt that the horses would be quite comfortable grazing on this open grass.

"We walk from here," William said. "Mr. Tipple is very particular about the library. He does not allow any Artician beasts near or into the main hall of the place for fear that they may nibble on his precious books."

Ava laughed at this statement, an image of the horses eating through the pages of a novel. "What, no scholarly horses in our realm?"

"Well, everything I read, Comet reads because of our mind link."

Ava looked at William and laughed. "You really do not understand subtle humor do you?"

William, who was just realizing that Ava was trying to amuse him, started to laugh uncomfortably. "Yeah, sometimes I am a little slow with the more subtle language of women," he said, trying to give a reasonable comeback to Ava's chiding.

William used the door handle to knock on the smaller door of the library and waited for a response. The door opened without a sound and an old man looked out and smiled a goofy smile as he said, "William, it is great to see you again!" The old man was wearing a contraption of metal and glass that covered both of his eyes. "And you must be Ava. Brendan told me many things about you and that he would be sending you to visit me eventually, though it took him far too long to arrange for you to visit this special place."

"I am not sure what Brendan's plans were, he surely did not share them with me. Nor did he tell me anything about this wonderful library or its keeper," Ava responded with a cheerful smile.

Mr. Tipple, understandably swayed by Ava's charm, led them into the main hall of the Great Library. Ava was dumbstruck as she entered a long hallway that led from the front door to the back of the building. In every side chamber were many levels of shelves full of books, there were tables and chairs scattered about, and at the end of each row, there were stairs that led to a level above. Light came into the library from a transparent arched ceiling that ran the length of the hall.

"I am overwhelmed" Ava sighed. "I did not believe that there were this many books in the entire world."

"There are even more books in other places, but this is the largest collection of historical and instructional texts in Articia," the librarian said with excitement.

"I could spend a lifetime here and not even read one tenth of these books," Ava said in awe.

"As much as I love to read, none of us is meant to read them all," Mr. Tipple said. "But come, I am sure it has been a long road and we have rooms for you to change and remove the soil of your travels."

...

Danny woke with a start, something was not right. As she tried to rise up from the chair, she saw a huge bag as it passed over her head. Then someone, something, struck her. The last thing she remembered in her struggle was the howl of a goblin as she caught it with a fist before losing consciousness.

...

Alec was worried about Danny. It was now well beyond the second full day since she had left and there was no sign of her. Jamal and Dustin were worried as well.

"We need to go look for her," Dustin said.

"I know she is in trouble," Jamal added.

"I am concerned as well. I will speak to Raphael and see what he advises," Alec said to the boys.

...

Ava sat and looked into the mirror in the bedchamber that Mr. Tipple had provided. "I look horrid. Just a few days on the road and I am a mess." She normally did not care much about how she looked, but these days on the road had shown her how pampered she was in Castle Articia.

Ava used the washbasin to clean her face and then brushed back her hair. The room clearly designed for a female visitor to the library, had an armoire with many outfits of various sizes. However, the style of the clothing was rather plain. Though there were dresses of many kinds, they were very simple. *Most of the female scholars who visit the library must be rather dowdy*, Ava thought.

She found one dress, though rather plain, that was acceptable. Though it would not pass at any formal ball, it was certainly practical for studying in the library. Ava dressed quickly, not wanting to lose any of the precious time that she would be able to spend in this wonderful place. She tied her hair back into a horse's tail with a blue ribbon, took one last look into the mirror and frowned, then left the bedchamber.

···

"I am concerned that Danny has not returned yet. The boys and I would like to go out to the cottage to check on her," Alec said to Raphael.

The elf was staring at the fire he had just kindled in the fireplace. A small tear was running down his face. Raphael was one of the few of the Vale who could see glimpses of the future. He had learned long ago, however, that you cannot prevent fate from taking its victims, and he saw the pain that would be on the road ahead for the king's children.

"Yes, but you will need help passing through our forest. Without Danny, you would easily get lost." Raphael wiped his face before he turned. "You need to go see my brother Michael. He will provide you with the means to find your way out of the forest to Danny's small farm in the east. You can find him at the main building at the center of our city."

"Thank you, Raphael. Jamal, Dustin, and I will be leaving right after we speak to Michael and I want to thank you for taking the time to teaching me about the healing arts," Alec said.

Raphael did not respond; instead, he turned back toward the fireplace. Alec realized that Raphael was struggling with the departure, so he decided to turn and leave the building. He walked down to the stable and entered to find the boys wrestling in the hay.

"What's going on here?" Alec asked the boys, stopping Jamal's punch in mid swing.

Jamal and Dustin looked up at Alec and said in unison. "Nut'in."

Dustin finished the sentence, "We always wrestle each other to improve our warrior skills."

Dustin got up slowly. Clearly, Jamal had the upper hand in this wrestling match. For a moment, Alec almost fondly recalled the regular beatings that Ava had given him, but then he came to his senses.

"Raphael told me that we must go and see his brother Michael to learn to find the trails from the Vale," Alec told them.

Dustin had a look of concern on his face and Jamal's eyes went wide. "We heard many elves talk about Michael. They called him the angry elf," Dustin said.

"Why do they call him that?" Alec asked.

"We asked an elf why he called him that and they said it was because he blamed himself for something the elves did somewhere not on Articia." Dustin answered.

"Well, if we are going to find our way back to Danny's house from deep in the Vale, we will have to speak to Michael. I do not believe that Raphael knows the way," Alec responded. "Come now, we have to see Michael in the largest building in the center of the Vale."

...

Danny drifted in and out of consciousness from the rough treatment she had received from the goblins. Tied and blindfolded, she could feel that they were heading west. She was not on any of the roads she knew. She could not hear the sounds of the familiar towns and villages along the roads west of her home. They had traveled many leagues. She could estimate the pace of the goblins and the time that had passed because she had felt the heat of the sun as it rose from the east and set in the west. The beasts were heading to the setting sun.

...

Ava walked down the hallway, reading the bindings of the books on the shelves. Some she understood, some she did not, but all the books seemed organized in groupings by the type or subject. She paused in a section that had a title she did not understand called *Agriculture*. She did not know that word, but as she flipped through some of the pages of the books stored on this set of shelves, she realized that these books provided information about farming and animal care. *Hmm, this could be very useful information for Artician farmers. However, we would need to teach them to read En-Glish or translate them into native Artician before they could benefit from this knowledge*, she thought.

There was a section called *Science and Mathematics*. She did not really understand the cryptic language written in these books. However, some very interesting drawings and shapes were pleasing to the eye.

The next section was the one where she decided to spend some more time. It was a section called *Fiction*. There appeared to be many stories translated to native Artician here. Mostly stories of heroes and monsters, of courage and valor, and some rather silly stories as well.

She read a few chapters of one the books translated into her language and thought it rather humorous. She stopped at the section that told a story about the painting of a fence by a young hero. The young man managed to trick many people of his hamlet to do most of the fence painting in his place. She noticed that there were many books here by the same author. However, she was not sure what to think of the author's surname, Mark of the Twain. It was a truly unusual family name.

She moved to the next section of the library, *History*. She was most interested in this section. Here were all of the books of the known Artician history. She browsed through the racks and saw the titles of many books that interested her. *E'ward and Arianna: A Love Story, The Royal Swords of Articia, Battle of the Haunted Hills, The First Charge of the One Hundred.* Ava was a bit melancholy at the title of the last book. She thought of William and the possible loss of her newfound sibling in some future battle.

She scanned the next row of books and saw a book, written by the elf Metatron. She opened the pages, but it was in an elfish script that she did not know how to read. "I wonder if Mr. Tipple can interpret this book for me," she said quietly to herself.

"Yes, I think I can," a quiet voice behind her responded. "Ah the 'Prophesies and Birth of the Children of the Dead.'"

Ava jumped and almost dropped the book she was holding. Mr. Tipple had come up behind her so quietly that she had been startled. "My goodness, Mr. Tipple, you must not be so quiet. You should never startle one trained in the warrior arts. We tend to react instinctively in such situations," Ava warned with a smile.

"I will remember that, my young Princess. Let me see what book you are having trouble reading," Mr. Tipple asked.

Ava handed Mr. Tipple the book.

"Well, It did not take you long to find this book, did it?" The old man stated.

Ava did not know what to think about that statement, so asked Mr. Tipple, "Is it a book of significance?"

"Well, yes," Mr. Tipple said. "It is the story of the prophecies about you and your siblings."

"Can you translate it?" Ava asked. "I think the reason I am here is to read this book".

"Well, I have read it many times. I can certainly summarize the story for you," Mr. Tipple offered. "Would that be sufficient? Metatron has forbidden me to translate the book into native Artician."

"Metatron, he is the author?" Ava said. "Why does he not want it translated?"

"He, like his elven brothers, feels that if too much of the elven knowledge is spread over this world, it would throw off the balance," Mr. Tipple answered. "The elves believe that the balance is the most important thing to maintain here in Articia."

"Then why write the books at all? Why build this library?" Ava asked.

"I asked them once," Mr. Tipple said. "Metatron's brother Raphael told me that sometimes an Artician would need to make a journey of knowledge. The library was created to provide a destination for some of those journeys," Mr. Tipple walked over to the tables and placed the book down before he continued. "He also told me that the library has a special magical protection. Once you leave the library, you will not remember the place until you are ready for another journey of knowledge."

William walked into the history section of the library and joined the conversation, "So, why then do I remember the library? I have visited it many times."

"I believe that you and your siblings may be immune to the rules of Articia," Mr. Tipple said. "It is probably because of the tampering that occurred during your conception."

"Tampering during conception?" Ava asked. "What does that mean?"

"Maybe it would be best if we sit here and I will tell you the story," Mr. Tipple said. Ava and William walked over to the chairs that were set up in this section for those who were reading and waited for Mr. Tipple, who opened the book and translated some of the writings.

> This is the recorded history as told by Metatron, the scribe of the elves. At the end, we lamented. For the war we started in our fervor to exterminate the evil in our domain, destroyed our entire world and its entire people. In our sorrow, we decided to have our final battle with the demons, which were responsible for the spark that started the cataclysmic fire. The demons finally influenced the people to use the ultimate power that ended their existence. However, demonkind escaped us by passing through a tear in the universe created by the power of the apocalypse.

Mr. Tipple turned the page.

> We followed the demons into the new world they invaded and found that a benevolent deity watched over the domain. She represented the light, and her mate guarded the balance, of their domain. However, there was also a being of darkness in this world. It was held at bay by the rules of balance that the deities put in place. The darkness was pleased with the arrival of the demons and the possible undoing of the Artician equilibrium.

Mr. Tipple paused to settle in his chair before he continued reading.

> The deity met us as we arrived and asked us to agree not to engage the demons directly. She also asked the elves to stay on this world so that our goodness could balance the evil that the demons had brought. It has been many centuries since we fled our home and settled here, and we stand committed to remain in fulfillment of our promise to counter the darkness of the demons.'

Mr. Tipple stopped here and looked at the two siblings seated before him. "I am going to skip a lot of history of the battles the elves have participated in for generations to talk about more current information. Mr. Tipple turned the pages until he reached the last few of the book and read:

> The demons have made a bold move and interfered with the natural order of things in Articia. They have implanted the queen with the seed of one of the dark beings from our dead world. Since it is not of the natural order, if this child were born and allowed to grow, it would be immune to the rules of Articia. My brothers and I went to the goddess to plead with her to destroy this abomination, but she denied our request. Instead, she herself tampered with the seed and caused it to multiply, thereby diminishing the evil within.

Mr. Tipple adjusted himself in his chair again and continued.

> She added an equal amount of light and goodness to the offspring and her consort influenced balance in the remainder of their spirit.

This revelation shocked Ava. "I am not of the blood of both of my parents? I am a child of the other world?"

"That is why the title of this accounting by Metatron is *The Children of the Dead*," Mr. Tipple stated. "You and your siblings did not benefit from a natural conception. The demons interfered and Adara and her mate corrected it by adding some of their own spirit to the mix. Therefore, you carry the light and the darkness. The demon world provided the seed; your mother provided the eggs. You are beings from both worlds.

"But, let me continue," Mr. Tipple said.

> My brothers and I do not know if this was the best solution, but the deity of this world was pleased. The balance of good and evil in the children will allow them to use their own free will to determine if they will lean to the darkness or the light. We will watch and hope that the children Queen Angelica will favor balance and avoid the escalation that occurred between the demons and our kind in the past.

This revelation dismayed Ava. *We are children of whom, or what for that matter. Are we demons or we gods? Are we something completely different?* She stared off into the distance, lost in thought as William spoke.

"If we all came from the same seed, why are we so different? Why are there two males and two females?"

"I am not sure, but it is all part of the randomness of life. Look around you in the world, no two trees, no two beasts are the same; even the rocks are not identical," Mr. Tipple instructed. "When we see identical twins, we see two beings that look completely alike, when in fact each has slight differences and are the mirror image of the other."

Ava had been listening to the conversation as she became lost in thought. She stood and looked toward Mr. Tipple. "There are four of us, each with part of the darkness and part of the light, if I understand correctly. But I surmise we all favor the light."

"Yes, that appears to be true" Mr. Tipple concurred.

"I have always considered myself to be good, but you tell me that the elves hope for us to restore the balance," Ava said. "Should we not take sides in the battle of the darkness and light, we already have made decisions that are counter to that neutrality that you have discussed." Ava finished as she thought of William and his decision to ride as one of the One Hundred. There is no nobler act for a warrior than to participate in a charge that does not retreat.

"All are hard things to comprehend. It is not a position that I would wish to be in. Because one of your siblings chooses to follow the light, does that mean one must follow the darkness to maintain the balance?" Mr. Tipple stated. "I do not think this is the case. As long as there is great darkness in the world, you can act for the good to maintain the balance. When the demons brought the four horsemen to this world, they gave you the opportunity to stand firm for the light."

...

Alec and the boys were standing at the doorway of the largest building any of them had ever seen. Guarding the entrance were elves that stood very tall, much like the elves that stood at the city gates. Dustin looked up toward the top of the building in awe, but Jamal leaned so far back trying to look up that he fell over onto his back.

One of the elfish guards smiled at the spectacle that Jamal had provided while the other opened the door for the new arrivals. Jamal jumped back to his feet and stood next to Dustin.

The elf spoke, "He is expecting you," as he waved the party through the door.

...

Ava stepped inside the vestibule and closed the door. William was already there, golden locks falling across his face. She looked at him, or rather through his illusion. "You no longer need to use that enchantment to disguise yourself with me. I want to look on my brother in his natural form," she said quietly.

William nodded and whispered the dispelling phrase, "*Esse quam videri.*" Black curls bounced on his forehead. He looked up at her, his gray eyes twinkling.

"Why do you hide your appearance from everyone?" Ava asked.

"When it was decided that I would be sent to Cyrus to live with the cousin of the king, it was also decided that I should appear to be of their blood," William said. "Brendan cast a spell that changed my appearance and so I'd be blond and blue-eyed like the rest of our cousins from Cyrus."

"I see," Ava acknowledged. "I guess it is hard to hide our family resemblance in Cyrus. Our appearance is not uncommon in the community around Castle Articia; but I can see where you would have stood out in a region of fair-complexion people."

William laughed at that. "Yes, I would have been a black sheep there for sure."

He walked over to a chair in the corner of the room and sat down. "I was the one who discovered I was different, though I was not told that I was one of Henry's sons. I started to get a feel for the practitioner's arts when I was seven and the first magic that I perceived was when I realized that others did not see me as I saw myself; they saw the appearance created by Brendan's spell. In a mirror I saw myself as I truly was; to everyone else I looked like one of my blond cousins."

"So you can see through other illusions or deceptions?" Ava asked.

"It is my magical specialty, and I can also create a few illusions as well," William replied. "I think it is my natural ability, though I have not had much opportunity to practice or train."

"What kind of illusions do you create?" Ava asked.

"Well, I can change my appearance," William responded. "It comes in quite handy in Cyrus where I need to blend in. However, my favorite is disguising my position when practicing battle tactics. My cousin says it is cheating, but when fighting goblins or other beings of the darkness, I do not believe we are required to play fair."

"How come you did not use it when we sparred?" Ava asked.

"It would not have been honorable," William said, quite perturbed.

Ava felt guilty all of a sudden. For years, she had used subtle magic to gain an advantage when sparring and had never considered that it might not be a fair contest when she used her powers.

"William?" She asked.

"Yes, Ava."

"Do you think we are gods?" she questioned.

William looked over at Ava from the chair he was sitting in. "I do not know. At least, I do not think so," he replied. "But we are certainly touched by the gods and unfortunately also by the darkness. But what concerns me most is what Mr. Tipple said earlier about our immunity to the rules of Articia."

"Why does that bother you?"

"Because the rules exist to keep balance, or at least that is what I believe Mr. Tipple was trying to explain to us," William answered. "If we are not bound by the rules, it means we could take some action that could throw the balance off."

"You are right. We could do something that would really make a mess of things."

"I don't know if our journey here is complete. But we certainly have learned quite a bit about ourselves," William stated. "Are you ready to head back to Castle Articia?"

"Not yet, William," Ava responded. "Mr. Tipple told me there are many texts here on invocations. We need to spend at least another day or two here so I have an opportunity to read some of them. We do not know when we will be able to return to the library and I want to make the best use of the time I have here. When we leave this place, we are likely to be pursued again by those dark riders and I would like to be better prepared to handle them."

...

Alec and the boys walked down a long hall toward what appeared to be a large altar at the end. Alec had never seen any building like this before. It had huge windows of colored glass, each window an artistic rendering of battle, or pain, or suffering. At the end of the chamber was a window that depicted a large fiery cloud with burning skeletons. They appeared to be trying to run from the carnage that a fire wrought.

On the floor of the hall were round symbols with various markings. Circling each, written phrases that Alec did not recognize. They appeared to be the same Latin script that Raphael had been teaching him earlier that day.

Standing on one of the circles, with his back to Alec and the boys, was an elfish warrior. He looked much like the guards of the city and of this building, who bore armor that looked like feathers. However, this elf was clearly one of the nobles of this city because his armor was adorned with gold and silver. As Alec examined the noble elf, he noticed that the symbol on his armor had the words *Saday sabaoth athanatos* in the old Latin language. Alec did not know what that meant but maybe it described an incantation that he was not yet ready to learn.

"Excuse me, sir," Alec approached the elf in front of him.

Michael turned to look at Alec and the boys, paused, and smiled. "Welcome to this place. May I be of service to you and your gallant escorts?"

At the words "gallant escorts," Jamal elbowed Dustin and smiled as he whispered, "We are gallant escorts."

"Sir, Raphael sent us here because he felt that you could help us to find our way out of the Vale," Alec responded. "We believe a friend of ours is in trouble and we need to go and render aid."

"I see," Michael said to them. "Come, young Prince. Let me show you the way then."

Michael walked over to Alec and placed his hand on his head. Alec could feel the power flow from this commanding elf into him; Michaels contact filled him with confidence and he now knew that he could find the way through Valemore Forest to Danny's farm.

"Now go, my young Prince, for the hour is late and your sister is in dire need," Michael instructed him. "Remember the balance and do not repeat our mistakes."

Alec did not fully understand Michael's last statement but he did feel the urgency to leave immediately to find Danny. "Come on, Jamal, Dustin. We have to leave now."

...

Ava hurried back to the main hall of the Great Library, searching for its librarian. She found him in a room that stored the texts that contained the phrases and motions of the various schools of magic. Mr. Tipple was sitting at one of the desks, reading avidly, and he looked like he was in pain.

"Mr. Tipple?" She whispered ever so softly, but he still jumped, managing to knock over some of the books piled on the desk. He hid a smile as he mumbled something, lifted a finger, and used magic that appeared to be the color of dark violet. The books floated back up and into a neat stack.

"You shouldn't scare me like that Princess Ava you'll give me a heart attack one of these days!" He sat back down where he had been sitting when Ava entered the room. "I had been expecting you to visit me this morning, but I did not guess that a princess of this realm would be such an early riser."

"I am not your *usual* princess," Ava stated quietly.

"I am enlightened," Mr. Tipple stated. "You told me that you are interested in gaining additional invocation knowledge while you are here. I am at your service and will assist you in any way I can. Please note that the section on the dark invocations is only available to read if you have specific written permission from the elfin authors. Those writings are considered very dangerous and have been put to paper only so that those who stand for the light can truly understand their foes."

Mr. Tipple stood up and started walking along the aisles of books as he described each section. "The first section here is on weather altercation spells, though I do not recommend spending much time on these. Very early in the time of magical discovery, sorcerers learned that one must not tamper with the natural environment here in our realm. Early practitioners got many lessons on balance when they tried to change the weather." Mr. Tipple shuffled through some papers on the table before he continued speaking. "The rules of balance pushed back very hard and tended to cause more problems than the limited good that resulted from the invocations."

"What do you mean by pushing back?" Ava asked.

Mr. Tipple seemed excited to tell a story of historical nature. "Well, there is one story about how very early in the history of Greater Articia; one of the monarchs chose to use weather as a weapon in a war with a neighboring country. He made it snow in the middle of the summer and destroyed all of the enemy's crops."

"Seems like a harsh way to defeat an enemy nation. The common people who would suffer most under such a tactic," Ava said with disgust.

Mr. Tipple smiled at her response and thought, *the goddess has chosen well in you, Ava.* He continued his story: "They learned quickly that the balance pushes back. The attacking kingdom then suffered three years of winter as a result of trying to use weather as a weapon." Mr. Tipple pushed his hair back off his brow and continued, "The people of that kingdom suffered from the lack of a good crop, which left them severely weakened. The famine that followed left the kingdom in distress and eventually opened it to invasion by its enemies. The war that followed their foolish action brought an end to that kingdom and left it in ruins," Mr. Tipple finished.

"Three winters for one, that seems like a rather extreme response in a world that maintains balance," Ava responded.

"Yes, it would seem rather punitive except to those who understand how the balance is maintained," Mr. Tipple answered. "Look over here. On the table there is a pendulum, a device that I constructed based on a description that I found in one of the historical texts. When all is balanced, the pendulum rests in the center undisturbed. But watch what happens when I pull the pendulum out of the center." Mr. Tipple pulled back on the weight of the pendulum and it started to swing back and forth, slowing in each pass, as Ava watched.

As it came to a stop, Ava asked, "So when it is disturbed, it passes the stable state of rest and goes to the extreme and then swings back past the point of rest to the other extreme. It continues this back-and-forth motion, lessening with each pass, until the balance is once again achieved."

"Exactly Princess, if the balance is not interfered with again, it will regain its peaceful state of rest. You are quite bright," Mr. Tipple responded. "The same is true for all magic that is created.

If you invoke magic in any form, the opposing magics will respond to bring back balance. This has kept the dark wizards in check for many years."

...

Alec, Jamal, and Dustin rode back through Valemore Forest heading east on the trail that had been hidden to them. It was not as difficult to traverse as on the previous trip they made with Danny.

Dustin broke the silence with a question. "Do you think she is all right?"

"I don't know, so let's move as quickly as we can to her house," Alec responded

...

Dominic looked over the hill to the edge of the forest. He could see the southern edge of the ruffians' camp. The men from the north seemed unconcerned they could be detected.

Dominic leaned over and whispered to Tristan, "What do you think—about a thousand men-at-arms?"

"That would be my best guess," Tristan replied.

"Pellius," Dom looked down the hill and whispered to the senior of the Third who was riding with them. "Do you think we can get closer to this camp or behind them without being detected?"

"I do not think so, Sire," the young warrior replied. "We cannot cross this plain without being detected by their sentries, even if we make the attempt at night."

"We could take the Pass of Uriel to the west of here," Tristan proposed. "It would allow us to get around behind the camp and we would be able to watch them from the high ground there."

"It will take almost a full day, but that is probably our best option," Dominic said. "I think you should stay here with Tancred in case the army camped before us starts moving south.

I will go west and around with Pellius to see what the northern side of this camp looks like." He mounted his horse and turned to the north. "Be careful, brother," Tristan said. "You know that our father would not be pleased if you did not return to Castle Articia safely," he finished with a foolish smile that Dominic returned by crossing his eyes at his brother before he rode to the west.

...

"After the section on weather, there are sections that cover other areas of the invocative arts." Mr. Tipple directed a question to Ava. "In order for me to suggest the best section for you to study, I need to understand what invocative arts you favor. May I see what your magical senses will show me?"

"Certainly Mr. Tipple, my current magical tutor has looked into my abilities many times, so I am not unfamiliar with the practice," Ava responded.

Mr. Tipple walked toward Ava as she calmed her senses, knowing that fighting a magical assessment only made it harder on the her and her examiner. He touched her temples as she closed her eyes.

In her mind, she opened her thoughts to her magical aura. Ava was in a familiar place, deep inside the source of her magical power. The pool of her magical energy was in front of her. It was massive, stretching beyond her mind sight. Mr. Tipple was standing on the shore looking over it, his mouth hanging open, looking thoroughly shocked and confused. "What is it, Mr. Tipple?" Ava asked.

The old man closed his mouth and said, "My dear ... This is, this is incredible. Your pool of magic seems limitless!" He took off his glasses and bent down. He touched the edge of the pool and scooped up some of its energy, cupping it in his hands. It was changing color in his hands; it was the same progression of her eyes as she used magic that is more complex.

"This is incredible," he whispered again, and then released the magical energy back into the pool. "Dear, my magical energy is insignificant compared to yours, and I have always been considered quite the conjurer. Your magical abilities seem to be boundless."

Ava expected his reaction. She had experienced the same response before. Still, there are things she wished to understand about her power. "Why have I been gifted so when my brothers Alec and William seem to have very little magical stamina?"

"There is no way to determine why," Mr. Tipple responded. "The goddess alone decides how her gifts are given. Even the type of magic is different for each practitioner. The texts in this library describe many forms of magic. But let us break this bond now and talk," Mr. Tipple faded in her mind's eye as she drifted out of her trance.

When Ava opened her eyes, she confided to the old librarian. "I am concerned that when I reach the peak of magical ability, I lose control. It has led to some very dangerous situations," Ava confessed. "Is there a book here that explains why that happens to me?"

Mr. Tipple seemed a bit distressed at that question. "Yes, I believe there is information about uncontrollable power, but I am not sure that it is a good idea for you to see it." Mr. Tipple started to walk down the rows of books.

"Why?" Ava questioned.

"It is very dangerous knowledge. To anyone else, it is just information, but to you and your abilities, it could be disastrous," Mr. Tipple said with a shudder.

"I would probably agree with you, but I think it is more dangerous for me to not know," Ava replied. "I have reached into that level of my power multiple times and have not been able to maintain control. I think knowledge of what it is would help me to control it."

Mr. Tipple looked at Ava gravely, and then walked slowly over to a shelf that contained a single scroll. He reached up with hands shaking and pulled it off the shelf. He paused for a long moment, considering the implication of sharing this information with the young princess. He sighed and turned to Ava as he said, "This is the most dangerous magic incantation in Articia. It can never be used because it would truly mean the end of us all."

Mr. Tipple handed the scroll to Ava and she opened it. She took a few moments to read the content of the scroll and then dropped it on the floor in shock. Ava put her hand over her heart as she said in anguish,

"It is a scroll for the incantation of the spell for Armageddon! This is the power of the four horsemen!" Ava said in shock. "Are you saying that when I lose control of my power, I am calling for the magic of Armageddon!"

...

Alec rode into the clearing that was Danny's home. As he scanned the farm, he felt that not all seemed right. The door to the house was open slightly and there was no sign of Danny.

"You two stay here while I check the house," Alec ordered as he dismounted Star Dancer. He drew his sword and cautiously went in the front door. As he scanned the room, he noticed that furniture was scattered as if there had been a struggle. It looked like Danny was taken from the house by force.

Alec quickly went back outside to tell the boys and found them scanning tracks on the ground.

"There were goblins here!" Dustin said excitedly. "At least ten of them went into the house and came out weighted down. They struggled with their burden. Danny probably put up a fight because they were knocked off their feet multiple times."

"What else can you see in the tracks?" Alec asked.

"They got control of her and headed off, to the west," Dustin added. "These tracks are at least a day, maybe two old. They have a head start on us but we should be able to catch them."

"Are they mounted?" Alec asked.

"No, no horses or other beasts of burden," Dustin replied.

"I'll split their 'eads!" Jamal shouted.

"We will catch them and free Danny," Alec said. "Quick! Let us get going. Can you follow those tracks if we are mounted and move quickly?"

"We cannot run, but I can keep them under eye at a quick pace," Dustin said.

"All right, Dustin, you lead then. Jamal, you ride with me and we will follow your companion." Alec finished as the group moved west after Danny's abductors.

...

Dominic looked beyond the hill and east past the camp. "They are building a road!"

"Yes, it would seem to be so. This could be disastrous for the king's army," Pellius stated. "If the forces of darkness bring their army down this road and avoid the Crystal Mountain pass, we will meet the brunt of the army on the open plains."

"We must get back to Tris and Tancred. We have to warn father and get support up for Lewisvel Keep. It will be more vulnerable from an attack from the west," Dominic said as he backed off the hill. "Let's ride quickly the way we came. I do not want the north men to know we have discovered what they are building."

...

Ava was distraught. "Am I a tool of destruction?" she said to Mr. Tipple. "Why would the goddess give me power to destroy the world?"

"Why do you assume the goddess gave you that power?" Mr. Tipple asked quietly. "That power may be part of what came with you from the other world."

"But the goddess diminished the darkness," Ava stated. "Why was the power not diminished as well?"

"For that, I have no answer," the librarian said. "But you should not concern yourself with the source of your of power. It has been given to you, and the choice to use it is yours alone."

"Not always," Ava replied. "I have lost control before and have only regained control because of someone else's intercession."

"What causes you to lose control?" Mr. Tipple asked.

"When I get angry or when someone I love is in danger, my magic quickly escalates to dangerous levels," Ava responded. "Am I to be the destroyer of this world?" Ava finished with frustration.

Mr. Tipple put his hand on her shoulder as he said, "Dear, dear, I do not believe that is what the goddess has in mind for you. With training and discipline and you should be able to maintain control of your power."

"But there is no time; my father's kingdom is in peril now," Ava replied with tears in her eyes. "How can I learn that kind of discipline in such a short time?"

"There are many ways to find inner peace. There may be a way you can achieve this peace in a short period. Come, there is a wonderful book I would like to show you. It was one of the first tomes that Metatron allowed me to translate into Artician," Mr. Tipple said as he led Ava into a section of the library with the title *Meditative Texts*. He reached up to a shelf and took down a book with the title *Tai Chi: Creating a Natural Balance of Self and World.*

"This book has instruction in a form of meditation that will help you to understand yourself and how to control your anger," Mr. Tipple added. "It is about a meditation method called Tai Chi that is a process of bringing the principles of the light and darkness back into harmony."

"Will there be enough time for me to learn these things before I have to face my anger again?" Ava asked.

"It is less about time and more about commitment, my dear," Mr. Tipple responded as he handed her the book. "You may take that book with you. When you have mastered what is within, I only ask that you return it to the library so some future patron can benefit from its information."

Ava returned to her bedchamber and started to read the book that Mr. Tipple had given her. After reading a section of the book on energy and discipline, Ava thought about her training so far. As she read more about how Tai Chi is a soft style of fighting. Ava stopped and thought about this statement. *Tai Chi is a soft style. Clearly, this is not specifically a fighting martial art.* Was it really just "brute force" fighting that she had been learning? How could she learn to control her actions in just a couple of days?

"How can I master such a method in just a few days?" Ava said with exasperation.

"Master what method?" William asked.

"Don't you ever knock?" Ava said irritably. "It is not polite to walk in on a woman."

"Your door was open, Ava," William said with some confusion.

Ava quelled her irritation and apologized. "Sorry, William, I have been preoccupied today." Ava closed the book she had been reading and placed it on the table.

"Is there something I can help with?" William asked as he walked over to sit on a small wooden chair under the only window in the room.

"No, I do not think so," Ava responded. "Mr. Tipple shared with me some knowledge that has me deeply troubled. It seems that the power that I have been given has the potential to be disastrous."

"I have no doubt that your power is unique, but how is it dangerous?" William asked.

"I have the power to bring about the Armageddon that destroyed the world from which the elves came," Ava said with trepidation.

William was shocked at this revelation. He was silent for some time before he responded. "Because you have the power does not mean that you will use it."

"I am not concerned about the power when I am in control. It is when I lose control that frightens me," Ava said.

"Then you should always maintain control," William stated.

"It is not that easy, I have already lost control many times already. Had there not been someone there to intervene, then I am afraid of what I would have done," Ava finished.

"So what can we do then?" William asked.

"Mr. Tipple believes that if I maintain my inner balance, as described in this book he has given me, I should be able to keep from being taken over by that horrible power." A tear was rolling down Ava's face as she revealed the curse that the demons had placed within her being. "But I do not know if I can master these techniques in time."

"In time for what" William asked. "What are you planning?"

"I do not believe we came here by accident," Ava confided. "I believe that this journey was for us to learn what is truly at stake. If the horsemen join the goblin force against our father, then Alec, our unknown sibling, you, and I may be the only hope that Articia has against such a foul force."

17
Marked

Danny woke in significant pain. She realized that she was leaning, if leaning was what you could call it. She was really hanging, since her arms were chained against a wall.

Danny slowly raised her head and tried to peer out of her swollen eyes. She looked around the large chamber; lined with the bones and skulls of humans, it was quite dark, and her eyes only barely adjusted to the blackness in the room. At the far end of the hall there appeared to be a wooden door. It was solid with no openings, no handle, and no other form of lock that she could discern.

She closed her eyes and tried to rest, still too weak to try to escape.

...

After talking for a couple of hours, William left Ava's room. It was late and she needed to rest. They had spent many days in the Great Library and he needed to get out into the open air and check on their mounts. He knew he was well overdue to tend to the horses.

He passed through the small entrance and out into the field in front of the library. He did not know why he preferred the open air to buildings, but he was happiest on the road traveling instead of cooped up inside one of the many castles, halls, or homes of the nobles he visited.

He saw Ava's horse off to the east, grazing in some tall grass, and looked around for Comet. He saw his companion to the northwest of the library on the top of a hill. Comet was facing west with his mane blowing into the wind.

William started to walk to the destri as it spoke to him. "*One of my brothers has told me of a story of some concern.*"

William climbed to the top of the hill and put his hand on Comet's neck. "What is the distress?"

"*He and his rider are pursuing goblins along a road north of here,*" Comet replied. "*But I am having problems communicating with my brother to get more information. There is some kind of interference with our bond.*"

"That is unusual. Have you ever had a problem like this before?" William questioned the destri.

"*Not personally, but I have heard stories of this happening in the past,*" the destri responded. "*It only occurs in the presence of a powerful demon.*"

...

"We are catching up to them," Dustin said as he saw Jamal sniffing the ground. "Jamal says that he can smell them now, which means that we are only about an hour or two behind the foul beasts."

"This seems too easy. You would think that the goblins would try to cover their tracks, even if they do not know we are in pursuit," Alec said. "It feels too much like a trap." Alec thought of the times he would play games of mental skill with Ava. She always seemed to be able to draw him into a loss or a stalemate. He was never good at that kind of strategy. It required an ability to think far ahead in the game, and he tended to play more of a reaction game with Ava. What would Ava do if she were in this situation?

"I think we are being led to danger," Alec stated. "My family's weapon master taught us about a contraption called a mouse trap and I think Danny is the cheese."

"Danny is not cheese!" Jamal said.

"It is a just a comparison, Jamal. I know Danny is not cheese," Alec clarified. "What I am trying to say is that I believe that the goblins are setting a trap for us ahead. If I am correct, we are getting close to the Haunted Hills"

At this statement both of the boys' eyes went wide as Dustin said, "They say that those hills have ghosts!"

"I have not personally been there but I am told there is a maze of caves under the hills that was left by miners many years ago," Alec told the pair. "A large battle was fought there as well and they say that the before they could retrieve the bodies of the soldiers that had died, they disappeared at night without a trace."

"Are there real ghosts in the Haunted Hills?" Dustin asked rather nervously.

"The locals of the area believed that ghouls took the men," Alec responded. "Recently, people have been disappearing again near the hills. My father believes they were foolish and went into the caves to look for riches and got lost."

"So you *do not* believe the hills are haunted?" Dustin asked apprehensively.

"Oh, I didn't say that. I am sure there are many ghosts in the area from the great battles that were fought," Alec answered. "But I believe that ghosts are benevolent. I think the real danger there is very alive and probably the goblins we have been chasing."

"Oh," Dustin said. "If that is where Danny was taken, then that is where I am going."

"Me, too," Jamal added bravely.

"We will have to watch for signs that we are closing in on the goblin trap. The best way to avoid this trap may be to spring it," Alec said.

"Traps are my specialty," said Dustin. "I have set many traps to catch game for us to eat. I should be able to see the signs of any trap a goblin would set."

"Good," Alec said. "I think we should slow down a little now. We do not want to rush into anything that is undetected. I learned that there are many signs to watch for in the woods to avoid being ambushed." Alec looked at the bushes and small trees ahead of them. "We should watch for tracks that turn away from the main group and watch and listen to the animals."

"Yes, animals are very skittish around men and monsters and they make a lot of noise when either passes," Dustin added.

"So we must be quiet to listen for the signs," Alec finished. "We also do not want the goblins to hear us coming, so we need to move very quietly in the woods now. We will walk our horses from here."

"*So you do listen in class,*" Star Dancer communicated to him humorously.

"*Not all of it is boring, you know,*" Alec thought back to the steed.

...

Ava felt she knew this garden, but she was sure she had never walked these grounds in her entire life. She sat down against a beautiful willow to enjoy the aroma of the surrounding fauna and pondered her arrival in the remarkable place.

I do not remember coming here, she thought, as she looked down the garden path into the distance.

She saw a shimmering light approaching. She knew what it was, of course. How many times had Brendan taught about signs of the Goddess? She tried to get up to meet Adara but her body did not respond to the commands that her mind was giving it.

Ava looked into the light as it formed into the image of Adara that she had seen at the Temple of Adara in Westwood. Clearly, the artisans who had carved that statue had seen the goddess because the statue was a perfect interpretation of what she was seeing in front of her at that moment.

Ava tried to lower her head in reverence, but again, she could not move. *Will Adara be displeased that I do not show respect? Would she punish her children for not lowering their eyes?* Ava had been on the receiving end of many lectures from her mother and father about earning and giving respect. They would frequently tutor her on why it was important for a person to know you were listening, and listening respectfully, by looking in their eyes. Her parents never told her how to behave when you interact with a goddess.

As Adara arrived in front of her, she sat down eye to eye with Ava. The goddess was everything that Ava had expected her to be, a definition of beauty and grace. Adara turned her head and smiled a little.

"Ava, I am your protector and guide. Someday you will stand beside me, but not today child. Many millennium ago I was once like you, a child of Articia before the light split from the darkness. Gods or goddesses earn a place in the heavens with their deeds. Very few are born with the ability to maintain the necessary power and pureness of spirit to achieve that reality."

Ava did not know why she was suddenly thinking of her brothers. "I will always be in Dom and Tristan's shadow. They truly are incredible, the noble ones. I am still just a child." She felt a pang in her chest as she remembered what she was missing back home. She looked up slightly astonished when the goddess laughed outright.

"Your brothers are noble, yes, but you, Alec, William, and the sister you have not met will do remarkable things. But sadly, you will also face incredible challenges."

Ava thought about what the goddess said. They were all so young. How could they do anything that would be so noble? She thought of the terrible power that she had just learned she possessed; Ava needed to know why the goddess had cursed her so. "Why have you given me such a horrifying power? I could destroy the world."

"Ava," the goddess said as she touched Ava on the temple. "I did not give you the power. As part of the chaos that arrived when the passage between our world and the world of the elves and demons, opened, the chaos that was created birthed the magical abilities in our realm. Articia did not have magical energies before the opening of the rift."

"But I have so *much* power; I do not believe I can control it!" Ava exclaimed as her eye welled with tears.

"The power you have was part of the seed when it was brought from the other world," the goddess explained. "I had hoped that when we split the seed, the power would be reduced. But I do not control the rules of the universes and where magic is concerned, chaos rules."

"I do not understand. You are a goddess. How can you not fix this?" Ava implored.

"There are very strict rules that even the gods have to follow. It is how everything around us stays stable and sound. Everything seeks balance, light and darkness, chaos and order. My consort stands in the middle watching and striving to maintain the balance of this universe," the goddess instructed, "but the demons of the other world scorn and maliciously flout the rules. They brought the seed from the place from which they came. In doing so, they were trying to create a being that was immune to the rules, a being that they could control."

Ava thought about the goddess's revelation. Adara did not give her power? Gods have rules? It was so much to absorb.

"Ava, you are one of the greatest works of fate. When my husband and I intervened with you and your siblings, we took a great risk to keep the demons from upsetting the balance", the goddess whispered.

"I am so afraid. I do not know if I can control the power I have," Ava said. "I am dismayed that I may someday use the power to destroy all that I love!"

"Be at peace, child," Adara soothed with a whisper. "I am always watching over you and will guide you when you or your siblings call. As long as you want my help, I will give it." Adara spoke as she put her hand on Ava's wrist. "I claim you as one of the light. You will always be under my protection and watchful eye."

Ava opened her eyes and felt her arm; something was different. She got up from the cot that she'd been lying on and

walked over to the mirror. A new mark, a brand, was on her wrist
in the shape of a half-moon circle. "Marked by the goddess," she
remembered. She was a chosen one. Her hair had also changed.
It was no longer the coal black that she shared with her siblings.
It was now the brownish blonde of her ancestral family. *Was this
a sign that the darkness was no longer in her?*

...

Danny was startled awake as she realized that something had
her by the neck, a demon!

"So, the spawn of the other world is awake. Did you really
think you could hide from us forever?" the demon barked.
Danny just looked at the beast and was struck dumb from the
sheer terror.

"SPEAK!" the demon commanded as it pulled her toward
him so hard the chains ripped at her wrists. The demon then
slammed Danny against the wall. The only thing keeping her on
her feet were the chains that held her leaning against the wall.
Danny managed to catch her breath long enough to squeak out
the words, "Where am I?"

"My dear," the demon sneered. "Don't you know? This is
your home."

...

"See, just over there, past that rock is some branches across
the road," Alec said from the bushes where he was hiding. "A
rather crude trap the goblins must not be very bright."

"Goblins are not very smart at all," Dustin replied. "They
tried and failed to attack our family farm many times. They
tend to be only dangerous in large numbers. Alone or in small
numbers, they are very weak."

"Well, let's not take any chances. We can go around the trap
and come ..." Before Alec could finish the sentence, Jamal was
running into the clearing, swinging his hammer in the air.

"Jamal, wait!" Alec called, but it was too late. Jamal had jumped the goblin trap and was swinging at a goblin hiding in the bushes just past the trap. It was rather stunned at the screaming boy and did not react in time to save its existence as Jamal's hammer came crashing down on its head.

More goblins jumped from the bushes and started to surround Jamal. He was swinging his bloody hammer over his head as he yelled his battle call. Alec quickly drew his sword and ran into the fray as Dustin started an incantation.

...

"This is not my home," Danny whispered.

"Ah, but it is, my young protégée. We thought we had lost control of the seed when the brood was split into a foursome," the demon admitted.

"I do not understand you," Danny said as she put her head down. The demon reached down and grabbed her chin hard and lifted her face to his "You are a child of the darkness; you shall serve us as many before you have served my kind."

"I serve none of your kind," Danny said with anger. "I serve no one."

The demon let go of Danny's chin and struck her across the cheek. She cried out, breathing heavily, as she put her head down from the excruciating pain of the demon's strike. She felt like she was hit by a rock on fire.

"You will learn to obey your new master one way or another!" the demon shouted as it stormed out the door.

...

"What is it?" Ava asked William as she opened the door of the room that Mr. Tipple had provided for her.

"Something is happening north and west of here. Comet has been hearing communication from another of his kind," William told her anxiously. "But he said there is interference from a demon. We need to go and investigate why there is a demon in the area. Are you ready to travel yet?"

As William was speaking to Ava, he noticed the symbol on her wrist and the change of her hair color. "What has happened to you?" he reached to touch a strand of her hair.

Ava held out her wrist. "It still stings a little. It is the mark of the goddess Adara. We have communed."

...

"Trespasser!" one of the goblins screeched in a tiny voice, running at Alec with a bludgeon and holding a head-sized shield. Alec swung Shadow Fang into the running goblin as he stepped to let it pass on his right side. The goblin never had a chance as the magically sharp blade of Alec's sword bit deep into its flesh.

Despite the aggressiveness of Jamal's attack, the goblins did not stop and Alec abandoned his hidden position to help the young warrior out of the predicament he had gotten himself into with his foolish charge.

Alec had not encountered goblins before, but these things were like a mixture of a hound and some of the spoiled children he sometimes saw at court. They howled and whined as they fought, which did grind a bit on Alec's nerves.

As Alec closed in on his next target, more goblins jumped out of the woods to attack the companions. If not for Jamal's magic, they would have quickly gotten the upper hand. Small balls of fire struck several of the goblins and lit their clothes on fire. In the confusion, many of the goblins fell to Alec's sword and Jamal's hammer. Still more of the goblins remained, but they were now a much more manageable number. Dustin pulled his staff off his back and joined the fray.

The goblins clawed at his thighs and pounded his chain mail with their little bludgeons. He had only killed one more of the beasts since they first engaged. The goblins were so flighty; he was having trouble connecting with his sword. If diminutive beasts were more organized, they would have taken down the trio easily. Their attacks were random and without a single purpose. Jamal was faring as badly as Alec was, with many scrapes and bruises. If they did not end this soon, they would be finished.

Just as Alec was beginning to lose hope, Star Dancer ran into the clearing and reared. The goblins turned to the destri and panicked. Two others fell immediately to Jamal's hammer as Dustin swung over and on top of the head of a third, ending its confusion. Alec then continued to swing underneath the club of a fourth and on the return swing took out two more gaping goblins. The destri came down on the last two, instantly killing them with its hooves.

As Alec looked around to see that the skirmish was over, the shaggy warhorse galloped into the clearing and snorted. It stepped over one of the dead goblins and relieved itself. Alec was stunned at the action of this diminutive pony, but then started to laugh at the display.

Star Dancer turned to look at the spectacle and communicated, *"It would appear that our shaggy friend is smarter that it seems."*

...

"Demons! How could they have gotten so close to the city of Articia without anyone knowing?" Ava asked.

"I do not know, but if a destri is in pursuit, then I am obligated to investigate. One of my comrades may be in danger and I may need to get word to our captain," William replied.

"Then we should ride to the northwest right away!"

"Ava, this is dangerous business. The demon may be one of the beasts that are pursuing us. It may not be wise for you to leave the sanctuary of the library," William advised.

"If you go, then I go. I will not be separated from you, brother," Ava said with firm resolve. "And besides, I have a feeling that if we separate, it will lead to disaster."

"Then so be it. When can you be ready to ride?"

"I want to go and say goodbye to Mr. Tipple first. I will meet you outside when I have gathered my things."

...

The demon struck Danny again. Blood was now flowing out of a gash on her cheek. She had never known so much pain in her life. She could not help but let the tears flow down her face. Despite the pain, she continued to resist; she refused to be a pawn in the demon's game. "I will not be yours," Danny stated, though she could offer no more than a whisper. "I will resist you till my end."

The demon knocked her head back in anger and Danny blacked out. "Well then, maybe your brother will have a weaker heart. We shall see if he is as strong when his sister's life hangs in the balance." The demon stormed out of the chamber, leaving the door open.

...

"The dark lord will not be happy," the imp stated.

The next voice that spoke was definitely human. "The dark lord does not have to know. The spawn of the queen must be destroyed. If they join forces, it would be disastrous for our army and our cause. Any interaction between them *must* be terminated before it even begins."

"But what you plan could spell disaster for the master," the imp replied. "If the citadel sorcerers engage Henry on the battlefield, it will throw off the delicate balance on this plane."

"So be it. With his power diminished, we will gain the upper hand in this battle for control of Articia!" the dark sorcerer said as he continued to read the tome.

You are a fool, sorcerer. You will bring the chaos we so desire! The imp thought with delight.

...

Alec climbed to the top of a tree overlooking Haunted Hills and surveyed the landscape. He saw no more goblins or any other life for that matter. Something was bothering him about this place. He felt darkness here. There was something dead here, but not buried. He could not put a finger on it, but he knew that great danger lay ahead.

He jumped off the last branch to the ground and spoke to the boys. "We should leave the horses here. Sorry, Star Dancer, but I think you would stand out too much on the open plain and would give us away as we approach."

"*I am not offended. Where you are going my kind cannot navigate well. I would be more of a hindrance than a benefit,*" the destri replied.

Alec pulled his bow and a pair of arrows from its strap on the saddle. He then motioned for the boys to come forward. "I considered asking you two to stay here, but I know you would not obey. Therefore, you must do everything I ask you to do as we enter the cave. There is something dangerous below and if you do not do as I ask, it could mean the end of all of us."

"I will do as you ask," Jamal promised, "as long as I can bash the heads of those who took Danny!"

"I will make sure that Jamal makes good decisions," Dustin told Alec. Alec smiled back at both of them and looked west. "Let's go then, quietly," he said as he started out of the forest into the hills.

Alec was not crazy; he could feel the power of what lay underground in the land of the dead. He had seen his first demon and the feel of it was fresh in the sickle-strike scar on his shoulder. Though he knew that the dark presence here was not one of the four riders, it felt much more dangerous.

He also felt drawn to it, almost by magic or some unforeseen power. He knew he would have to face this demon if he was going to get Danny back. "A pawn in one of Ava's games," he whispered.

"What?" Jamal asked.

"It's nothing important, Jamal. Let us keep moving. When we get to the caves, stay behind me," Alec instructed the young boys. He knew that the course was leading straight to the demon, but like it or not, he was going to find Danny.

...

18

Broken plans

Dominic and his escort from the Third rode on the eastern road to return through the Pass of Uriel. They pushed to reach the observation point where Alec and his escort were waiting.

"Sire, your brother, and Tancred have had to move off to the south," Pellius informed the prince. "They are riding to the gates of Lewisvel Keep."

"What do you know?" Dominic asked. "Why did they stop observing the northern forces?"

"They were surprised by an advance scout," Pellius responded. "Tristan dispatched the scout but not before he got off a warning call from his horn. " The destri has communicated what we learned about the road. Lewisvel will be warned of the pending attack from the west."

"I will assume that we can no longer head back to the east to rejoin my brother," Dominic stated. "With the invading army alerted to our presence, we have but one choice."

"Yes, Sire," the young rider, replied.

"Please communicate to your brethren that we are heading south back to Castle Articia to warn my father of these changing developments," Dominic commanded. "And tell him to tell Tris to hang tight. We will return with the army of Articia!"

...

"Mr. Tipple," Ava said as she walked into the chamber where the librarian did most of his reading. She found him studying some of the tomes he had pulled out the day before. At the sound of her voice, the Mr. Tipple turned, saw Ava, and smiled.

"Yes dear, how can I help you?" His eye widened as he took in the color of Ava's hair and noticed the mark of the goddess on her wrist as she brushed back her hair.

"I am afraid I must be leaving your wonderful library," Ava told Mr. Tipple with regret. "There is trouble away from here and I believe I must respond." She laid a book down on his desk. On the cover was a one-word title of *Sonnets*. "I truly enjoyed that book. I hope to come back very soon to read many more."

"I am sorry to see you go so soon, Princess. I truly appreciate your love of the written word." Mr. Tipple got up and gave the princess a very tight hug. "I have faith that your journey will be safe and the road ahead will be smooth beneath your feet."

"I shall return as soon as I can," Ava said, somewhat teary-eyed as she walked out of Mr. Tipple's reading room.

William was waiting for her in the hallway. He could see immediately by her body language that it was hard for her to leave this place. He knew by watching her for the last few days that the library was the one place in the whole world that Ava was destined to reside.

They walked down the long corridor to the small door, and Ava saw as she stepped out into the garden and saw their mounts saddled and packed. William, a veteran traveler, knew how get ready quickly for the long road. Ava sighed as she climbed up on Aurora and kicked her into a trot. They headed out of the western gate without speaking and turned to the northwest.

"*I have heard no more updates on what is happening in the hills,*" William's mount stated.

"Then I guess we are riding blind," William replied as his mount stepped onto the gravel road that led toward the Haunted Hills.

...

Alec, Jamal, and Dustin quietly moved up to opening of the cave. He could see two goblin sentries standing and jabbering with each other as they were guarding the entrance of the cave that Alec knew they must enter.

"We need to take these two out *quietly*," Alec whispered more to Jamal than to Dustin. He reached for the bow on his back and pulled two arrows from his quiver. As he held one of the arrows in his teeth, he cocked the other and drew the bow back. He listened to make sure that there was no beast in the area, and then he let the arrow fly.

As soon as it was on the way to its target, he grabbed the second from his mouth and cocked, then let it fly as his first shot struck a goblin true. The other goblin, confused by the event, made a fatal mistake as it turned to look at its comrade. The second arrow struck its ear, killing the foul beast instantly.

The trio walked from their hiding place at the edge of the bushes and moved slowly toward the cave. The two goblins lay dead on the ground in front of them.

"That was remarkable shooting," Dustin said to Alec as they walked.

"I have been told I am pretty good with a bow," he responded to the young boy. "But we need to move cautiously now. I am sure there is some kind of trap or danger waiting for us in these caves."

...

Bryn came into the war room and rather excitedly called to the king, "We have a problem in the north, Sire!"

The king turned and saw the expression on Bryn's face and frowned. "The last time I saw that expression, we were on the verge of disaster. Please tell me that it is just indigestion, my friend."

"I am afraid not, Sire. We just had a message from one of the Tyros of the One Hundred. Dominic and his escort are making haste to return to the castle," Bryn reported. "They carry bad news as our scouts in the north. The ruffians have been building a road north of the Crystal Mountains. We need a new to rethink our battle plans."

The king looked at the map. "This is disastrous; we need to mobilize the army now. If we do not meet the ruffians' army head-on as they leave the northern forest, the city of Lewisvel will be lost."

"There is more news, Sire. Tristan and one of the Third were cut off by the ruffians and they were forced to head east to Lewisvel Keep," Bryn informed him. "At least, they will be able to warn the city of the impending invasion."

The king was very worried about Tristan. He would be trapped in a city that was likely to be destroyed. He turned to one of the knights of the One Hundred and said, "We need to get word to Prince Ericson that he must meet the main body of our army in the plains south of Lewisvel Keep."

"It is already done, Sire. We have assigned a Tyro of the Third to the prince so that we would have the ability to communicate with his forces," the knight replied.

...

"Have you noticed that we have not been pursued?" Ava asked William as she surveyed the countryside.

"I would not expect any trouble this far south in your father's kingdom," William replied, not understanding Ava's concern.

"Yes, but where have the riders gone that were pursuing us?" Ava asked.

William almost hit himself in the head for his foolishness. The riders! The protection that the Great Library had provided caused him to forget the darkness that had been chasing them. Where had they gone? *Comet, I am confused by this change of events. Do you have any insights?* He thought.

"*No, William. I felt that the darkness had diminished but did not realize that they had moved on,*" the destri relayed.

William thought of this and looked at Ava. "We should take this as a blessing from Adara. The road should be a little less weary now."

Ava should have been reassured but started to get a sickening feeling. She was not sure what caused it, but she was starting to feel that one of her siblings was in considerable pain. She turned to William, a tear starting own her cheek, "William, we must make haste. I believe that Alec is in great danger."

...

The king mounted his warhorse, its barding gleaming in the sun. The army cheered at the grandeur. The whole of the army and most of the simple folk of Articia loved their King. When the king sends the call for aid to the countryside, there had been no hesitation by the common person take up arms in support of the kingdom. Henry was always there to help every village in times of trouble and the kingdom had seen many years of peace under his reign.

As the king rode forward and out of the gate of Castle Articia, the cavaliers of the One Hundred pounded their fists into their breastplates. It was in perfect unison for the well-trained knights acted as a single unit. They mounted and fell in behind the king in the procession. Their squires, charged with carrying their lances, rode behind and beside them.

As the king and the nights of One Hundred reached the open field where the regular army had formed, two thousand of the Artician cavalry fell in behind the One Hundred. Falling in behind the cavalry was three thousand longbowmen, mostly hunters by trade, but a critical component of the Artician army.

The pike men followed the archers. Their primary role was to pitch in against any charge of the goblin army. They were two thousand strong and would be a formidable force against the dark army. Behind them the regular men-at-arms, four thousand swordsmen ready to engage should the battle go hand to hand,

and it looked like they were going to used heavily now that they would have to face the army of darkness on the open plains west of the Crystal Mountains. Despite this dire prospect, they marched resolute behind the pike men of the army.

The last group was the infantry, which consisted of able-bodied townspeople. They had the most to lose in this upcoming battle. Failure would mean the loss of their farms and their livelihoods. The largest of the force, standing at twenty thousand, they marched with pride to be part of King Henry's army. The king looked back at the pheasants, farmers, bakers, and other townsfolk. These people were the Articia that the army was marching to protect. Their enthusiasm to stand for their families and homes raised his hope and gladdened his heart.

The queen watched from the window of the tower. The Queen of Articia would not march with the army of Articia. She was now responsible for the rearguard and the defense of the castle. She looked around the ramparts; old men who could no longer do the long march, and young boys who were too young to die on the battlefield stood guard. Some of the junior officers remained to command the castle defenses.

She saw the carts used for provisions, tent carriers, rolling smithies, and the remaining logistical support for the army now pulling into formation behind the infantry. Funny how similar things would be here, but the army that remained consisted of old men, women, young boys, and girls of the surrounding villages. The queen was well aware that if the regular army should fail on the field of battle, what remained here at the castle would not last long against the army of the darkness.

...

"Should we tell the master that the army is moving?" the younger imp asked.

"Hell no, this is going to be fun! Come on; we have to head to the north to see what mischief we can cause," the elder of the two answered.

19
The Sword of Fire

One will enter, one receives,
the sword of flame retrieves.
He may enter on the final eve,
but warning, he may never leave.

William was examining the bodies of the dead goblins for any sign of what had happened. He wrinkled his nose as he was leaning over one of them. "A horse peed on this one—first time I have seen that happen in a battle."

Ava was searching got tracks in the ground, "They appear to have headed off in this direction," she said to William as he came over to confirm what Ava saw.

"You are right. Come on. Let's mount and follow the tracks."

They rode on the path for another hour when Comet communicated with William. "*Star Dancer, my brother, is ahead of us. I can now hear him clearly.*"

William responded with concern. "Star Dancer was assigned to Alec. Is he with him?"

"Who is Star Dancer and where is Alec?" Ava said as William realized he had questioned Comet verbally.

"Star Dancer is a destri that was assigned to keep your brother safe" William answered.

"WHAT! Alec has been selected by a destri?" Ava was not comfortable with this news. The destri only bonded with cavaliers, and all cavaliers became the riders of the One Hundred.

"My mount tells me that it is an unusual bonding, and that Alec is not destined to be one of the riders. The destri broke their rules of bonding to make this happen, with the blessing of the goddess," William told her. He knew that she was distraught from this revelation.

Ava was relieved. She already felt like she was going to lose one brother. She could not live with the thought of losing Alec as well. They reached the clearing where Star Dancer and the "warhorse" of Jamal and Dustin were hiding.

Ava walked up to Star Dancer and put her hand on his neck. "Please tell me where I can find my brother."

"*Your brother has entered the cave to face the evil one,*" Star Dancer replied. "*He has gone to rescue your sister.*"

"My sister?" Ava asked.

"*Yes. Goblins kidnapped your sister Danny and brought her to a cave at the end of those bushes. He left with the boys to go rescue her,*" the destri responded.

Ava had not thought of her fourth sibling until this moment. She turned to William, tears forming in her eyes. "They have our sister. We must follow Alec to render aid."

William had been communing with Comet and knew the whole story. He was as shocked as Ava was at the description of his newfound sibling. "We are facing a demon in those caves," he said as he drew his sword from its scabbard.

Before William finished drawing his sword, Ava turned rapidly and sent a bolt of energy at a branch on a tree. There was a high-pitched scream as an imp appeared and fell to the ground, writhing in pain. William ran over and grabbed the imp by the throat. "What do we have here?" he said as he walked the beast back over to Ava.

"That is an imp," Ava responded. "I have felt that we were being watched for some time now, but I was not able to figure out what was observing our progress. The creature became visible when I reached out with my senses to find Alec. The magical nature of the imp lit up like a lamp," Ava finished.

"So what do we do with him?" William asked with the imp struggling in his grip. Star Dancer came over and replied, "*We question him.*"

...

The dark sorcerer watched as his evil army started to march through the northern pass of the Coal Mountains. The force, with the addition of the men from the north, was over one hundred thousand strong and moving to battle the army of King Henry. *This time, Henry, you will not prevail*, the sorcerer thought to himself.

...

Alec and the boys were huddled outside the door of the main chamber. Though it was only slightly ajar, they could hear the conversation clearly from their position.

"I will not serve you! Kill me if you must, but I will never do what you ask." They heard the feeble but determined voice of Danny from the room.

Always stubborn, Alec thought as he grinned just a bit.

"YOU WILL SUCCUMB TO MY WILL!" He heard as a whip cracked. He could hear Danny groan, but she did not yell out. Then he heard a sound like a bolt of lightning and Danny screamed in pain.

Jamal could contain himself no longer, as he grabbed the hammer off his back and burst through the door. Dustin was close behind. Alec followed more cautiously, relying on his training. *Never burst into a room. Move carefully into every situation*, he remembered Bryn's regular lecture. He certainly was not prepared for what he saw when he entered the murky chamber.

The first thing he noticed was the size of the demon's hands. It was holding up Jamal by his head, now buried in the demon's palm. The demon swung Jamal as if it would a stick and threw him up against the wall. The small warrior hit the ground groaning, but at least he was still alive, though he was clearly out of the fight.

Dustin fared no better. The demon's whip lashed out and wrapped around his neck. Unfortunately, he was in the middle of his incantation; small flames shot from his hands and burned his incantation sheet to ashes. The results of his actions were a scorched face and hands. The demon laughed at this and sent a chill down Alec's spine. Then it pulled back hard on the whip and sent Dustin spinning into the wall opposite Jamal.

What shook him up the most was the condition of Danny. Chained to the wall, what remained of her clothes was in tatters. Her stomach was so bloody he could not even see the individual cuts. Her arms were the same, and all of her fingers bent at odd angles. On her shoulder were ugly gashes. Both her eyes were blacked and swollen almost shut. Her nose was dripping blood, her lips cracked and bleeding as well. In the demon's hand, Alec saw a tailed whip, a vicious weapon with ends tipped in steel.

Alec was very concerned for her; all he could see though the matted in blood was her black bouncing curls. *This has been going on for a while*, he thought to himself.

He could feel the anger well up in him as he faced the demon. The dark lord turned with his blood red eyes and greeted Alec,

"You're late. We have been expecting you."

. . .

Tristan stood at the edge of the table in the hall of Lewisvel Keep. The elder of the keep and leader of the people shook his head at Tristan's news. Lewisvel Keep was the first line of defense against the continued raids of the goblins of the northeast. However, its strength has always been the stronger wall that faces east against the goblins' persistent attacks.

"This is an unusual tactic for the goblins. They must have new leadership to act so boldly." The weapon master declared.

"Yes, but I am more concerned that they were able to build this road undetected." Tristan replied.

Lewisvel Keep's weapon master turned toward Tristan, misunderstanding his statement, and challenged, "Are you implying that we have not been alert here, young Prince?"

Tristan thought before he spoke since he had not intended that at all, nor had he expected this reaction and the misinterpretation of his observation. "No, I have no doubts about the strength and diligence of this keep or its master-at-arms."

The weapon master nodded and looked back to the map on the table.

Tristan continued, "I believe that the goblin horde has had considerable magical help to hide their latest activities."

The elder of the keep looked at Tristan with concern. "Do you believe that the army we are about to face has sorcerers at its helm?"

"I am afraid so. There is no other explanation as to how the goblins could build this road under the noses of the scouts constantly scouring that area. To build a road of that magnitude would have required years of construction," Tristan replied.

"So, expect the unexpected then." The elder statesman responded as he looked at the weapon master. "Let us see if we can devise some surprises of our own."

...

Alec moved cautiously into the room, keeping his distance so that he would not be within range of that vicious whip. He tried to think how he could come out of this situation alive because he was no fool and knew that he alone would be no match for this demon. His best option was a tactic of distraction. Alec looked for any weakness demonstrated by the demon. If he could get the demon to lower its guard, he might be able to land a successful, *No*, he admitted to himself, a *lucky* strike.

"I have no quarrel with you, demon. Let my sister go and we will leave this place to you."

The demon laughed at Alec's proposal. "My young Prince, I didn't drag your sister all the way here so that you could just march away when you arrived. I wanted you here. You have forgotten who you are and where your home is. I wanted to bring you here so you would remember."

Do not strike first, Bryn had told him. *Let your opponent show you his weaknesses.* Alec was sure that a demon would have no weaknesses. He knew little about them but knew enough from the tales that no one ever survived a fight with a demon. The best you could do was to strike them often enough and hard enough to cause them serious harm; only then could you banish them from Articia.

What had the demon said? Alec thought. *I have forgotten where my home is?* The demon's statement made no sense to him. "So what is it you think I have forgotten?" Alec asked the demon in front of him as he heard Dustin groaning against the opposite wall from Jamal. Alec shivered, as the demon looked him directly in the eyes with those crimson orbs.

"You are a child of our creation," the demon said glaring at him. "You have a duty to perform. You were born to destroy, and you were born to annihilate, to bring about the end to this miserable world."

Danny looked up at Alec, through all the pain she was in, and sent him a half-smile that said, "Do not believe him, Alec. He is a deceiver." It also held a hint of triumph, as if Danny were saying, "I made it, I lasted. Now it's almost over." Danny had the look of a wounded soldier at the end of a long war. She would soon be going home to Adara. Alec hated knowing he was going to let her down.

"You will never turn us!" she yelled at the demon, which quickly turned around and struck Danny. Alec knew this would be his only chance. He jumped at the demon and raked his sword diagonally across the demon's back. A sickly hissing sound came from the wound that Alec's sword had opened, but it seemed to have no effect on the fiend.

The demon turned quickly back toward Alec and drew its sword so fast Alec barely saw it leave the scabbard.

"So Alec, Shall we duel?" the demon asked with a tormenting snarl on his lips.

Alec gritted his teeth knowing that he had just made what was likely to be his last strike on the demon, but he refused to yield even though it would mean the certain end of Danny and himself. Alec resolved to fight as long as he could, even though he had no real hope of winning, of beating the demon.

···

Ava and William arrived at the cave's entrance and saw the dead goblins strewn on the ground.

"Quickly, William, or I fear we will not be able to help them." The pair ran down the hall to a battle that was already raging.

···

It was quite clear that his strike had not truly damaged the demon, but the same could not be said about his sword. Alec knew immediately that the power of the Shadow Fang, diminished after it struck the demon as the spirit of the sword was completely depleted. Their bond seemed gone as well. He no longer felt a soul in the sword. With this new realization, Alec felt unarmed against such a powerful foe. The beast did not need the sword that it carried, for Alec no longer had any power to wield one against the monster.

With his nasty grimace, the beast stepped forward to strike him. Alec had to be quick; he knew this attack but was not sure if his defensive move would be effective against this foe. Alec stepped under the sword arm of the demon as he would step under the sword arm of a mounted rider. It almost worked, but he realized his error as he attempted to strike the demon once more. This time the sword found no purchase; it merely glanced off the creature's hard skin.

The demon's reaction was far superior to Alec's feeble attack as it brought its hand back down from the earlier swing and caught the back of Alec's head, which sent him flying toward Danny on the back wall. He hit the floor so hard that it knocked wind out of him. Alec raised his head and was blood around him that he knew was from his now broken nose. Alec refused to quit and got back on his feet. As he turned to the demon, it grabbed him by the neck and lifted him in the air. Alec dropped his sword and grabbed at the demon's arm with both hands, trying to loosen its deadly grip on his throat. Danny was kicking furiously at the demon, but the demon just laughed and struck Danny across the face. This time it knocked her unconscious.

Alec was desperate. He tried to hit at the demon's face while he held the hand at his throat, but he could no longer draw the necessary strength to make any difference. As he was starting to black out, he heard a noise in the hallway.

...

Ava and William burst into the room to see the demon holding Alec in the air. The foul beast turned, startled by the latest arrivals. It had not expected any other being to enter the chamber. Its orbs went wide when it realized that these were the last two siblings of the quartet. The demon had previously been confident, but now it was anxious. It absentmindedly let go of Alec, who fell in a lump on the floor. Ava stepped forward as she raised her hand and sent a wave of power at the demon. Unlike its mounted brothers, this demon did not budge from the force of Ava's magic, but it was motionless as if it were standing against a gale force wind.

"I don't think I can do this indefinitely!" Ava shouted to William.

Alec slowly got up from the floor having realized the demon was frozen in place, apparently held by some unknown force that he hoped was wielded by a new ally. The demon stood between Alec and his new allies so that his view was blocked. He did not see Ava or William across the room. Alec reached up and pinched his nose to stop the bleeding; he knew he had to hurry over to help Danny before it was too late because she was almost gone. He stumbled over to her and leaned one hand against the wall to steady himself as he whispered, "Adara, help us!"

Danny lifted her head slightly and looked at him through the one eye that was not completely swollen shut and managed a weak grin as she said, "You look horrible."

"Don't we both," Alec replied. "Let me see if I can ease some of your pain." He reached up to touch her temples as he whispered, "*Lumen sano maximus.*" The power left his hands as a small trickle of reddish flame and then grew to engulf Danny. She sighed as the pain subsided and the smallest of the wounds started to heal.

The demon spun its head around to Alec and Danny and raised its sword. At that moment, it realized that the force of the human witch only kept it from moving forward. It would be able to escape the stream of her power by moving sideways. Her power was immense, *I will have to be careful when I deal with that one*, it thought. The demon stepped toward Alec as it said, "Oh no you don't, young whelp. She is mine and you will not undo what I took so long to create."

Alec turned to the demon and raised his hand to grab its sword arm. It would be fruitless of course, for he knew he did not have the power to stop the demon's swing, but something unexpected happened as his hand grasped the demon. It screamed. The demon stopped its attack, dropped its sword to the ground, and backed away from Alec holding its wrist in agony.

As the demon moved back, Alec saw Ava and William standing across the room. Believing that Ava had attacked the demon, he called to her in desperation "Ava! I am glad you came to deal with this foul demon."

"I did not do that, Alec. It was you. The demon is vulnerable to the healing arts!" Ava shouted back to him. The demon whipped its head toward her. *What treachery allowed her to obtain that knowledge?* It thought. *No matter, they still do not have the power to defeat me.*

Alec thought of Ava's words as he looked down at the hand that had touched the demon. The red healing glow was still there. When he used healing magic on the demon, it was like striking it with a sword. He looked over at it and realized the demon had rebuilt its confidence and was moving toward him again.

Adara, help me! He thought as he ran toward the demon yelling "*SANO QUAM MAXIMUS!*"

As the last words left his lip, his hand struck the demon's torso. The healing power surged through Alec's hands into the demon full force. It screamed a horrible sound that shook all four of King Henry's children to the bone. The demon jumped away from Alec and hit the wall hard. The whole room rattled from the impact as the demon fell to the floor breathing heavily. It looked at Alec with hatred in its eyes.

"So, young whelp, you have discovered the depth of your power, a shame it has manifested itself in such a disgusting manner."

Alec picked up the sword that the demon had dropped and felt the bond immediately. *The Sword of Flame!* He thought. *How did the demon get one of the royal Artician swords!* Alec heard the soul bond from the sword reply,

"It is a long story, young warrior, one that will have to wait until you make another journey of discovery."

Alec looked back at the demon. It was clearly near death. "Do you have anything to say before I finish you?"

Ava gasped from the other side of the room. She knew that Alec must destroy the demon, but she had never seen her brother so resolute and certain. She had never seen this kind of anger in him. *The sorrows*, she heard echo in her mind.

The demon laughed out loud, "You? Destroy me? You are a funny one." The demon tried to get up but no longer had the energy to rise. "You may banish me from this world, but I will find a way back. We will duel again, my young whelp."

Alec stepped up to the demon and laid his hand on it again, repeating the incantation he had used to fell the demon. *"Sano quam maximus!"* The demon screamed louder this time and Ava had to cover her ears as William put his head down from the pressure of it. Alec stood his ground and watched as the demon faded into the ether.

Moments of silence passed as Alec stared into the space before he heard Danny groan again from the wall. He moved quickly to her and continued the work to heal the worst of her wounds. William went over to help him free her from the irons that had restrained her to the wall. As they did this, Ava moved over to Dustin, who appeared to be in the worst condition of the gallant young pair. The young boy had badly burnt face and hands and there was a bloody ring around his neck as if someone had run a knife completely around it.

Ava put her hand on his temples to feel the depth of his injuries, and then opened her eyes. What Ava found in the sensing surprised her. She would have to ask Alec about it another time. For now, she would do her best to heal his burns and revive him. She looked around the room and toward Alec's other companion. She saw that he had started to regain his wits on his own.

Ava watched William and Alec gently place the now unbound young woman on the ground. *We are sisters*, Ava thought to herself. She could see in Alec's eyes that her sister would be all right.

Her newfound sister was starting to speak but it would be at least a day before she could travel. Ava did not want to spend another minute in this cave. "We should get out of here as soon as we can, but this young man is seriously burned and cannot be moved. Alec, can you help him?"

At her pleading, Jamal came to his senses and jumped to his feet. He ran to his brother and knelt beside him. "Dustin, please Dustin, do not leave me alone." Ava saw a huge teardrop from the young man's cheek as Alec moved quickly to Dustin's side.

He looked at his wounds and laid his hands on his chest as he whispered,

"*Lumen sano*." A reddish glow emitted from his hands and enveloped Dustin. He started to breathe easier, a scar around his neck and remnants of the burns were all that remained.

"Alec," Ava asked as she turned to him, "why did you not complete the healing?"

"Our wounds and our scars are what define us. They tell the tale of our experience," Alec responded. "These scars will always remind Dustin of his brush with death. They will make him stronger and wiser so that he will make better decisions the next time he faces danger."

"Seems kind of harsh," Ava said to Alec.

"It is something I learned while I was in the city of the Vale," Alec responded.

Ava raised her eyebrows, "You visited the Vale?"

"Yes, a long story, but like you, I do not want to stay in this place. We must leave the Haunted Hills and find someplace safe to spend the night," Alec said. "I think we should head straight back to Castle Articia as soon as we are fit to travel. Danny will need to rest after suffering this ordeal. And then you can tell me about your hair."

Ava looked at her brother silently; of course, he would notice the change. He left her side to help a very confused young man to his feet. He asked the young man, she believed he called him Dustin, if he could walk. The young man nodded. His other young companion pulled Dustin's arm up over his shoulder and helped guide the injured boy to the door and down the passageway.

Alec was walking over to her new sister. *What was the name he said? Danny? What an unusual name for a girl.* Mostly Ava was impressed with how mature Alec had become, but she was also concerned with how stoic her brother had been after this ordeal. She rose to her feet, brushed off her clothing, and followed William and Alec out of the cave. Alec had Danny in his arms, with her head on his shoulder as he followed William, who had taken the lead.

...

The imp was rolling on the floor laughing. Its companion, still a little uncomfortable, was smiling at the spectacle. "We should not celebrate the banishment of one of or brothers with so much ... zest," it said to the imp on the floor.

"Oh, but we should," the older imp declared. "It brings the beautiful chaos. It is the rapture of uncertainty. You will soon learn how important the randomness of chaos is to this world."

"But we will have to face the demon lord again. Are you not fearful of his wrath?" the younger imp asked.

"Those demons have such a short memory. It will be a millennium before it returns to this realm. We have nothing to fear from that one," the elder of the two replied. "Come now, we must head north to the battleground. There will be so many more opportunities for mischief in the days to come. This place is finally getting interesting!"

...

The two destri, Ava's horse, and the shaggy warhorse were waiting for the four siblings outside the cave. Ava helped Danny change her tattered clothing into one of the library smocks that she had packed for the road. "I am sorry, it is not very stylish," Ava said to Danny.

"It is all right," she said. "At my cabin at the edge of the woods, we dressed pretty simply. Fancy clothing is very hard to keep clean when you are farming."

Ava thought about this for a bit and then said, "I wish I had an opportunity to live on a farm. Life at the castle gets too complicated sometimes. I have often thought how it would be nice to have a simpler life."

"The grass is always greener…," Danny murmured.

"Huh? What does that mean?" Ava commented.

"It is something I read in book that my master kept in his house. It means that we are never happy with the life we have and are always coveting the life of another," Danny instructed.

Ava smiled at this. "Yes, I believe you are right. I am so glad to finally meet you. I only recently learned that I have a sister."

"I only recently learned that I am a princess," Danny said with a bit of a struggle as she winced from her injuries. Ava helped Danny to get comfortable before they continued talking. The girls sat talking for only a short time before Danny drifted off to sleep. Alec and William spent that time constructing a litter to carry Danny. "They seem to be getting along well," William said to Alec, who had been quiet until now"

"Yes, I think it is a girl thing," Alec replied.

"She will not be able to walk or ride a long distance for at least a day," William stated.

"I know, brother," he thought about that statement and queried William. "Have you known for long that we are siblings?"

"I have known that I was a member of the royal family since I was eleven," William responded. "I eavesdropped on a conversation between our father and our uncle and heard them talking about it. When I confronted my uncle about the facts, he told me how important it was to keep this secret, and I have kept that secret until just recently."

"You are riding a destri. Are you one of the One Hundred?" Alec said with some concern.

"Not yet, but I will be one day."

"Now that I am riding a destri, will I be expected to ride with the One Hundred as well?"

"No, you have not volunteered to be one. Those who chose the path of the One Hundred have done so voluntarily," William replied. "You are not required to ride with those who may not return."

"But I thought only cavaliers rode destri," Alec inquired.

"Yes, that is so. A destri chooses a rider when they have committed to the duty of the One Hundred," William said. "But I think you are a special case."

"Well, I am glad that I got to meet you before you are called to your fateful ride," Alec said with some trepidation. "Let's finish this and get out of here. I think that demon is certain to have servants and I do not want to be here when they arrive."

Once the litter was completed, Alec laid the hoist over the shaggy warhorse's rump as it snorted. "I am sorry, boy; the other horses are too tall to pull the litter. You are the only beast who can handle this properly."

Dustin rubbed the horse's neck and whispered, "It is our duty boy, and it is a great honor to transport a princess of the realm."

As they started to ride to the north, Alec asked Ava and, "So, tell me about the crescent moon on your wrist and your new hair color."

Ava looked turned to him. Of course, Alec would notice the obvious changes. "The goddess has marked me as hers."

Alec smiled at her and the news she had just revealed. He then turned his view back to the north and the direction that they rode and thought *the goddess will not mark me now that I have been tainted by the touch of the demon.*

20

All Alone

Ava had not slept well for many days. She just could not get comfortable with the fact that she felt so alone. Ava was the only one of Henry's children still left at Castle Articia. As she lay in her bed, she drifted into a restless sleep.

It was the third night since her brothers Tristan and Dominic had left on their First Excursion of the kingdom and she already knew that she would have a restless sleep tonight. Her eyes had dark circles around them, and for the first time in her life, she used makeup to cover her fatigue. However, she mostly needed to hide the signs of her distress.

Sighing, Ava rose from the bed and pulled a robe on over her sleeping gown. The halls were dead silent, as they always were that time of night. Ava was not sure where to go. Walking through the halls, she could feel a cold draft flowing through the castle, but she could not quite take her mind off what was troubling her senses. William had left yesterday to return to Cyrus to continue his training. Her parents were particularly busy managing the Artician estates during the harvest season and now preparing for the harsh season, when the snows fell and you lived off the labors of the growing season. Her classes filled her day, but they still felt … hollow, without meaning. Empty.

She had been lying on her bed thinking of William. The time she had spent on the road with him, she had discovered that he was honorable, honest, noble, and a talented warrior and swordsman. He was a lot like Alec, though more stoic. A sob escaped her throat, followed by another. Tears started to stream down her cheeks and Ava felt childish, but she could not stop it. She tried to wipe them away, but fresh ones only replaced them. Why was she crying? Something was wrong.

Ava ran to the nearest window. She looked out to see a burnt wasteland in the place of what were once a green meadow and a forest. "Oh no, I really did it. I destroyed my world. What happened? How did this happen?"

As she scanned the barren landscape, she saw a man standing in the distance. He was holding a walking stick and was sketching in the sand. Ava ran down to the courtyard and out of the castle gates. She ran toward the unknown man. As far as she knew, he was the only other person still alive in Articia. She called out to him as she continued to run toward him "Sir!" but he did not turn. He just kept writing in the sand.

As she reached the area where the man was standing, she noticed a symbol on the ground. It was circular with one dark and one white teardrop wrapping around each other. She had seen this symbol before, but where? Her mind was a fog. She could not remember how she got here.

"Sir, what has happened here?" The man looked down at Ava; it was then that she realized how tall he was. He stood a full head and shoulders above her.

"The balance was disrupted and the end came." He continued to draw the symbol in the sand.

"But how? We just left the demon's lair; I do not remember what happened?" Ava asked desperately.

"It has not happened yet, Ava; you are looking into the future," the mystery man said plainly.

Ava was floating in a cloud of forgotten dreams and lost causes. She turned to the man. "I can't change this?" she asked, almost in tears. Ava's vision of the scene was slowly fading as she heard his last words.

"No future is set in stone."

...

Ava woke with a start and realized she was still sitting by the fire of the small camp. She had been sitting, meditating and just had a waking dream. Ava had never experienced this before. Was it a message from the goddess, and who was the man drawing in the sand?

"What is that you are drawing on the ground Ava?" William asked.

Ava looked down at the ground and saw the same symbol from her vision. However, this time she recognized it. The *yin* and the *yang*, it was the symbol from the book given to her by Mr. Tipple. She put her head up and looked at William. "It is about balance. I believe that everything we have done and learned is about maintaining balance."

William paused and thought of Ava's words. He then replied, "It is clearly important. It is a message that has been part of the training that all of the One Hundred receive. When I was a young boy, our uncle decided that I should squire to one of the cavaliers of the One Hundred to learn responsibility and discipline. The first lessons they teach their squires is about balance. Balance in everything, from staying on a horse to standing a lance. We learned about the balance of battle."

"Is it only about fighting that the young men in the Third learn in their training?" Ava said with sadness.

"No, we also learn about the importance of every citizen of Articia and the contributions every person makes to a civilized society." William sat down on a log next to the fire. It was still a full day's ride from the castle and they had to stop for the night. Ava looked briefly at Alec, who was standing watch over Danny, who now slept comfortably on a roll on the ground. It had taken her a long time to drift into the dreamless sleep that she was now enjoying. William started speaking again and Ava turned to listen to him.

"I spent time baking bread down in the ovens with the kitchen hands as well as mucking out the stables with the stable boys," William told her with a smile. "I actually enjoyed that time because I learned that common folk have a simple life. They live and they die at their designated times, and they are mostly happy. They work hard. They reap the fruits of their labor. They have fairs and festivals, attend weddings and funerals."

Ava thought of fairs and festivals; she was starting to miss life in the palace. William continued, "I learned of the sacrifice that a cavalier makes when he decides to ride with the One Hundred. They will have no family, no weddings, and no heirs. They know that the decision they make is to serve the realm and protect the people from the beasts that disrupt the balance of life."

Ava looked William in the eyes; she had not known that the cavaliers gave up so much.

"From village to village a squire travels with his cavalier. They get to know the people for whom they are fighting. I followed my cavalier as he journeyed to more than fifty villages." William paused.

"I bet you were treated like heroes by the villagers. It must have been hard to remain fit with so many feasts," Ava said jovially.

William smiled. "That would have been a sight, but no. When a cavalier of the One Hundred rode into town, he took off his armor, laid down his lance, and helped the villagers with their everyday toil. We paid for our meals with our labor," William continued. "And in doing so, we came to know the villagers. Because I was younger, I met more of the children of the village."

William looked off into the distance, then continued, "I can remember their names: Katherine and Jack from a small village near a river where they showed me the best places for fishing. I remember a girl named Lauren; she was so athletic; she taught me how important it is to run and play. I learned about music and song from a boy named Nicholas and a girl named Natalie. However, most of all, I learned about loss and grief from a little girl named Emily. She had lost her best friend when a bull had broken its gates and trampled the little girl."

"How sad," Ava replied.

"I still remember all of their names. I know what I fight for; I know who I fight for; and I know why I fight," William said as he turned back to Ava. "The cavalier I traveled with told me to remember all of their names and to remember all of their stories so if I decided to join the One Hundred, I would know the people for whom I would, through my service to the king and the kingdom of Articia, be pledging my life and my honor."

"I understand," Ava said. "My father often told me and my siblings how important it was for us to protect the people of Articia because they were the most import part of our nation. We, as monarchs, are only here for a short time but the nation remains when we are gone."

"It is part of it, but there is more," William stated. "The strength of our nation is its people, not our armies, not the One Hundred, and not our royal family."

"So where is the balance?" Ava asked.

"Each individual squire makes his own decision to join the One Hundred," William said. It is at that moment of decision and commitment that the destri come to you. I remember well the day of my vow." William thought back to the day of his initiation.

"For whom do you stand" The cavalier asked the young squire as he put the flat of his sword on William's left shoulder,

"I stand for the light against the darkness," William answered.

"For whom do take this vow?" the cavalier asked as he moved the sword over William's head to his right shoulder.

"For my king and my country," William stated.

"For whom will you give your life?" The cavalier asked.

"For the people of Articia," William completed.

"Rise young rider of the Third. You now are committed to the One Hundred. From this day on, you will commit your mind and your heart to train for the day you will be called by the king to defend the kingdom of Articia," the cavalier finished as he sheathed his sword. "Go now to the yard and meet the mount that has selected you for a partner."

William warmly remembered the first time he saw Comet ride into the training yard. He looked at Ava and continued, "What remains when the One Hundred act as defenders of the light to destroy the beasts of the darkness, are the people. It is little Emily who held my hand as we brought flowers to place on the stone that they put near a meadow to memorialize her friend."

Ava thought about this for a while. She watched Alec wake Danny to redress her wounds. He had grown quite a bit in the last couple of weeks, but so had she. Ava certainly felt less secure because of the grave knowledge she learned about herself at the Great Library. She thought of her vision of the destruction and the loss of all the people she loved. Was she strong enough to resist calling on that horrible power? Somehow, she knew that the curious yin-yang symbol from Mr. Tipple's book was the key.

She thought of what Alec had said; that he would not completely heal Dustin because the experience would make him stronger. Our scars and wounds are constant reminders of the mistakes we make when we are young. *Does Alec truly know that these boys were not human?* She thought. *He must.*

William was the most mature of the four siblings; he had grown up early, learning humility and honor, as he was moving from village to village. What about her newfound sister, what had the demon put her through in the cave? They all had their scars, of one form or another. What about me; when have I been truly tested? What will I be asked to sacrifice? Is this our destiny, to give until our scars become our end? Life used to be so simple, a game, sparring, playing, singing, dancing. We have not been asked to grow up until just recently.

Ava thought of Emily. *Who was the little girl, the friend, in whose remembrance Emily puts flowers on her stone? She had clearly touched William's soul.* Ava saw the sun starting to rise above the hills to the east and rose to saddle her horse.

"We should get moving as soon as possible," she said to her siblings. "We need to warn father about the riders."

Danny looked at her and smiled. "I have never been to the castle. I have nothing appropriate to wear for such an occasion."

Ava chuckled and responded. "Oh come on. We are very fashionable in the smocks that the library provided. We should be ready for a full gala ball."

They all laughed at Ava's comment as they packed their saddles and mounted for the ride. They were just shy of a day from Castle Articia and would need most of the light to complete the trip.

...

The goblin army had started marching as soon as the winter melt reached its surge. The road that the dark citadel wizards had pressed into creation allowed them to march at a much quicker pace than the soggy trail would have allowed before the construction of the route through the northern woods.

"The goblin army will be on the western plain in two, maybe three, days" the acolyte exclaimed. "They will be caught completely by surprise."

"You are very optimistic. The royal family of Articia is very good at this game," the sorcerer Koschei said to the young wizard. "They are probably well aware of our approach now. It is not easy to hide an army this large with such a dark intention from those who stand for the light."

"But surely the sorcerers from the citadel are more powerful than the practitioners that Henry has at his disposal?" the young man asked.

"That is *King* Henry," the sorcerer looked at the young lad sternly. "Though he is our enemy, you will treat the title with respect. We have strict rules about such things in the enclave. Remember your place, my young apprentice."

"Yes, Master. I understand that we respect our betters," the young man said. "But why should we give respect to the leader of our enemy?"

"You must always respect the position and rank your enemy," Koschei replied. "Lack of respect leads us to make foolish and arrogant decisions. If you do not respect your opponent, you will not defeat him."

"I think I understand, Master."

"Now, take this to the dark lord in the citadel. He must know that we are close to the keep at Lewisvel," the elderly sorcerer commanded.

"Immediately," the young man said as he put the scroll in his satchel, mounted his horse, and rode off to the northeast.

As the sorcerer Koschei watched the young man ride off to the citadel, he thought of the lord of the sorcerer guild. *You hide in your tower and leave the real fighting to the sorcerers of the elements. Someday that will be your downfall. As we gain power from our experiences, you will no longer be the most powerful sorcerer amongst our brethren. Soon the guild will call Fire Sorcerer Koschei the master of the guild.*

...

In the early morning, the army of Cyrus marched into the valley where King Henry's forces were camped. The king's army was impressive. The brownish-red tents, the colors of the flag of Articia, lined the entire lowland of the southern valley.

The supply carts were set up by the river so that the filter nets could be kept wet. Bryn possessed a remarkable amount of battle experience. The opposing force will detect an army that does not take precautions. Bryn knew that the opposing army would just have to count the rising smoke plumes to estimate the forces that they would face in battle. Therefore, Bryn had the logistics and supply carts build their fires under a wet cloth. This caused the smoke to whiten against the sky, making the army much harder to detect from a distance, and many fires would be needed to cook enough food to feed an army this large.

"We must not tarry long here, Sire. If will consume our supplies too quickly, we will have to tap the winter stores to maintain the army," the young soldier was concerned about the village of his origin and the hard winter they faced ahead.

The king looked at the young man, who clearly did not have enough winters to understand the true impact of a battle like the one they were about to face. "We hope to engage the enemy soon, son. However, do not worry about us eating the winter stores. We will eat much less after the first day of battle," the king told the young soldier.

"I do not understand, Sire. Why will the army eat less food after the first day?" the sergeant asked.

"Because, many of our brave soldiers and their beasts will not survive the first day of battle," the king responded grimly. "You will learn many difficult truths of life and death when we meet the forces of darkness."

The young soldier stopped as he realized the meaning of the king's statement. This was clearly the first time he realized that many of the men would not be returning to their homes when the business of war was completed. He saluted the king and left to attend to his duties.

The king thought about all of the young men of his army who had never faced death. How would they hold against the army of the goblins? How would they stand when many of the One Hundred fell against the charge of the wolug? Only time would tell.

...

Tristan stood watch on the wall of Lewisvel Keep with the platoon that is his charge. They were all clearly nervous and he could see the fear in their eyes. Like him, none of these soldiers had really faced a battle such as this one promised to be. Like him, they were unsure of how they would perform when they actually had to fight.

He looked across the fortification and saw the master of the keep inspecting the line. They all knew that the king's army was over the ridge, waiting to set a trap for the goblin army. The masters of the keep used Tancred and his mount to communicate with its destri brothers to coordinate the details of the pending battle.

Tristan thought about the destri and their ability to communicate with each other from great distances. He also thought about the fact they were not natural to Articia. He shook his head as he realized he was actually missing his classes in the tower with Brendan. Would he learn the rest of Articia's history, or would his demise become part of what will be taught to the students of the future?

He was a prince of Articia. Despite the fact that he was only sixteen, he had responsibility. He would have to be a leader on the wall of the keep. Stand tall and strong and not show the fear that was inside him. *I have to set an example for the other men on the wall so they can make a stand with me*, he thought. *What would his father do? His father would speak to his army to give them confidence.* He looked along his section of the wall. The keep's weapon master gave the youngest and least experienced of the soldiers this section because it is the least likely to be attacked. It was clear that he did not want the king's son to be at great risk. However, there are no guarantees in war.

He collected his thoughts and spoke to his men. "Soldiers, I know you are all anxious to get on with this. Nevertheless, we must be patient. Our weapon master knows his business well and the wall is strong. We are here to ensure that the enemy does not breach this stronghold!" He paused as much to gather his thoughts as to allow the soldiers on the wall to collect theirs. "We will fight soon. We are ready; we will stand on this wall and the enemy will not pass!"

There was a subdued affirmation from the troops as Tristan continued. "Before today, we were boys with little responsibility or care. Tomorrow we will be men. We will be the men that stand for the light against the darkness! We will prevail to see the sun rise over the eastern wall and to bear witness to the retreat of this army of the night!" Tristan paused to allow the soldiers to cheer the battle call. "Tomorrow we will march out of the western gate to join the forces of the king and drive the goblin horde back into the darkness of the Coal Mountains!"

A roar erupted from the younger troops on Tristan's section of the wall. The weapon master turned to look at the spectacle and nodded in approval. He knew the king's son was the cause of the improved morale. The rest of the hardened veterans looked over to the youngest of their ranks, drew their swords, and pounded their shields to show solidarity.

The soldiers of the keep were ready, but all depended on King Henry's army remaining undetected. Tristan drew his sword as well and struck his shield repeatedly with his men.

The weapon master of Lewisvel Keep smiled as he thought *that is right. Let us get them to focus on our little keep. The more they do, the better it is for the whole.*

. . .

King Henry looked at the hill that separated his army from the keep. He could hear the clang of swords banging shields and smiled. *Sly one, I know what you are doing. Clever my old friend, very clever. If we all survive, I will have to decorate you again, weapon master of Lewisvel Keep. You will soon run out of room on your mantel."*

. . .

The sorcerer heard the racket from the keep. "Well, so much for our missing scout. Looks like we are expected," he said as he walked toward the other practitioners. "We will have to adjust our plan a bit. They are locked up tight and ready for our advance."

"Do you think they were able to get the scout to talk, Master?" one of the younger acolytes asked.

"No. I am sure that he did not survive. He would not have allowed himself to be taken prisoner," the sorcerer said as he pored through the scrolls. "Here we are. Come and review our objective. This is a plan of the ground embattlements for the keep. See here; this is the weak point of the wall. The builders of the keep never expected an attack of this scale from inside the kingdom, so they did not put enough thought into how they assembled the walls. It is the narrowest part of the keep and it has very little wall for archers to stand and fire. If we push one of our siege engines here, we will breach the wall easily.

"But, Master, to get to that section of wall we will have to pass through a protected alcove. Our men will be decimated by archers as we approach the narrow section of that route," the acolyte stated.

"It is time for you to learn a little more about the power of the darkness," the sorcerer sneered. "We are about to teach the king and his army about the fog of war."

21

The Quiet before the Storm

Death is like that moment right before sunrise.
At first, it is dark, and scary, and you feel utterly alone.
But slowly, as the sun rises,
you come to the realization that death is just another form of life,
and what you left behind is only temporarily lost.

Ava, Alec, William, and Danny rode through the village that was east of Castle Articia. The countryside was completely deserted.

"I think the army has already marched to meet the goblins," William said as he examined tracks on the road. He looked along the road leading away from the castle. "There are too many for me to count."

Yes, the One Hundred have ridden off to Lewisvel Keep," Comet communicated to him. *It would appear that the enemy army has built a road through the forest of the northlands.*

"What!" William said, alarmed.

"What is it, William?" Ava asked with concern.

"The army of darkness has outmaneuvered Henry's army. They have built a road through the forest north of the Lewisvel Keep."

"That's horrible news. Does our father know?"

"Yes, our father's army is camped south of Lewisvel Keep," William responded.

"We must hurry to the castle and see who is there. I suspect that my mother is now responsible for its defense," Ava said as she remounted her horse. "Come on. We must make haste."

…

"Make sure the remaining amount of last year's dry stores is covered. Though I have confidence the king will be successful, there is no excuse for us waste the fruit of our labor," the queen said to the retainer who was sealing the casks of grain.

"Yes, my Lady. I will ensure that the grain will be sealed and dry," the retainer responded. "The kitchen hands have also salted and dried the meat. We will not want for protein for at least a month."

"Very good," the queen responded.

A call from the east tower stopped the inhabitants of the castle short. *This was early for word from the battlefield,* the queen thought.

"Six riders from the east approach," the guard on the tower called. There was silence for a brief period before there was an update to the queen.

"Two of the riders are the youngest of the royal children. They ride with two other youngsters of the same stature and what appear to be two young boys," the guard called.

"There are six," she called up to the tower guard.

"Yes, Ava and Alec and another young gentleman and a young woman, and two young lads" the guard called down. The queen's eyes went wide and she went to the entry ordering, "Open the gate!"

The warden heard the urgency of her call. He enlisted help to turn the gear of the portcullis as fast as they could. The royal children rode in under the gate before it completed its rise.

"Mother, I have great news ...," Ava started as she saw her mother running over to her and her siblings.

"William! Daniele! It is wonderful to finally here where you belong!" she called out. "And, Alec and Ava," She said, giving them the 'stare,' "I am very happy that you made it home safe as well."

Alec and Ava looked at each other with that I-guess-we're-in-trouble-again look. It was a look they had shared many times in the past and would likely repeat many times in the future.

"It's good to see you as well, mother," Ava said quietly. The queen looked at her and started to smile when she noticed the color of her hair. It was then that the queen knew that Ava had communed with Adara.

William and Danny started to dismount but the queen barely let Danny touch the ground before she gently pulled her into a hug and said, "So many times I almost sent soldiers to bring you and your family to live in the castle. It has been unbearable that I could not be able to hold one of my children and watch them grow. It was only some comfort that I saw you William. It has all been unbearable." Tears of joy were running down Queen Angelica's face. "It is so good to finally have you home where you belong."

Danny did not know what to think of the whole thing. In fact, she was somewhat uncomfortable with it all. "Thank you," she said apprehensively.

The queen smiled at her and released the hug. She could feel Danny's pain and recent injuries. It would be many years before the girl would be comfortable with the thought of her new family. "Normally, I would schedule a feast for such an occasion. But with the war, we must ration the food until we know where we stand for the winter ahead."

"Oh dear, I almost forgot about the war," Ava said. "We cannot stay long, mother. We must ride out to meet the army on the field of battle."

"What? Are you delirious?" the queen said. "You will all stay here where it is safe. Well, at least for now."

William, who had been quiet until now, spoke next. "Mother, we must ride to meet the army. It is the will of Adara. We have been chosen to maintain the balance." At these words, the queen's face turned from its bright pinkish glow to ashen white.

"I know the legend, it cannot be so. I will not give you to her," the queen said with some firmness.

"Mother," Alec said. "We are no longer the innocent children that once ran the halls of this castle."

He reached out and took his mother's hand in hers. She looked at him and tears welled up in her eyes. She could feel the touch of the demon in him. It had not corrupted him, but it had left a stain on his soul. She started to realize that what she felt in Danny was the same. She thought Danny's pain was just the injuries she endured. It was clear now what had happened.

"What happened to the demon you faced? Is it still in the area?" she asked.

"How did you know about the demon?" Alec asked, reliving in his mind the memory of his encounter.

"I sensed his taint on you. It is a familiar to me since I was inflicted with the touch of a demon before you were all born." The queen remembered well the day the demon ravished her and planted its evil seed. She had begged Adara to destroy the child that was growing in her; but the goddess had other plans and turned the queen's fear of corruption into the hope that the children would be a force for goodly things.

"Does the effect of that evil encounter ever go away?" Danny asked, as she thought of her own encounter contact with the demon. Danny had spent the most time under its influence and wanted to know if the darkness inside her would ever subside.

"It … diminishes over time. But it does not completely go away," the queen informed her gently. "The hardest thing is to not let its influence control you."

"The demon has been banished and can harm them no more," William said. "Alec recovered one of the royal swords as well."

The queen's eyes went wide. "Which sword did you recover?" As Alec drew the sword, she immediately recognized it. "I am relieved; I had thought it was a sword from your brothers or your father. When we have settled, you will have to tell me how you obtained it, Alec."

The queen addressed one of her groomsmen, "Please stable and feed the horses."

Ava started to protest but the queen raised her hand to stop her. "We will need to provide a sturdy meal to my children and give them a night's rest before they join the king on the battlefield."

Danny smiled at the commanding nature of the queen; she could not help but like her demeanor. She suddenly felt guilty of her feelings for the royal family, resentments that had been festering for years because of an outcast duke. *What was it Raphael had said? "If you only see the world through eyes of hatred, then all you can see is hate." I have only seen this place through eyes of hate*, she thought.

"So, who are these young gentleman that are traveling with you?" the queen asked. Jamal and Dustin knocked each other over to be the first to approach the queen and bow. As they both got up from the ground, they bowed and banged heads. Danny just sighed as the boys introduced themselves.

"I am Dustin, a wizard of some power," the young man said as he dropped to a knee in front of the queen. "Um, my Lady."

"I am Jamal a warrior." He put one arm on his chest and bowed, "mi lady."

"Well, two fine gentleman. Please enjoy the hospitality of our castle while you stay here in Articia," the queen responded. No sooner had she finished than the two scurried off to the kitchens.

Alec grinned and said, "I hope you have an abundance of food stores because I suspect they will make a large portion of it disappear today."

"Well," the queen said, looking back at the children. "You must go wash the road off yourselves and dress for dinner."

...

The king looked off into the distance at the forest edge. The goblin army had not yet attacked the keep of Lewisvel. *What are they waiting for?* He thought as he looked up into the night sky. *Surely, they are ready to march on the keep by now.* He saw a scout returning at a gallop from the western road. "Well, Bryn, what do you think?" the king asked his old friend.

"The goblins have never been known for their patience, my Lord" Bryn rubbed the stubble that was now forming on his chin. "I think there is some powerful leadership this time. We must be facing be a goblin chief or some other war master driving this army. In fact I think the road is clear evidence that the army of darkness has new leadership."

As Bryn was finishing his statement, the scout was riding fast up the hill to the king. "Sire! Sire! There is a heavy fog rolling through the forest from the northern mountains!" The scout stopped and caught his breath.

"When do you estimate it will reach the valley?" Bryn asked.

"It should arrive on the sunrise," the scout said grimly.

...

"The fog is rolling, master. We have moved the siege towers into position, these will allow our goblin warriors to scale the walls of the keep when our army is ready to march," the goblin reported to the elder sorcerer. "We do not believe that they know of our full numbers yet"

"Yes, I believe they are still unaware of the second army that formed farther north." the wizard said. "Get the army ready to move. As soon as the fog hits the wall of the keep, we will march on our enemy."

...

"Sir, a fog is rolling into the valley and toward the western gate," the tower watch called down to the Lewisvel weapon master.

"How long before it reaches the wall?" the weapon master called up to the tower.

"It is moving very slow, unnaturally slowly. Not until morn at the light's rise, sir."

The weapon master looked around the wall and ordered. "Get some sleep, boys. The attack will come in the morn!"

...

Ava could not sleep; her dreams were too vivid, too real. She kept seeing a nightmare of the future, a future that would occur if she lost control. Ava chose to spend the rest of the night sitting on a cushion, staring into the wood box in the central hall. There was no fire in the hearth, as it was no longer necessary. The warmth of the spring had arrived and warmed the stone of the castle. She turned her head and looked out the large central window at the night sky.

The twin sisters, Rebe and Cathe, were passing high across the heavens, as they kept watch on the night. Both moons were full, a very unusual circumstance. It took many centuries for the right alignment in the sky. It was rare that both could fully reflect the light of the goddess. Is this a good omen or a bad one? She did not know these things.

Ava wished she could talk to Brendan but he was on the battlefield with her father. He would be able to help her understand the burden of the horrible power that she had. While she was thinking, she heard a noise by the eastern door. Light from a candle trickled into the room ahead of Alec.

"It seems like I am not the only one who could not sleep this night." He walked to the mantle and lit the candles there from the one he held in his hand. Then he sat next to Ava. "The night is warm. I think the summer is coming early," Alec said as he stared at the unlit fire as well. "From what I learned, I think it was the tampering of the elves that made it so."

Ava studied her brother. *Yes, there was something different about him,* she thought. *You have been to the city of the elves.* "What is the land of the elves like, Alec?"

He smiled at her affectionately. It was the first time Ava had seen him smile since they were sparring in the yard the day before this journey. "It was remarkable, Ava. You would have loved to see it," Alec said. "I hope someday you will get the chance."

"Things always seem so grim these days," Ava said.

A light flickered in from the west entrance to the hall. Danny walked in holding a small candle. "Well, is the inability to sleep when stressed a family trait?" Danny asked smiling.

"No, but it is understandable," a voice from the eastern door added. William walked in and sat down with his siblings. "We all worry about what will transpire tomorrow. I have spent many hours meditating but still have not figured out what our role is to be for the battle."

"I have been thinking about balance and about destruction," Ava said with a sigh. All three of her siblings waited for her to provide an explanation. As they were staring at her, Ava looked up and squirmed uncomfortably.

"So enlighten us, Ava," Alec said.

Ava looked at the trio and her eyes started to tear. How do you tell your brother, your newfound siblings, that you are destined to destroy the world? Alec looked at her with confusion; he did not know what she had seen in the Great Library. William looked at her and nodded his head, giving her the approval she really did not need. *Speak now Ava or you may never find the courage again*, she thought.

"In the Great Library I discovered why I lose control of my magic," Ava said, mostly to Alec and Danny, who did not have the benefit of spending that time with her for the last couple of days.

This is good news, Alec thought. Ava was a powerful practitioner and with her power under control, she would be a valuable asset to the Artician nation. "So what did you learn?"

"I learned that I have the power to destroy the world," Ava responded.

Danny frowned and Alec's eyes went wide.

...

Queen Angelica watched the sunrise over the Crystal Mountains. At first, there was just a shimmer of gold against the white caps of the teeth of the world. Then it gained momentum as it lit the valley below. On a clear day, she could see to the valley where the king's army would be camped, but today seemed unnaturally hazy.

She had not slept that night. The prophesy haunted her and kept her from the comfort of dreams. *"One will die, but live within the sky,"* she recalled. The seer had been vague and would not tell her which of her children would die, just that one of them would. If she let them go, one would not return.

She learned very young never to deny the will of the goddess; it could only lead to ruin. The queen had paid a harsh price for turning her back on her responsibilities. Adara had commanded her to embark on a quest soon after Tristan was born, but selfishly she chose to stay close to her family. When she did finally travel, she shuddered at the thought of what had happened. A rider from a small village came to the queen to report an unexplained illness. The queen rushed out of the castle to aid the village and did not wait for an escort. It was because of this that the demon had intercepted her on that road. Even as she suffered from the treatment of the demon, the goddess still came to her and made the wrong right. Adara also warned her of the balance and that a price to be paid because of her stubbornness and the interference of the goddess. Which one of her children will pay the price of her sins? It was unbearable.

As she thought of the possible consequences of her past actions, a chambermaid called into her room. "Milady, you asked me to wake you at light's rising."

"I am up, thank you, Millie," The queen answered. She went to her closet to select an outfit to see her children off to war. *To war*, she thought. *"I am sending my children off to war.*

She left the chamber and headed to the main hall, where she found her young children dressed and packing for the road. The queen smiled as she saw Ava and Danny in tunic and trousers. This would not be enough for the children of Henry. "Come" she said as she led the children to the wall of the room. She touched a pattern of stars on the intricate drawing and a chamber opened to the surprise of the children. "You will not go off to war without some protection. We have many gifts from our allies, the dwarves, which could be useful in your endeavors today."

Ava and Alec looked at each other; they thought there was no place in the castle that they had not yet found. It seemed that there were a few surprises left for them yet. The queen outfitted Ava and Danny with light armor, fitting for female warrior princesses. The cut was perfect; a little adjustment of the straps and it fit snug. Ava drew Last Kiss to get a feel for movement with armor. The dwarves were remarkable. It was a perfect fit.

"How could this fit so perfectly? I have not stood for an armorer to be measured for this fine suit," Ava asked.

"It is the nature of the dwarven armor. It adjusts to its wearer," The queen responded. "I am afraid, William, that I have no dwarven armor for you to wear."

"It is of no matter, mother. My armor is still back in Cyrus on the rack in the barracks. I traveled only in my lightest garb since I had to make haste to Castle Articia to fulfill the destiny that the goddess had set in front of me."

"There are many destinies to fulfill, William. Your uncle knew that this day would come and has been prepared all along. Your squire waits in the stable with Dustin and Jamal. They will help you into your armor," the queen said smiling.

"How is that possible?" William asked, somewhat confused.

"Your uncle sent your squire to Castle Articia with your things before he marched to meet your father," she replied. William said to his siblings "I will meet you in the courtyard when you are ready." William walked out of the room and down the hall.

Ava, Alec, and Danny finished gathering their things and bid farewell to their mother. However, the queen asked Danielle to stay a few more minutes. Ava smiled as she turned down the hall. Her mother and newfound sister had whispered conversation away from the palace twins and both giggled as Danny walked toward them smiling.

"What is it?" Ava asked, she was surprised how jealous she was that her mother and Danny were conversing and held secrets and she was not included.

"Nothing, really, just us getting to know each other," Danny replied as she walked by the stunned siblings.

In the courtyard, they found the groomsmen waiting with their horses. Star Dancer was over by the mill, doing what appeared to be sharpening of his hooves. Alec walked over to inquire, "What is it that you are doing to your hooves?"

We may get an opportunity to engage the wolug today. It would be disgraceful for a destri to miss an opportunity to deal one of the dark beasts a fatal blow, the destri responded.

"Do you think we will engage the wolug directly?" Alec asked Star Dancer.

We cannot predict the future, but we are heading into battle. One should always be prepared in such situations, the destri replied.

As the destri finished the conversation, William's squire opened the stable doors and William, in full armor, walked to the destri that had chosen him. Ava and Danny stopped conversing and gazed at William. The armor of a cavalier was ornate but functional. It shined brightly in the sunlight. He was a warrior of the goddess, a warrior of the light.

Ava was surprised by her reaction to William in his knightly garb. The sight of a true cavalier left her light-headed.

Danny knew the feeling. "It is something, the biggest tease in the land. Many ladies have swooned at the sight of a cavalier but are quickly disappointed when they discover that they do not sire families."

"You do not sound like much of a farm girl with such knowledge," Ava said in reply. "I would think you would not have seen any of the One Hundred on your farm."

"My mother told me many stories of her childhood, including a story of her unrequited love of a cavalier that she met as a young girl," Danny told her as she tightened the saddle straps on her horse.

As they were finishing their discussion, Jamal and Dustin rode out of the stable on their 'warhorse'. They were wearing armor that they had fashioned out of kitchen pots and pans. It was quite the comical display as they formed up beside William, who was amused and touched by the earnestness of the young boys.

"I wish they would stay here were they would be safe," Danny said under her breath.

"Dwarves are funny beings sometimes. They jump into a fight without thinking, but they are some of the happiest races in our domain. It would be impossible to keep them cooped up in the castle," Ava responded.

"Dwarves?" Danny asked.

Ava looked at her a little confused. "You did not know that Jamal and Dustin are dwarves?"

"No," Danny said, somewhat surprised. "I just thought them rather sturdy and remarkably lucky boys,"

"Well, they are rather young dwarves. Probably just reaching their twentieth year," Ava said as she tightened the cinch on her saddle.

"They are twenty!" Danny said with shock. "They do not act like men of that age."

"Dwarves, like the elves, live very long lives," Ava explained. "A dwarf of twenty would be a child of eight or nine years to us."

"So young, that explains a lot. So should we make them stay here for their own safety?" Danny pleaded.

"We do not have the power or resources left in the castle to restrain two determined dwarves, even two as young as Jamal and Dustin. They are unnaturally strong and have remarkable stubbornness." As she watched them maneuver their shaggy horse in behind William to wait to march, Ava continued. "They, even at this young age, would be the equivalent of two or more men in battle," I think it is the will of the goddess that you met them, and that they travel with our party."

As the two sisters finished speaking, William nodded to his squire, mounted, and rode toward the gate. Alec mounted Star Dancer and rode up beside William. He slung his longbow over his shoulder as he took his brother's hand in greeting. Ava and Danny mounted their horses as well and rode to the gate as the squire pulled a cart of supplies and William's lances behind. Bringing up the rear were Jamal and Dustin, clanging and banging with every step of their pony.

22

The Charge of the One Hundred

As the sun completed its rise between the Crystal Mountains, the king looked over the hill into the valley that was to the west of the Lewisvel Keep. The fog was so thick now that the keep was not visible from the field. Bryn walked up to the king's side and pondered the current situation.

"What do you think, my friend?" the king asked his longtime confidant on the matters of battle strategy.

"I am convinced they have sorcerers at the head of this army" Bryn responded as he was drawing formations on the ground. "So I suspect that what they are hiding is a much larger army than we anticipated."

"How large?" the king asked.

"It could be many thousands more, though I am more concerned about the keep right now. With this fog, the men at the keep cannot expect effectively thin the attacking forces with their archery. "

"We need to do something about this fog. Maybe Brendan can cook something up to eliminate the effect."

"I will look into it, Sire. However, I think we should get ready to march now. Things may move faster than we expected."

"Agreed." The king replied. "Muster the troops. We ride when the sun reaches the Lewisvel peak of the Crystal Mountains."

Bryn called to the captain of the army. "Muster the run. We go at the peak of the sun over the mountains."

...

It was quiet on the walls of Lewisvel. Tristan had not gotten much sleep the night before. He thought of the pending battle.

It could mean disaster to the soldiers on the wall. They had an important task; they were the diversion so they needed to stay in the fight as long as they could.

The fog engulfed the entire keep and the soldiers guarding the walls had reverted to voice signals to report from each section. Tristan listened to the calls of the watch, waiting for his turn to respond. They could no longer use the system of flags for messages. The fog had eliminated that form of silent communication.

As Tristan sat and listened to the call of the watch, he started to get a feeling that something was not right. Off in the distance. He sensed the darkness. He tried to listen for a noise over the wall but heard nothing but the calls of the watch. He was concentrating so hard on the feeling that he missed his turn, and the weapon master of the keep called to his post for an answer.

As he pondered the feeling, he realized what was bothering him. It was the silence. In the distance, it was silent—no insects, no dripping of water from the dew of the trees in the field. No sound at all. He reached out with his senses and his magic to feel around the mist. Then he hit it, the tower was thirty feet high and solid. It had an aura of magic about it. What was it? He concentrated harder. *Silence. They have silenced a siege tower with magic!* he thought as he jumped to his feet and called "To arms! We are on the verge of breach. They have rolled a tower into the western break!"

Tristan ran along the wall to where the siege tower was now dropping a bridge over the edge of the western break. Goblins started running over the ramparts from the tower and onto the upper walks of the keep."

...

Bryn heard the call from the wall as the forces of Articia moved quietly across the valley west of the keep. The One Hundred had taken a position to the west of the regular cavalry, ready to make the charge at the wolug horde when they countered. One thing was certain—the sorcerers of the dark army would not be able to control the beasts when they saw the army of the light. The wolug could not help but attack. It was part of their being, their makeup, to destroy the heroes of the light, and the cavaliers of the One Hundred stood for the best of the light. When the beasts saw their armor shining, reflecting the light of the goddess, they would charge in a frenzy.

...

Brendan was now deep into the valley with a small contingent of soldiers. What he had planned required him to move to the edge of the fog. The kings' strategy was to start his incantation as the main force of the army arrived so that the army of darkness would have less time to react to the maneuvering of King Henry. The downside of this, of course, is that the keep would have to hold the forces of darkness at bay for a couple of hours. This would definitely be a difficult endeavor.

He looked off to the west, the first battalion of longbow men and pike men were deploying behind the rise, out of sight from any force that would approach from the north or east. They were the pincer against any troops that manage to get behind the main force. To his right was the main body of the army. They would engage east of the cavaliers. Well-trained men, but he was still concerned about the number of them that would fall today.

No loss was good for the nation. These were the best and brightest of Artician soldiers. How can the nation afford to risk them in battle? Nevertheless, he knew his duty and knew how important it was to end this battle here. It would be an hour before the forces were in place when the signal would come for Brendan to eliminate the fog. He listened to the sound of fighting at Lewisvel Keep with concern.

...

Ava looked ahead toward the east. Still an hour from the battlefield, even with the quickened pace they kept, they dared not push their horses any harder. It was already near impossible for Dustin and Jamal to keep up with the larger horses and the destri. She reached out with her magical senses, trying to feel the battle that had surely begun. She could not feel anything but a slight tingle of darkness. Dark magic is present, but she could not discern its source or purpose. "William, have you received any updates from the battlefield?"

"Yes, but only that the army is moving into position," he responded. "Though there is some confusion. There is a mention of an unearthly fog."

"We must hurry. The army of darkness has sorcerers at its head. They need to be neutralized or our father's army is in great peril," Ava said as she turned Aurora into a gallop to the northeast.

Alec looked back toward Dustin and Jamal, who were falling behind and called, "We must ride ahead. Catch up to us on the battlefield as soon as you can. Look for Bryn; he will help you find the place where you can be of service to the army of Articia."

Dustin looked at Alec and promised, "We will see you after the battle is done and we have a victory!"

...

Tristan drew Silver Bane and called out *"Tartarus inferi."* The magic of the sword cleared about fifty yards of the fog around him, making the siege tower and the goblins that were now charging off the tower completely visible. The men-at-arms guarding this part of the wall, mostly young men like him, met the goblins as they streamed down the walkways of the wall. Tristan was the first to engage, bearing Silver Bane down on the unfortunate goblin closest to him. The magic in the sword cut through the poorly forged scimitar that the goblin used as a weapon and severed its arm; on the backswing, Tristan finished the pitiful creature, stopping its cries of pain as it fell from the wall.

Tristan looked around to see if the rest of the young men who served on his section of the wall were successfully repelling the goblins off their sections of the embattlements. They all seemed to have things under control, but sounds of chaos echoed from parts of the wall not lit by his magic. He looked at the fires that lit the wall for the watch; they had no benefit against the magical fog.

He thought about the effect of his sword on his section and almost kicked himself. "Of course, you can only defeat a magical fog with a magical fire. He was concentrating on the flames of the oil torches that lined the wall of Lewisvel Keep and called out *"Tartarus inferí maximus."*

Slowly the torches flickered and started to burn with the magical fire that Tristan ignited. Around the new magical fires, the fog started to clear, revealing many goblins and many dead men-at-arms.

The goblins must have been ensorcelled against the fog, he thought. *Well they no longer have the advantage!* He saw two additional towers up against other parts of the keep wall. His section of the wall had not allowed the beasts to gain a foothold. His contingent of men-at-arms was keeping the goblins at bay.

The other locations where the other towers were on the wall did not fare so well. They were caught unaware as the goblins continued to stream to the upper walls of the keep. *I must do something to help those posts,* he considered but knew it would leave his post severely weakened. His section was assigned three platoons of men-at-arms. He knew that in order for the keep to have a chance, he would now have to manage with just one.

"First platoon, go to help secure the wall to the west; third platoon, to the north," Tristan called as he fought off another goblin that tried to jump the sword wall the second platoon had formed against the tower. "Second platoon, we must stand strong until the northern and western spurs recover." The men-at-arms of the second platoon sounded an acknowledgement of his command.

. . .

Mr. Tipple stood on the western road, watching the battle start to form. He had chosen to wait at this location. It was most likely route that Ava and her siblings would take on the way to the battlefield.

I am sure that I will pay a high price for this action; he thought as he looked again at the scrolls he had chosen to share with Ava prior to her joining the fray. He knew that the children of the dead were immune to the rules of balance on Articia and Ava would be able to make use of these scrolls, but he was not. There would be a high price to pay for his interference today. It may come in the form of a fire destroying some of the classic works in the library, a disaster in the library garden that would leave him without food, or perhaps blindness. "Oh my, I hope I am not struck blind. It would make it very hard for me to do my job!" he said aloud.

. . .

Brendan stood with his apprentice at the edge of the fog, readying his incantation. The king's army would be in position in just a few moments. Timing was everything for this action. They needed to surprise the army of darkness, so he would have to be successful with what he planned to do about the fog.

"Master, how can you make the fog from the dark sorcerers disappear? Even the light of Adara does not clear this unnatural haze," the young apprentice said. Brendan knew the boy was nervous. He did not usually take an apprentice, but this boy showed remarkable talent and intelligence at a very young age.

He was clearly nervous because they were going to be very close to the opposing army when the fog cleared.

"Maximillian, the light of Adara would usually burn off this fog, but it has clearly been ensorcelled against the heat of the sun," Brendan told the young boy. "So we will counter that enchantment with our own sorceries. I will add some magic of our own to Adara's light." Brendan looked up to the sky, the orb was already well above the crystal mountains. "Now is the time." Brendan looked to the east and raised his staff, as he yelled *"Magis lumen aduro maximus!"*

Power streamed from Brendan's rod and his hand toward the light of Adara. The army of darkness hesitated; they could feel the wave of power that crossed the field of battle and knew that things were about to change.

Brendan turned to his young apprentice and yelled, "Now is the time to run!" He started to jog toward the flag at the head of the king's army. Young Maximillian looked through now thinning fog and saw the leading edge of a goblin battalion about three hundred yards off, he quickly turned and ran after Brendan.

The young acolyte quickly passed the older sorcerer and ran into and through the front line of pike men, who laughed at the sight of the boy outrunning his master. After Brendan had passed, the pike men stood and planted their long weapons as the first barrier to the opposing army.

...

William and Alec crested the hill overlooking the valley where the battle was about to begin. As Ava and Danny caught up, it was clear that something was changing on the battlefield. They all felt the wave of power as it radiated out from the center of the valley.

Danny, William, and Alec had looks of concern on their faces but Ava was smiling. She knew the feel of Brendan's magic.

"Come on! They have started without us!" she called back as she rode by them. Alec looked at her and shook his head "Come on. The way Ava is, she is not likely to leave any of the enemy for us to fight."

The remaining siblings rode off after Ava. Danny looked back to see Dustin and Jamal approaching about thousand yards back. She rolled her eyes and caught up to her siblings.

...

Tristan surveyed the walls of the keep; by some miracle or magic, the fog had almost completely dispersed from the walls and remained thick only in the shaded sections of the ground where the light of Adara had not risen high enough in the sky to burn it away. Though the men of the keep had suffered many casualties, they were still in the fight. He was sure it would have been a completely different outcome, had he not raised the alarm.

Tristan looked at the three towers. Still pushed up against the wall, Tris could see that the other two towers were now under control. The men-at-arms he sent to augment their defense ensured that they would make a stand. His group, however, was now in dire straits. Only four of the original twenty remained of the second platoon. If they did not get reinforcements soon, they would lose control of this section of the wall. He needed to do something now to aid his remaining soldiers.

With his magical senses, Tristan reached into the tower. This would buy time, but only a little. He pointed his hand to the opening of the tower and shouted the spell that he knew would exhaust his limited magical ability. "*Flamma edo edi essum!*" Flames shot from his fingertips and filled the inside of the tower. Surprised by the power of his spell, the heat was remarkable and the whole tower erupted in flames. The remaining men stationed with him cheered, as it was clear that the tower was now unusable. No more goblins would threaten the wall from this tower.

"Go to the eastern tower to provide support. I do not think they will be able to use this device to attack Lewisvel anymore today," Tristan said and the men at his command turned and ran to the eastern tower. Tristan watched them go, unaware of the burning goblin that ran from the tower with a spear in its hand.

Tristan relaxed a bit, confident now that they would win the day against the army of darkness. He did not realize the gravity of his error until he looked down at the spear that had pierced his heart.

...

Ava stopped Aurora short as she saw Mr. Tipple sitting on the side of the road. "Mr. Tipple," she said as she got off her horse and went to him. "I am pleased to see you, but this area is about to get very dangerous. Is it wise for you to be here?"

"My young lady," Mr. Tipple said quite annoyed, "just because I am presently a librarian does not mean that I have never seen the horrors of war." He stood up from the log he was sitting on and pulled three scrolls from his bag. "I felt that I did not truly prepare you for what is to come, so I have these items that I translated for you to use in your upcoming endeavor. The first one is a historical discussion of some value. You may find it will help you come up with some unique ideas."

"Thank you," Ava said as she unwound the scroll and read it. It was a rather short accounting relating to the situation at hand. Clearly, Mr. Tipple had given her a summary of a much longer accounting. She read within the scroll a single statement that gave her pause.

It is not known precisely where angels dwell, whether in the air, the void, or the planets. It has not been God's pleasure that we should be informed of their abode.

Arovet Li

The void, Ava thought. *I have seen that phrase before.* She thought about this as Mr. Tipple was handing her another scroll. This time when she opened it, she understood what Mr. Tipple was showing her. She looked confidently into his eyes and said, "Thank you, Mr. Tipple. I understand."

"This last one is most important. You will release chaos when you take that action, young woman. You must return everything to a balanced situation when you are finished or you will leave us all in quite a miserable state." Mr. Tipple handed her the last scroll. Ava looked at the scroll and quickly understood the sage's advice. "Thank you, Mr. Tipple. Until this moment, I had only considered violent action as the means to solve the upcoming battle. This will help to reduce the casualties if the proper event occurs and the time is right."

"Remember, young Princess, there is only one time that this action should be taken. Things must truly be desperate before you unleash this chaos." Mr. Tipple gave Ava a quick hug and started east back toward the southern road and the Great Library.

"Who was that?" Alec asked Ava as they approached her passing Mr. Tipple who was humming an unfamiliar tune.

"It is a librarian!" Ava said with a laugh, "a powerful ally for whom I have great respect." Ava remounted Aurora and turned east toward the battlefield. "Come on! We have no time to waste." She moved with more spirit. The scrolls had given her some hope that she may be able to help her father's army without destroying the world.

Alec looked back at the old man who was walking east and shook his head. *I think you have gone completely mad*, Alec thought of Ava. *You have changed so much since I saw you last.*

...

The fog was starting to clear quickly and the forward pike men were the first to call the alarm. They had clearly underestimated the number of the dark army's forces. Bryn rode quickly to the hill where King Henry sat on his mount. "Sire, I think I have to change our estimate of our opposing force," Bryn said as he turned his horse toward the battlefield. "I am afraid the force we face may exceed one hundred thousand strong."

"Yes, I think you are correct. Your recommendations," the king asked his longtime friend.

"Our original battle plan is sound. We can move on the force and trap them against the keep wall. I am sure our friends in the keep can aid us in significantly reducing their numbers," Bryn responded. "But we will lose many of our men in this engagement; the kingdom may never recover from such losses."

"Bryn, I must signal a new strategy," the king looked toward his eldest son in the distance.

"What is your command?"

"Bryn, you will have to lead the eastern forces, since our enemy has a much larger force than we anticipated," the king said. "I need to send Dominic a signal to take the lead for the western flank. They must hold the ground so that the goblins and their allies cannot flank our army from the west. We must keep them in the river valley."

"I understand," Bryn stated. "I will signal his forces in the western battalion immediately." Bryn turned his horse, rode toward the signalmen, and sent the word to the western forces of the king.

"May Adara be with you," the king whispered as he turned toward his captain of the army. "The wolug seem to be far back in the force. I expect that whoever is currently controlling them knew the mounted monsters would be of no value against the walls of the keep since there power is on the ground and thank Adara, have not shown the ability to climb walls."

"Yes, I noticed that too. Do you think the dark sorcerers have found a way to control the beasts?" the captain said with some concern. "It could be disastrous for our forces if the wolug were able to concentrate on our main army."

"No, I do not. I think they have only the ability to keep the wolug from charging outright once they see the cavaliers of the One Hundred," the king responded. "They are too wild and have too much hatred for things of the light to be fully controlled. We have learned from our many engagements with the wolug that we can depend on the behavior of the wolves of the darkness."

The captain surveyed the army in the distance. "Something is amiss, my King. I am not sure what, but I believe there are still surprises for us here today."

"Well, then, there is no time like the present. It is time we get into this battle with our division," the king said as he turned and waved to his signalman. The young man nodded and put a horn to his mouth and blew the battle call.

...

The siblings heard the horn blast of the battle call as they reached the top of the last rise before the valley of Lewisvel Keep. As Ava surveyed the battlefield, she saw the cavaliers of the One Hundred lined up and ready to ride to the west of a turn in the lower bank of a dry riverbed.

"A good tactic," William said. "They are using the cover of the berm of the dry river to disguise their actions. When they rise above the hill, the wolug will immediately start their charge. The cavaliers will be able to meet them in even force on the narrow flatland where they will have the advantage."

"Why is that a benefit?" Alec asked.

"When they charge, the cavaliers will try to lance the wolug in the heart. This will instantly kill them. If they miss their mark, the wolug can get close enough for a strike. Their poisonous bite is always fatal," William explained. "If they can get the wolug to charge close to each other, it is harder for the wolug to dodge the lances. That is why the One Hundred charge in so tight a line."

"Seems wise," Alec said. "Why are there only One Hundred cavaliers?"

"There are only a limited number of destri on Articia. No other mount can stand against the wolug" William responded. "For generations the One Hundred have charged the wolug to keep their numbers at bay. Adara has blessed humanity by not letting the beasts breed in great numbers. After a battle, it can take many generations for the wolug to build up enough numbers to threaten our people again and it takes many generations for the destri to sire enough mounts to respond"

"Seems like a stalemate to me," Ava said as she had heard most of the conversation between Alec and William. "There must be a better way to deal with the beasts."

"Many have tried and failed," William said. "They are the spawn of the darkness and are protected by the one who created the beasts. No magic or other means can eliminate the wolug. Piercing their hearts has been the only way to bring about their destruction."

Ava was frustrated. She knew what would happen to the cavaliers in this stalemate. Many brave knights would fall. There is no magical power in all of Articia that could prevent their fate. She could feel the serious tone of William's explanation and knew it to be true. She turned to look at Danny, whose eyes were now welled with tears that would soon fall in distress.

The Cavaliers of the One Hundred reached the crest of the hill. Their squires were pulling their carts quickly west toward the road that will bring them back to castle Articia. They had done their jobs and now have the responsibility to survive with the hope of becoming future cavaliers of the One Hundred. Despite their desire to be knights, the great steeds will not choose most of them and they will leave the service of the knights to become members of the Artician army.

It was clear that the army of darkness had seen the knights because goblins were quickly scattering north and south of the main force. They knew that the charge was coming and any foolish enough to stand in front of the charging wolug would be ripped apart by their hunger.

Alec, Danny, and Ava, shaken by the ferocity of the howl that echoed from the core of the dark force, watched in horror as the beasts started to charge at the knights of Adara. However, William sat stoic in his saddle. He waited for the action that he knew was coming. The One Hundred knights of Adara started moving slowly at first, but soon were in full gallop with lances forward. It was then that Ava and her siblings saw for the first time the beast that the cavaliers would battle. She now understood why they had to defeat the wolug. They were horrible creatures of the darkness; the drool from their maws destroyed everything it touched. The ground smoked where they passed and a trail of blackened ground was all they left in their wake.

Ava watched the wolug advance and was the first to recognize that things were not as the cavaliers expected. "William! The four horsemen are riding the four lead wolug!"

...

The young knight, honored to charge at the center of the line, knew that was given was crucial role. He and his mount would set the pace of the charge, and would make the first strike with a lance. As he looked ahead to assess the wild charge of the wolug, he noticed something that he had not expected from his training. The wolug in the center of the pack did not have goblin riders. There were four unfamiliar beasts on the back of the dark wolves. The young knight faltered as he saw that one of the riders had a ghostly white skull for a head. Because of lost concentration, his lance dipped too low for a true strike. The action was fatal when one of the lead wolug jumped the lance and ended the young cavalier's life with its jaw at his throat.

...

Ava watch as the forces of light and darkness clashed. The sound of this battle was horrifying, the howling of fatally wounded wolug, the screaming of men and destri echoed with the evil howl of the dark beasts. It broke her heart to see so many of Articia's young heroes die in such a way. "William, how can they just ride to their deaths? Is there no hope?" Ava asked him.

William turned to Ava, a single tear running down his cheek. "If they don't, who will? If no one made the sacrifice they are making today, the beasts would run wild over the whole of Articia. No man, woman, or child would survive the onslaught of the wolug."

"Is there nothing we can do?" Danny asked desperately.

"We can join the fight," Alec said. "The four horsemen do not belong here. They are throwing of the balance."

"What do you mean?" William looked over the battlefield to see what Alec had already surmised.

"The One Hundred have faltered," Alec said. "The middle of the line fell apart where the horsemen charged through. Too many of the wolug are running past."

The wolug had broken through the line and were turning to the main body of the army. The front line was not prepared to deal with this kind of fight.

"We must ride to meet them," William said. "The horsemen have been hunting us and may still come to intercept us. It will give the army time to get prepared to deal with the new threat."

"We have a better option," Ava said. "Mr. Tipple has given me a way to deal with the riders. I believe we can banish them back to their dead world from which they came."

"Can you truly perform such an act?" Danny asked Ava.

Alec smiled as he turned to Danny, "I think our biggest concern is that she does not overdo it."

"Regardless, we must ride now if we are to bait the dark ones to us." William pulled down the visor on his helmet and, like the One Hundred who had charged before him, lowered his lance, and yelled, "For Adara!"

Comet reared and jumped into a run. Alec grabbed his bow off his back and followed. Ava and Danny pushed their mounts in pursuit. Ava yelled ahead to her brothers, "You must not engage them. We must turn and run them into the dry riverbed behind the line. It is there that I can use what I have learned!"

23
The Battle Rages

Terra expositus vorago irritus

On the eastern side of the battlefield, Dominic's battalion was struggling to keep the goblin horde from outflanking the battle line. He looked along the eastern mark for an answer and noticed commotion from the behind his guard. As he turned, he saw what appeared to be two young boys on a shaggy mule running toward the line of battle. He watched, as they slammed into the goblin line close to the weakened edge. The men of that section were about to be shattered by the opposing force. He could not believe what he saw next. As the young men reached the front of the skirmish, the stockier of the two jumped from the shaggy mule with a carpenter's hammer. He landed on a group of the goblins yelling some kind of odd yell. The young boy hit the goblins so hard that they scattered in all directions.

Dominic's men-at-arms stood in stunned silence for a brief moment, but as soon as they realized that the young "warrior" had given them an advantage, they regained the ground they had just recently lost.

His companion was having an equal effect on another group of confused goblins with an odd kind of fire magic that he was casting. The boy on the shaggy mount rode through the goblins shooting fire from his fingertips, striking random goblins, and causing them to lose their footing as they tried to pat out the fires on their fur and clothing.

Their mount was the most effective of the troupe as it engaged the goblin force with more ferocity then any warhorse Dominic had ever seen. It ran through a large group of goblins, biting, kicking, and trampling every goblin it passed.

Dominic's men took advantage of the chaos that the two boys and the shaggy beast created. It allowed them to push the eastern line back into formation. Dominic could only wonder at the actions of this new addition to his force of men.

He turned back to see the condition of the main army, where his father was facing the brunt of the goblin horde. Many men had lost their lives as the army was slowly pushed back from the battle line. The pike men were holding strong, but it was clear that they would soon collapse from the onslaught of goblins that they faced.

Thousands of goblins lay dead or dying from the barrage of arrows, the king's men had sent their way. The bodies of goblins piled up on the battlefield, causing the pike men to retreat to maintain a good position with their long pikes. The army of Articia was pushed back to the valley rise. Any farther back and they would lose the advantage of the high ground.

Dominic looked off to where the cavaliers were to engage and what he saw in the distance broke his spirit. Most of the One Hundred had fallen and there were still a large number of wolug. Something had disrupted the balance and weakened their standard tactics. Soon they would turn on the main body of the army and it would be finished. Dominic drew Ghost Touch and called out to his section of the army. "Today is a good day to die, for Adara and for the light!" Dominic yelled as he started to gallop toward the line.

Before the prince reached the line of battle, he heard unearthly screams from the west. The wolug had abandoned what was left of the One Hundred cavaliers and started to run to the western hills. Dominic pulled the reins on his horse and stopped to watch the change in fortune.

He did not know what had caused them to flee, but he would thank Adara properly later if they survived the day. If not, he would thank her in person. He turned back to his forward line and saw that his men had gotten an advantage. The two young boys were still causing quite a stir in the middle of the opposing force. He was heartened as he joined the line to push the goblins back to the Coal Mountains.

...

Ava called over to Danny, "Follow me to the top of the rise. We have to wait for our brothers to draw the riders into the dry riverbed!" Then Ava turned Aurora to the hills and road to the northwest. Away from Danny and Ava, William and Alec were bearing down on the four riders and remaining wolug.

William, Comet sent to him. *I can see your thoughts. You must not engage the riders. Did you not hear your sister's request?*

"I heard my sister," William responded. "But I am honor bound to avenge the death of my comrades."

That you will do, but at its proper time, Comet communicated to William. *Now is not the time for you to stand for Adara.* Comet paused in his communication as William turned to look toward Ava. *For now, you must trust your sister. This is the time for Ava to make a stand against the darkness.*

William gathered his thoughts to consider the words that Comet had sent to him. The destri added, *it is the will of Adara.*

William called to Alec, "We must turn toward the dry bed now. They must follow us to the place where Ava has designated!" When he got acknowledgement from Alec, they turned in unison to the west with the riders and the remaining wolug in pursuit.

...

The king looked across the battlefield. It was not looking good for his army. There were just too many goblins in the horde. Henry turned to Bryn and said, "Well, looks like this may be our last battle together, my old friend."

Bryn looked across the field and over to the keep—all three towers were in flames. "Looks like the keep is still standing and your son Dominic is doing a remarkable job holding our eastern flank. Bryn then looked off to the west and said, "The wolug appear to be running to the west. Not like that is the only unusual thing that has occurred today."

"Any ideas left?" the king asked his weapon master.

"I may have a few," Brendan said as he walked up to the pair. "But we will pay a price for the action I plan."

"I think we are out of options, Bren. What do you have up your sleeve?" the king asked.

"The goblin army's main force is in the dry riverbed," Brendan began. "I have already prepared a spell that will shake the earth and release the Rothian Lake trapped in a high bowl of the Crystal Mountains. That will allow it to flow back into the bed and wash the goblin army away."

"That's brilliant!" Bryn said. "I will signal the troops to head to the top of the hills to escape the onslaught.

King Henry looked toward his weapon master. "Bryn, if we take this action, our army will be destroyed with that of our enemies when they are swept by the rushing water. We are in the lowlands here and if the whole lake flows down, there is no place we can run to escape from the rushing water."

Bryn looked up at the mountains and thought of the lake that had been contained for many generations. "You are right, my friend. This action will be the end of our army, but it will protect Articia as a whole." Bryn thought of this for a while. "Well, at least Tris will be spared to take your throne and your other children are away from the worst of this action."

The king looked over to Dominic's line. His men would be the first hit by the wall of water. The hills behind them would provide refuge for a short while, but soon the water would overcome all of them. "Brendan, work your magic. I am sure there are none among us who would regret the lives we give today to save the people of Articia from a world of dark oppression."

"Bryn," the king turned to Bryn and said "Blow the horn for the men to fall back to the crests of the hills once Brendan starts his conjuring. We may not live to see tomorrow, but at least we will live long enough to see the goblin horde drown before we go to Adara!"

Bryn smiled as he started to understand the order of the king. He nodded to his aide, who brought the horn to his lips and blew the call to fall back.

...

"My Lord, the army of King Henry is retreating," the fire sorcerer's apprentice said. "And the wolug have started running wild to the west toward the castle of Articia.

"Good, good. We must not let up. Not until all of Henry's forces are destroyed," the red-robed sorcerer said. "Then and only then will the forces of darkness rule this land." The enchanter walked to the edge of the northern forest and looked across the battlefield. "Signal our troops to move and hold the riverbed. Once our forces are in place, we will prepare for the final push."

...

"Ava, they are almost upon us," Danny warned as she drew the sword she had borrowed from the armory in the castle.

"Yes, I think now is the time." Ava looked down the hill as Alec and William were riding up to meet them. The destri were truly amazing beings. They outran the wolug and the dark riders with ease. There was more than enough time to do what she was planning.

Ava opened the scroll one more time. She needed to be sure of the image of her conjuring so that there would be no error in the mission she was about to accomplish. She looked out toward William, who gave her a look of concern. She knew that he was unaware of the event she had planned ahead. She gave him a confident nod and started her incantation, then yelled, "*Terra expositus vorago irritus!*"

. . .

Brendan looked toward the Crystal Mountains. This would be the last action he would perform for his king. So many men would perish here to save the people of Articia. He looked over to where the king sat on his horse. *I wish there was some incantation to transport you back to castle Articia. The people will truly miss your leadership.*

Brendan collected his thoughts and concentrated on the spell that he was about to perform. Slowly he built up the magical energy for its casting. This would be the most powerful magic he ever performed. He thought of Ava, how magical power flowed so easy for her. *She could perform this incantation with the slightest thought, and probably could hold in the water with one of her force spells.* He often wondered how she was able to perform some of the magic she accomplished without incantation.

He focused on the task. He looked to the west and saw that Dominic's men had reached the top of the rise. He looked to the mountaintop and started his incantation.

"Tremo terra maximus!"

. . .

In front of Ava, the earth opened. However, it did not open to the heart of Articia as her siblings expected. It opened to another world. Looking into the chasm, they saw a dead place that had a red sun rising over the horizon. In the sky, a grey moon hung sadly over a barren desert. Nothing lived on this world; there were no plants or animals. It was incredibly disheartening to see the state of this place.

The gap opened under the wolug and their dark riders. They did not have a chance to react before they fell through gap and into the other world. The death rider screamed with hatred as it looked back at Ava with flaming eyes. She had sent them back to the place where they had come from.

Ava was preparing to release the portal spell when the earth started to shake. She was terrified. Ava had not known that this spell would have such an effect. The ground shaking was so intense, that the siblings and their mounts were thrown to the ground. Ava struggled to her knees as she looked off in the distance to see rocks fly from the Crystal Mountains, and the water rushed from the Rothian Lake. It is as if the cataclysm she created had freed the mountain lake!

"Oh no, what have I done" Ava said. She reached with her magic to try to stop the disaster that was occurring. Though she strained as hard as she could, she could not reach through the wave of power that was between her and the flood.

Ava paused, confused, she stopped trying struggling with her magic. She was stunned to find out that Brendan had caused the flood. She could feel his magic. *Why, why would he sacrifice so many of Articia's soldiers* she thought? Ava got to her feet. She had to stop this disaster now. She prepared to reach with all of her power, but before Ava could act, a powerful voice in her head caused her to pause.

Be at peace, child. This has all been preordained. Focus your power to keep the portal you have created open until the healing waters of Articia can pass through the portal and restore the land of the place previously destroyed.

Ava heard the words of the goddess and realized this was the first time she had heard the Adara's voice while she was awake. It was all very confusing but she knew that this was important by the tone of the direction she received.

She looked at the world through the portal. The wolug and riders that fell through were no longer visible. The distance they fell would certainly have been fatal for the wolug, but she was not sure about the demons that fell with them. She could tell that the power of her magic was fading. The goddess had ordered her to keep the portal open so she reached out again with her mind and held the path to the barren place open.

...

Dominic and his men were the closest to the center of Brendan's incantation. The ground shook so violently that all of his men and the goblins that were advancing from the riverbed below were knocked to the ground. Miraculously he managed to stay on his horse, though it was quite spooked by the shaking of the land.

Dominic heard the thunder of the water exploding from the mountain lake. It did not take him long to realize that this action would destroy the goblin army and the army of the king. Dominic looked east toward his father. The king smiled at his eldest son, and saluted him. In this small action, he told Dominic how proud he was with his action today. Dominic saluted back to his father and then looked to Lewisvel keep. At least Tristan would survive. The walls of the keep should be high enough to keep out the rushing water. Dominic looked at his men, who were getting back to their feet. They all were quick to understand that their time on Articia was ending. He sheathed his sword and called to his men.

"It has been my honor to serve this day with you all! Many will remember our actions and they will sing of our sacrifice and record our heroism in the annals of Artician history. None will forget the men of this army and what we have done here today for the people of Articia!"

His men cheered in response. They turned to watch the goblin army fall as the first rush of the water covered the ground in front of them. Dominic could barely hear the sound of the screaming goblins over the onslaught of water; it did give him satisfaction to know that before he and his men had met their fate, they will witness the destruction of the forces of darkness.

...

Ava watched as the water flowed through the portal she had opened in the riverbed. She saw the horde of goblins, most now drowned, flowing over the edge and into the dead world and understood why Brendan had cast his spell to release the water. This goblin army was endless; it would have truly destroyed all of Articia.

She watched as the water continued to flow into the portal and eventually diminished to a trickle. When there was no more threat that the rising water would affect the Artician army, she released her control of the portal and it started to close. The four of them watched as wisps of white clouds started to form around the dead world. The water that she had sent through the portal seemed to be making a small change to the place that spawned such horrific beings like the four horseman.

Ava looked over the battlefield as she took the reins of her horse.

"There are still some goblins on the field of battle," she said. "It is now our duty to join our father's army to protect Articia. Ava mounted Aurora and watched as the portal finally closed. There was no longer any sign of the dead world and its small grey orb. Danny, Alec, and William mounted their horses as well as they prepared to ride. Ava pulled out Last Kiss and called her siblings into a battle charge.

"For Adara! For Articia!"

...

King Henry watched the goblins swept away by the raging river. He did not understand why they were still in existence. *Brendan must have overestimated the amount of water in that mountain lake,* he thought. Across the battlefield, the king saw that there were still some goblins remaining. King Henry met Bryn's eyes and said,

"It seems that Adara is with us today, but there is still work to do here. Call for the charge and let's finish the dark beasts."

The king mounted his horse and drew his sword. The horns blew as he started his charge. The men, who had been standing in stunned silence, drew their swords and charged with their king into the wall of the remaining goblins.

...

Tancred held Tristan in his arms as his spirit started to leave the confines of his body.

"I have failed you my prince," he said, as he knew there was nothing he could do to save Tristan's life.

"No, Tan, you were a perfect warrior. You sent many goblins to their demise. It was an honor to serve with you, honored of the Third." Tristan paused and winced in pain. His heart struggled to beat with the wound that the spear inflicted. He spoke one final time, "Tell my family I died with honor." As his final words left his lips, his spirit loosened its bonds and he was gone. Tancred reached up and closed Tristan's eyes as he bowed his head.

...

The four siblings fought through many goblins as they moved east to join up with the king's army. William made sure that no goblins remained to cause them trouble. Ava put all of her training and her magical skill to work as they fought against their adversaries.

They clashed with the foul beasts on their way east, but Ava felt something change from the north, a sensation of great power. As she searched its source, a ball of flame erupted from the northern woods and headed toward the hill where her father was fighting.

Ava reached up and out with her magic and changed the course of the projectile. It smashed with a large explosion into the side of the Crystal Mountains. Ava turned her horse toward the source as she felt the second wave of power forming. She kicked Aurora into a charge and toward this new threat in order to engage the sorcerer who was attacking her father.

Alec saw that Ava had turned to the north and he yelled to William, "Join up with father and let him know Ava is going after what I believe is the leader of this army. I think she intends to cut the head off the snake herself!"

William nodded to Alec and called over to Danny to let her know what was happening. Danny looked over to Ava and smiled. She pulled hard on the reigns and turned her horse to follow William.

Alec rode hard and caught up to Ava. "What's the plan, sister?"

"I felt the presence of powerful sorcerers at the edge of the northern forest," she replied. "I do not know why they have not shown themselves before, but they are now threating our father's army. I mean to keep them from focusing on us rather than our men-at-arms."

"Ava, are you crazy! You cannot seriously be thinking of taking on an experienced group of sorcerers. We should find Brendan," Alec responded.

"There is no time. Alec. They have already started attacking," Ava responded as another fireball exploded from the woods and headed toward the king. Ava concentrated on redirecting this one and managed to cause it to explode as it slammed into the ground behind them. "I may not be able to defeat them, but maybe I can delay them until Brendan notices that they have started attacking our army."

"Well, then, let's harass them as much as we can. I will tag along, though I am not sure that my martial skills will be any value against sorcerers of any form," Alec said as they continued to charge toward the northern edge of the battlefield.

Star Dancer sent to Alec *I am in communication with Comet. We will relay information between you and William so your father can coordinate a response to this new danger.*

...

"Their sorcerer has unleashed his powers on the field of battle," the adept said to the practitioner of fire sorcery. "He has destroyed most of the goblin army."

"Well, the door is opened then." The sorcerer of fire said. He looked at his companions; the other practitioners of the elements were the most powerful group of sorcerers from the dark citadel. They were the most experienced practitioners for each of the elements they represented. Together they could do considerable damage. However, the king only had one sorcerer at his service. If they all joined forces, the balance would be tilted and the spirit of Articia would push back. He had strict orders from the master of the dark arts not to throw off the balance. They could ill afford the result that would occur when the essence of this plane responded. Now that the king's sorcerer had acted, he could respond in kind.

"My brothers, there is nothing left for you to do here. I am confident that I will be able to do some considerable damage to the king now. Return to the citadel and wait for my return. The master of the citadel will want to know how things are progressing on the battlefield." The fire lord finished.

As the three other sorcerers left the battlefield, the fire sorcerer looked across the plains to find where the king's flag was flying. He scanned the valley until he spied it waving on a rise to the southeast. "Well, Henry of the plains. It looks like your days end here." The sorcerer raised his hands and moved them in a spherical motion as he shouted, "*Orbis incendium volatus magnus!*" As he finished his incantation, a ball of fire formed, grew, and flew from his hands toward the hill where King Henry was commanding his army.

He watched with a self-satisfied smirk, waiting for the explosion that would occur when the fireball hit the hill where the king and his closest advisors were located.

It was not long before the sorcerer's smirk turned to a frown. The fireball he had cast veered off to the east and struck the side of the mountain. He formed his hands again and angrily shouted, *"Orbis incendium volatus magnus!"* as a second fireball flew from his hands toward the king. Again, it went awry and struck the ground halfway to its target.

The sorcerer squinted and saw the shadow of two riders in the exploding fires. They were racing toward him. "Well, Brendan, I did not think you had the courage to confront me directly," he said as he prepared another incantation. "Let's see if you are still as clumsy as you were when we were boys." The fire sorcerer put his thumbs together as he moved his hand up and down in a waving motion and yelled *"Fluctus incendium volatus magnus!"*

A wave of fire rolled across the field, burning everything it passed. It moved quickly toward the two riders and would soon consume them.

...

Alec saw the wave of flame form and rush toward them. "Um, Ava," he said nervously.

"I see it," she said. This was not going to be as easy to thwart as the previous spell. She put a wall of force around her and her brother as she pulled her horse to a stop. She looked around for ideas and then grinned.

"You always make me nervous when you smile like that Ava," Alec said as he watched her ready some unusual spell.

She reached to the riverbed, still filled with some of the water of Lake Rothian, and shouted the spell *"Inrigatus impetus incendi!"*

The flames already surrounded them and Alec was getting uncomfortable from the heat. However, it cleared when the water Ava called passed over them putting out the fires, and continued in the direction of the northern wood. Ava turned to Alec.

"Come on, we must get closer to deal with the sorcerer directly!"

"Ava, are you crazy! You cannot possibly think of battling a sorcerer of that much power," Alec said with exasperation. "I know you have powerful magical skills but that sorcerer has experience that you do not yet have."

"I am hoping that Brendan will see the magical activity and come to our aid," Ava responded. "But we must protect our father from this wizard, especially if Brendan has left his side to assist us!"

...

Brendan looked to the north as the ball of fire left the trees and headed toward their position on the battlefield.

"Well, it seems like the leader of this army is now making an appearance."

The king saw the danger and looked toward Brendan. "Should I order a retreat or do you have this, my friend?"

"Let me see what I can do about this new development," Brendan told the king. He concentrated on the rapidly approaching ball of fire as he prepared his spell. Before he could start his incantation, the fireball turned sharply and rammed into the side of one of the Crystal Mountains. Brendan raised an eyebrow as his whole face registered his surprise. Brendan watched as the trees on the mountainside exploded into flame.

"Well," Brendan said.

"Great job, Brendan, Can you keep him at bay while we finish off their army?" the king asked.

"I am afraid, sire, that I am not responsible for our fortune here. It would appear that we have another sorcerer or maybe sorceress in the game."

"Ava?"

"It certainly feels like her," Brendan replied.

"May Adara be with them!" the king prayed as the second

fireball shot from the woods and struck the ground between the forest and the king's position.

...

"We need to get in close," Ava said to Alec.

"What, Are you crazy!" He responded.

"I will distract him with counter-sorcery, and then you see if you can finish him with your bow."

Alec shook his head, and nodded to his sister. He was doubtful he would be able to kill a sorcerer of this much power. He thought of Brendan, he was not as fit like the soldiers at castle Articia. Brendan studied his sorcery all the time so the martial arts were not part of his training, and it showed in his physical frame and fitness. Alec hoped that this practitioner was the same. He tightened he legs on his saddle so he could release the reigns and knock an arrow in his bow as he saw Ava mutter a spell while she looked back at the newly formed river.

...

Dominic's forces had fought the goblins back against the southern wall of Lewisvel Keep. The archers on top of the wall used that opportunity to decimate the remaining goblins and other men from the dark forces. It would soon be over on this part of the battlefield. Dominic would then be able to turn to help the main army. As he looked across his section of the battlefield, he was distraught at the number of men who lay dead on the hills where he stood, despite their good fortune and valiant efforts.

These would be the only dead and wounded that would be returned to their homes since the rest that were in the riverbed would have been washed away when the water struck. He looked over at the two odd young boys, certainly endowed with dumb luck or the favored by the goddess. They were still fighting as wildly as they had when the battle started. However, now they had to run after the goblins, all of which were running in sheer terror from the crazy pair and their shaggy warhorse. He looked at the fallen again. He wished he had had a chance to get to know them better, before they gave their lives for the people of Articia.

· · ·

The fire sorcerer chuckled darkly as he saw the two riders engulfed by the wave of flame that he had sent their way. "Brendan, you fool, you never were prepared to use your sorcery in response one of my attacks," the sorcerer of fire stated. "You were such an easy target back in school and you are still one today."

He turned back to the hill where the king was and started to form another spell, but he never got the chance to ignite the fireball. A wave of water rolled over him and knocked him to the ground.

· · ·

Ava and Alec were only one hundred feet from the edge of the wood when they saw the sorcerer fall as a wall of water hit him square. She turned to Alec and yelled, "There is no better time than now. Aim for the heart of that fire beast, Alec!" As she finished her words, the fire sorcerer stood back up. His anger was clearly visible by the flames flashing in his eyes.

Alec pulled back on the bow as the practitioner of fire started a spell to counter Alec.

"Alec, we are running out of time," Ava yelled.

"On the way," Alec said as he let the arrow fly.

Ava put up a wall of force around them to protect against the sorcerer's next attack. It never came.

The red-robed practitioner had a look of confusion on his face that ended when Alec's arrow hit true and ended his existence.

Ava pulled Aurora to a halt as the fire sorcerer fell to the ground. "Good shot, Alec."

"I thought for sure he was going to destroy me with a spell, but he seemed unable to conjure his fire," Alec said as he stopped next to Ava.

There are many things about magic you do not understand, Alec, Star Dancer sent to him as Ava looked at him with pride.

"If you spent more time with me in Brendan's class, you would have learned much more than just history," Ava said to him as she scanned the forest. "The fire sorcerer was drenched from the water that hit him. He could not produce a spark to make his spell work. Your shot flew at him when he was the most vulnerable."

"Well I think we got lucky," Alec replied.

"Yes, we did." Ava responded. "I think the forest is clear. Let's go back to help finish the enemy to the south." Ava turned to the south as Alec followed. They rode quickly to assist their father.

As they got farther and farther from the forest edge, a dark shadow stepped from the edge of the northern forest. Duke Marquin looked at the pair riding to the south. He sneered as he knocked an arrow in an ornate bow and pulled it back. He released the string and let the arrow fly in the direction of Alec and Ava.

...

Dominic's division joined the king's main army as they pushed what remained of the goblin horde farther and farther north. The cavalry of Cyrus maneuvered around from the west to contain the retreating forces of the goblins. It was not very long before the goblins threw down their weapons and ran full out to the northeast and back toward the Coal Mountains.

The king's army stopped a few hundred yards from the front gate of Lewisvel keep. The siege towers were now just smoldering rubble up against the walls of the great fortress. Dominic turned to the keep and saw that the large gate was now open. The remaining forces of the keep were joining the pursuit of the retreating army.

As the last of the keeps men left the castle, a single soldier led a destri through the open gate. Dominic saw was something that he thought he would never see in his lifetime—the destri was pulling a litter.

He looked to the distance to see if he could recognize the man leading the horse but could not discern the young knight's identity. However, he could tell that the litter had a shroud over a body. The young knight led the destri and its charge toward the king's position.

Dominic thought about this situation. Clearly, destri were noble steeds and were not be used to pull wounded men. Suddenly he realized what was wrong. Dominic wailed "No!" and turned his horse to meet the soldier, destri, and their fallen comrade.

...

Ava saw the goblins running off to the northeast and it lifted her spirits. She knew many men had lost their lives today, but it could have been a lot worse. She paused briefly as she saw her father's flag in the distance and turned her horse toward it. That simple action saved her life for the arrow that was tracking her missed its mark and hit Aurora in the thigh. Her horse screamed as it rolled down to the ground, throwing Ava from the saddle.

The last thing that Ava remembered before she lost consciousness was Alec calling her name.

...

"Ava, open your eyes," Tristan said to her as she was resting on the ground. He was smiling at her as her eyes fluttered open. She heard Tristan speak to her again. "You have had a remarkable day, sister. I can honestly say you earned a knighthood for sure."

Ava sat up and looked around. She was very confused by the surroundings. They were on an open field of green. She did not understand what she was seeing.

Tristan was wearing white shining armor and his hand was at his hip on the hilt of a large sword. She blinked her eyes and asked, "Am I dreaming or am I dead?"

"You are not dead," Tristan told Ava. "And I am not sure I could call this a dream."

Ava thought of what had recently happened and looked around again. There was a grassy plain, a slight breeze, and the smell of honeysuckle in the air. It was truly heavenly. Ava came to a horrifying realization. "Tris, are you dead?" Ava eyes started to well up with tears.

"I no longer have a physical body," Tristan responded gently. "But I am not dead. My spirit survives and is now in the service of Adara."

Ava broke down crying as Tristan reached down and touched her shoulder. "Ava, be at peace. It was the exact time that I was meant to depart from our world. It was predestined that I would give my life in the defense of our people."

"Why? I do not understand why," Ava said with the tears streaming down her cheeks. "I would have given my life to save you."

"Yes, I know, Ava. That is why you are still alive." Tristan helped Ava to her feet. "The people of Articia need me here to watch over them. They need you there to protect them."

"It's not right, Tris. I cannot live without you," she moaned.

"Ava, I will always be with you, watching over you," Tristan promised as he touched her forehead "Now you must awake. Our family is worried sick about you."

...

"Ava, darling, wake up," the queen whispered as she brushed back Ava's hair.

Ava's eyes fluttered open. She was no longer lying on the grassy knoll, but was looking at the ceiling of her room. She tried to sit up but the world started spinning.

"Take it easy, dear. You have been unconscious for three days," the queen said to Ava as she gently laid her back down. "You had quite the spill out there."

"Mom, Tris is gone," she said with tears spilling over her eyes.

"Yes, he is gone," she said with a sigh. "Adara warned me that our family would pay a heavy price for the good of Articia and that one of my children would not return from the field of battle." The queen took a wet cloth and wiped Ava's head. "Adara will look after your brother. His actions saved many lives at Lewisvel Keep."

"I spoke to him," Ava said. "I knew he was gone, but I could not accept it."

"His spirit was strong and will live on beyond its bonds to our world," the queen encouraged. "I still feel his presence and I am sure he will be watching over us now."

"The battle, is it over?" Ava asked.

"Yes, the forces of darkness have been defeated," the queen assured her. "And Brendan would like to have a word with you about the rather risky sorcery you performed on the riverbed." The queen's lips curled a bit as she thought back to Brendan's' reaction when Alec told him about the portal that Ava had opened to the other world.

"I suspect that you will not likely fare well with the chastising he probably has in store, despite the fact that your actions actually saved his life and the lives of many men on the battlefield. In fact, the captain of the army has requested that you be knighted for your contributions to the routing of the dark army."

Ava responded weakly, "That seems a rather unusual."

"Yes, it is, dear, but after William, Alec, and Danny spoke of your actions, there was no one in the room who argued against it."

"So I guess I will have to suffer through all of those ridiculous rituals that I see the men perform when they are knighted." She paused for a moment to gather her wits, then gasped, "Oh my, am I going to have to get and train a squire?" Ava said. She rubbed her forehead. She knew there would be a bump from the tumble she took.

"I am afraid your father has already assigned you a young gentleman," the queen said smiling. "But I think he has ulterior motives. I think he wants to make sure you no longer take off on your own."

"Who" Ava asked with curiosity?

"His name is Evan. He is quite the charmer."

"Are you sure my father isn't just trying to find me a husband to tie me down?"

The queen laughed at this, which caused quite the commotion in the hall. The news traveled rather quickly throughout the castle that Ava had awoken and her siblings, her father, and two rather nervous young dwarves came rushing to her room. They conversed for some time.

The queen quietly slipped from the room; there were still soldiers that she needed to tend. The queen commanded that an infirmary be set up in the courtyard to allow her to participate in the healing of Articia's soldiers.

After a short discussion, Ava gasped, "My horse! Is Aurora all right?"

Alec responded first. "That horse of yours is a true warrior. After you were thrown from her back, we were overrun by the fleeing goblins. Your horse stepped over you to protect you from the stampede, kicking and biting every goblin that came close to where you lay. I stood and fought off the rest of the goblin horde that was foolish enough to come near us, but most of them avoided us altogether because of the frenzy your horse made and the fiery blaze that emanated from Fire Storm."

Ava giggled at the thought of Aurora acting that way. "But she took an arrow. I saw it as I was thrown."

"Yes, it caught her in the rump. She was rather annoyed about that. It took some time to calm her down so I could pull it out and heal the wound. She tried to bite me many times in the process."

Ava burst out laughing at Alec's description of her mare's activity.

24

Reprimands

M r. Tipple was whistling as he approached the gate of the garden that surrounded the Great Library. He lifted the latch, proceeded through, and before he turned to close the gate, he saw Raphael and Michael sitting on the rocks surrounding the fountain in the middle of the walkway. They turned when they heard him and rose to their feet.

"Metronome, I wish to speak to you," Michael said in an irritated tone using the librarians' real name.

"What could possible move you out of your palace of pain and bring you to my beautiful garden on such a fine day?"

"You know how dangerous this game is that you are playing with the people here on this world. Did you learn nothing from our previous mistake?" Raphael asked.

"Yes, I most certainly do know the danger, and so I kept the promise we made with the deity of this place. I helped the favored one find a way to help restore the balance that was in place before the interloper intervened," Mr. Tipple responded calmly.

The garden gate slammed open. The three elves turned toward the commotion and a man dressed in the garb of one of the locals walked into the garden.

It was Metronome who spoke first as the visitor approached the trio. "Scratch, you have no power here in this garden. And for that matter, you have no power on Articia."

"Please, call me Duke. It is the title I have chosen for this place," the man said. "Now tell me, I thought you were all going to remain neutral on this new world we have discovered."

"Always the deceiver," Raphael said. "You know better than we do that our neutrality is restricted by our bargain with the omnipresent power of this domain. We have promised to maintain that balance and we have chosen to do so without directly interfering with the daily lives of this world's inhabitants."

"Unlike your actions, Lucifer" Raphael said as Duke Marquin turned to look at him.

"Oh, but you wound me so," he said in a mocking fashion, one that he frequently used when conversing with his brethren. "I am bound by no such rules, so therefore I will continue to interfere as I see fit." The duke walked toward the library. "Right now, I need to do a little research, for I must start planning my next adventure."

Raphael frowned as he watched the deceiver walk toward the library. Metronome turned to his siblings Raphael and Michael and reminded them, "You know our agreement. She told us not to interfere with his actions. She sees him as but a child on this world and hopes he may one day change his tune."

Michael had been clenching his fists because of the encounter but relaxed as Metronome walked to the library. "If we are not interfering, why are you heading his way?"

"Because, my brothers, the doors of the great library are locked, being the librarian, I do possess the keys necessary for him to enter the place." Mr. Tipple smiled back at him, "and besides, the last time he was here, he ripped the pages out of so many of my best works. I need to keep an eye on him to ensure that he does not repeat his previous behavior in my library."

Raphael shook his head then turned to his brother Michael. "What do you think will happen now that the waters of Articia have fallen on the barren lands of our home world?"

"I do not know," Michael said as he started to walk back to the open gate of the library garden. "I think it is time for us to return to the Vale. We can discuss this more in the morning."

...

The grey orb rose over the red sands of a barren desert. Rain was falling heavily now and causing small tributaries to form in the lowland that surround many outcroppings and rock formations. It was the first time rain had fallen in this barren place in many millennia.

Some of the water filtered through the reddish sand and disappeared from the wastes, but around the rock formations, the water collected in the shadows to form pools and small streams. Alongside one of these pools, a small green shoot of a long-departed forest burst through the sand to reach for the light of a forgotten sun.

25
Light Rising

Ava was back on her feet a couple of weeks after her ordeal. It had taken her a many days to regain enough balance and strength to ride and practice swordplay again. Brendan had explained to her that she was concussed, which is the reason that she had the horrible headaches and was dizzy when she walked. Eventually, even it cleared.

The loss of her brother Tristan did not resolve. Long after the memorial and funeral, she spent day after day thinking about what she could have done differently to save her brother. She thought about whether she could find a spell to turn back time itself, all so she could intervene. Every thought she had ended with the same result. It is the will of the goddess Adara and Ava did not have the power to change what had already passed.

She walked along the rows of books of the castle library, searching for something new to read. Mr. Tipple had agreed to have more books sent from the Great Library to Castle Articia so that more of the city's people could enjoy the stories and expand their knowledge. Ava worked out an arrangement to have Mr. Tipple deliver a cart full of books every season so that there would always be new books to enjoy. The librarian merrily called his new cart a "book mobile." Ava thought it was a funny name for a horse-drawn cart.

She had always loved reading; it allowed her to escape into different worlds and softened the pain of loss that she now felt whenever she thought of Tristan.

When Mr. Tipple made his last delivery of books, he brought a whole set of Graek myths. Ava had just finished the story of a place called a labyrinth. The story was about a great prince from a faraway kingdom who fought and defeated a great monster called a Minotaur. She was looking for another volume from this set of myths when a voice from behind startled her.

"My lady, I have been looking all over for you. You have made so much of an effort to hide. It is very difficult for a squire to perform his duties when his knight avoids him in such a way," Evan said.

Ava turned to see the young squire standing there with his hands at his side as he bowed. She put the book back on the shelf and put her hand over her heart in a responsive salute. Ava was not avoiding him; it was more coincidence that they never crossed paths. She had been thinking a lot about the prospect of training a squire.

Despite her recent adventure with William and the stories that he told of his training, she really did not know what she was supposed to do in regards to training a squire to become a knight. Women never really became knights in Articia and certainly did not train squires.

"Well," Ava said with a sigh, "I guess it is about time we start your training. She looked at the row of books in front of her. "There are many things that are important for a knight of Articia to learn. You will need to read many works of honor and bravery," she said to the young boy. "You will need to train in the martial arts." She stopped and faced the young squire to look him over. He was just past his eleventh year, but fit. He would do well in the games. She observed him squirm at the suggestion of reading, Ava thought of the knights at the royal events. How the ladies in waiting reacted to them whenever they arrived. She smiled a devilish smile. "But all in good time. First, I believe I will teach you to dance."

"There's no music," Evan objected somewhat nervously.

"Ah, but there is always music in your soul," she laughed aloud as she raised her hand for him to take. He timidly took her hand as she grabbed his other and put it on her waist. They danced around in circles with Ava laughing as Evan tried to make the correct steps.

Ava realized her entire character was transforming. The old Ava would not have started dancing with her squire in the middle of a library with no music. She would have dragged him straight out to the training yard and thrashed him in combat repeatedly until he got it right.

She was missing her brothers dearly at this moment. William and Alec had gone with Dominic on his First Excursion. It was not as it should have been; Tris was going to ride with Dom. Now Tris could only watch over them. "Try to keep them from getting in too much trouble, Tris," she whispered to herself.

"What?" Evan asked as his two left feet struggled to keep a steady rhythm.

"Nothing, Evan. Let's try the dance again," Ava responded with a smile. For at this moment, Ava only wanted to dance …

Epilogue

Danny enjoyed her time alone. She walked the halls of the Castle Articia in the early morning when nobody was stirring. It was her favorite time of day.

She did not know what to think about her new life with all of its grandeur. And of course, the servants, she still could not get used to other people doing everything for her. It was all right to have servants around, especially when she didn't know when and where she was supposed to be in the castle. However, Danny had the sensibilities of a farmer. Hard work and perseverance were necessary to live when you toiled the land.

Living as a member of the royal family was a completely new experience. She was not sure that she would ever get comfortable living in the home of the royals. As she turned the corner to walk down to the courtyard, she heard a quiet voice.

Danielle.

She came to a halt and turned to see who had called her name. She had not heard this young man's voice before and she was concerned that there was an intruder in the castle. However, there was no one there.

She slowly turned back and started to walk again when she heard,

Danielle, come to me!

This time she could not resist the call; she turned to the door of the royal armory and opened it. As she slowly walked in, she said,

"Hello? Is someone there?" She entered the room and the door slammed shut. She was shrouded in darkness.

"Danielle, we are a pair. We are predestined to be bonded!" She heard these words in her mind. "As it was at the instance of the forge, heart to hand and hand to heart, the soul of the sword chooses its wielder."

Danny was struck dumb. She tried to speak but no words would come. On the northwest side of the room shone the bright light of a glowing sword, with a hilt that resembled a beast of the sea. It lit up the chamber and she felt drawn toward it.

"From warrior to warrior, heart to heart, and soul to soul I have passed. I am the song of the sea and the hurricane that cleanses the world. I am independent and free. I have fought the darkness and uncertainty of the deep. I am Rigid Water! I am your confidant, your partner!"

About the Authors

Katherine "Katie" Delia Enos lived her last wonderful days in Westford, Massachusetts. She was born on Good Friday, April 5th, 1996 in Silver Spring, Maryland, where she spent the first three years of her life. Her family moved to Westford in 1999. During first grade, she began playing soccer and this became one of the major focuses in her life. Playing for town, club, and district teams, she had the opportunity to play with and meet many young women in the region and made many friends in the "soccer society." Katie was an accomplished goalkeeper (quite an achievement for a player only 5 feet 2 inches tall). Her teammates and opponents described her as "a little crazy" and sometimes they called her "the brick" or "the wall."

Katie was also very musically inclined. She played or tried many instruments including the piano, viola, saxophone, and guitar and was actively taking lessons at the Indian Hill Music School in Littleton, Massachusetts. She also wrote her own music and planned to take voice lessons in the summer of 2010.

Even though she was only just fourteen, Katie had already chosen that her life profession was to be a writer. She wrote constantly, with many story ideas plastering her room, on her computer, and stuffed in drawers and containers. Katie was also an avid reader, with a small library in her locker at school and a much larger one in her room at home. She would have been a freshman at Westford Academy in the fall.

Katie died on June 30th, 2010, as a result of an automobile-pedestrian accident on one of the many dangerous country roads in Westford, Massachusetts. She is missed dearly and remembered by her family and by countless friends, teammates, and fellow soccer players. Katie's last noble act was to donate her organs (by her own request), which saved or improved the lives of four people. Katie was honored for this act by being selected as a floragraph honoree on the Donate Life float in the Rose Parade in 2012.

Edward Anthony Enos is a systems engineer by profession and a writer born out of grief, remorse, and regret. As part of his own grieving process, he decided that he had to bring to life the stories and characters that his daughter Katie had created.

My daughter Katie wrote many works but did not get to complete any of her writing. This book is based on one of her earliest efforts to write a full novel.

Katie had hoped to become immortalized by the power of the words that she had written. This book is the first of many that will be derived from the thousands of pages that she penned before her death. I have decided to publish this and many books to follow in this series in Katie's name only. Even though I had to complete a lot of this work for her, (and though it was heavily edited as I discovered that I am not an English major!), it was her spark that gave the world of Articia and its people life, and it was her life that I used as inspiration for building the characters, their personalities, and their stories.

Ava represents Katie's love of books and stories and her unwillingness to be told "You can't because you're too short, a girl, too young, etc." William represents Katie's nobility and her caring for people. There are many stories of her standing up to bullies for a friend. Alec represents Katie's remarkable empathy and her ability to find a friend just about anywhere. He also represents the love of competition and unwillingness to quit, even when she wasn't the best, the fastest, or the star. He also represents the times when no matter how hard she worked, she would frequently find herself finishing second, as Alec could not find a way to beat Ava in the martial arts. Danny represents most of Katie's insecurities. She represents the times when

Katie felt invisible, unnoticed, and unknown. Those who knew Katie well will see the many parallels between her life and the personalities and actions of the characters in this book.

Enjoy and God bless.

CPSIA information can be obtained at www.ICGtesting.com
Printed in the USA
BVOW011219301112

306948BV00003B/9/P